Books by Kay L Moody

Truth Seer

Healer

Lie Maker
Coming July 1, 2019!

Want a free short story by Kay L Moody? Join Kay's email list for exclusive news and updates and your FREE sci fi short story collection!

www.KayLMoody.com/collection

HOW MUCH HISTORY CAN SHE CHANGE?

HEALER

KAY L MOODY

MARTEN
PRESS

Healer
Truth Seer Trilogy Book 2
By Kay L Moody

Published by Marten Press
3731 W 10400 S, Ste 102
South Jordan, UT 84009

www.MartenPress.com

Cover by Shawnda Craig
Edited by Deborah Spencer and Emily Chambers

ISBN: 978-1-7324588-2-6

To Mark
You are there every day to encourage,
inspire, and believe in me. This book
wouldn't exist without you.

ONE

TEN HOURS AFTER ESCAPING CERTAIN death, Imara Kalu jumped back in harm's way. It had been natural to rescue her sister from crazed terrorists, but now she put her life on the line for a complete stranger. A little boy running from a slave cartel.

She adjusted the thermostat on her temperature-controlled underclothing as she ran. So much running, but at least this time she wasn't in underground catacombs with no service.

"We're almost there," Abe said as he tapped a message on his hologram screen. "Edrice says it's two more blocks, and then we're there."

Edrice was Abe's business partner. With a hila of photographic memory, she knew the city of Cairo like the back of her hand. Maybe even better.

On the plane ride to Cairo, Abe had explained how Edrice tracked the little boy for several days. He'd been caught by Sef, the slave cartel leader, but somehow the boy had escaped. Maye, one of Abe's employees, had been sent to rescue the boy. For some reason, he was unwilling to be rescued.

7

Imara jumped over a pile of glass shards in the street. Looking over her shoulder, her eyes traveled from the glass to the empty window from which it had clearly come. Through the window she saw a small group of people with heads bent, exchanging whispers. They stood near the broken window but did nothing to fix it. Was that normal?

As her feet pounded the pavement, she looked back at Abe, hoping he would have an answer. He shrugged. "That happens a lot. Most buildings have impact-proof glass now, but it's too expensive to install in homes."

They turned a corner and kept running. Imara shook her head. "But why?" she asked. "Why would anyone break the glass? And who did it?"

Abe's shoulders twitched as he grimaced. "Sef. It's always Sef. Or some of his men, anyway. He's the leader of the slave cartel. He kidnaps orphans. He deals drugs worse than death. His gangsters are more feared than venomous cobras."

His ran his hand down the side of his face, and everything about his expression seemed foreign. She had seen Abe experience fear, determination, anger, and love even. But never had she seen him so devoid of hope. Since hope was the quality that had attracted her to him in the first place, her heart ached to see him without it now.

His copper skin looked lighter under the street lights than it had in the catacombs. He ran his fingers through the generous portion of dark hair on his head, and then a small twinkle appeared in his eye. His feet slowed as he brushed his hand over her elbow and gave a squeeze. "We can save the boy if you're here," he said. "My employee, Maye, is with him now, and Sef's gangsters are closing in. They'll kill Maye and kidnap the boy if we can't convince the boy to come with us. But you'll be able to convince him. I know you will."

With a smile, she increased her speed. She had made a lot of mistakes in the past. She saw the worst in people and pushed everyone away. Her sister, Naki, she had hurt worst of all. But in the catacombs, Abe had believed in her. He believed she could change if only she tried. All she wanted now was to make things right with Naki and find a way to help Abe. If he had believed in her, she could believe in herself. No matter what happened tonight, she would save that boy.

In the past week, she'd lost her job, her mentor, and her hila. Once a truth seer, now she was nothing but a hollow shell of a person. One desperate to make things right.

"This way," Abe said as he pointed down an alley.

Around the corner, a small boy of about ten stood with his back against the alley wall. His fingers clenched around a knife hilt with the blade facing toward them.

A young woman with billowy clothes and big eyes stood a meter away from the boy. She stared at her hands as her breath shuddered in jagged puffs. Blood dripped from her palms down to her elbows. Abe had his bag open and gauze out before Imara had a chance to blink.

"It's almost curfew," the young woman said as she held her palms up for Abe to clean. "He cut me twice! The first time wasn't bad, but this time…" Her breath rattled as she tried to suck in air.

"I've got it, Maye," Abe said. "The cut isn't deep, and I have my ointment with pain killer. You'll be good as new in no time."

She hissed at him and stomped her foot. "How could you leave us like that? You've been gone for five days. Five!" Her shoulders shook as she glared at Abe.

A slew of angry retorts bounced through Imara's mind, but she tried to push them all away. Surely, Maye had no idea that Abe went to the catacombs to rescue his dad. She obviously had no idea how many times his life had been in danger. If she knew, she wouldn't yell at him like this. The anger still bubbled in Imara's chest, but she took a deep breath to calm it. She wasn't this person anymore. She was going to see the best in people, not the worst. Besides, this was no time to be making judgments about Maye.

Curfew was approaching, and that meant anyone under eighteen had to be off the streets. Right now, they had to save this boy before they ran out of time.

Ignoring Abe and Maye, Imara took careful steps toward the boy. His face may have been hardened and his knife pointed, but his arms trembled. She automatically searched for the colorful shapes depicting his emotion. With her hila, she'd been able to see emotions, truths, and even intentions. Even though she knew her hila was gone, her eyes still searched for the colors. She saw nothing.

The boy growled as she stared, but his chin quivered at the same time. Yesterday, she would have seen wine-colored spikes coming off his skin, but today she saw body language. Body language that indicated fear.

She needed this boy to trust her. If he was scared, she had to show him she wouldn't hurt him. She dropped to the ground and crossed her legs. As an extra measure, she clasped her hands behind her head. "Can I hurt you when I'm sitting like this?" she asked.

The boy blinked back at her. He narrowed his eyes, as if thinking. When Maye let out a sigh from behind her, he raised his knife higher and moved his face into a glare. "This is a trick," he said. "You're trying to hurt me."

Imara took in a slow breath. When she spoke again, she used a soothing voice. This time, she tried a different kind of question. "Why do people trick others?"

The boy blinked at her again. His knife lowered a centimeter as he screwed up his face in thought. "You want to hurt me," he said.

She kept her hands clasped behind her head and again sought her soothing voice. "I've been hurt before too. It's hard to trust people after that happens, but you know what?"

The boy watched her, looking more confused than anything.

She decided to give him a little smile. "I just learned that most people don't want to hurt me."

The boy's eyes shifted around from her to Abe, to Maye, and back again. He'd held his knife out with a rigid hand, but then it relaxed, and he cocked his head to the side.

"I have an idea," she said. "What if you come with us but we let you keep your knife? If you feel threatened, you can stab anyone. Even me."

The boy stared for several seconds before he started to nod. Once the nod began, he stopped and asked, "Where do you want to take me?"

She glanced back at Abe, realizing she didn't know the answer.

"To my headquarters," Abe said.

This made the boy tighten his grip on the knife and bare his teeth in a scowl.

Abe took a step back and raised his hands up with his palms out. "We have a nice place for you to eat and sleep until you can go back to the Egyptian Council."

At those words, the boy's shoulders relaxed. "The Egyptian Council?"

"You already know about the Egyptian Council?" Imara asked.

The boy stared with a blank expression, so finally, Abe answered. "His parents died three months ago. He was in the care of the Egyptian Council until Sef's gangsters kidnapped him a week ago."

"How do you know that?" the boy asked as he narrowed his eyes.

"It's his job to know," Maye answered with sharpness in her tone. "We work for the Egyptian Council, and it's good that you trust them. The sixteen council members are the only part of Cairo that hasn't been infiltrated by Sef."

"I want to go back to the Egyptian Council," the boy announced.

"We can take you there in the morning, but right now we need to get you off the streets before curfew," Abe said. "Do you trust us?"

The boy coiled.

Imara looked into the boy's eyes and held his gaze until his shoulders relaxed. With a smile, she said, "We might need your help if there's trouble on the way. Can you use your knife if you have to?"

The boy's head bobbed up and down, and he rolled his shoulders back.

"Would you like to stand in front of us or behind us as we walk?" she asked as she got to her feet.

12

He considered for a moment and then said, "Behind."

"That's a smart choice. Then you can keep an eye on us and make sure we don't do anything tricky."

Without her hila, she couldn't see the tangerine glow of pride coming off his skin, but she noticed other things. His lips twitched into barely a smile, and his chest puffed up. Her heart ached for the loss of colors, but with body language, she found she could still interpret his emotion.

A loud *whoop* sounded from down the alleyway. Maye shivered, and Abe jerked his head toward the entrance of the alley. "We need to get out of here," he said under his breath.

Imara nodded and glanced back at the boy to wave him forward. When she turned back to march after Abe, she noticed Maye staring at her. Her face had relaxed, though her shoulders were still tense. After a moment, Imara noticed she started to smile. Just a little.

Not sure exactly what to do next, Imara smiled back. It was such a tiny thing, but it made her heart swell. Maybe now that she was determined to stop seeing the worst in people, she could have friends. Real friends. For the first time in years.

Soon they were on their way, with Abe in the front and the little boy in the rear. Everything went smoothly for about a minute, but then, the boy sucked in a breath. Even without seeing him, she knew he was afraid once again.

When she turned to face him, he stared at the ground. Maye gasped even louder than the boy had and started backing away with short steps. Abe appeared at Imara's side and grabbed her arm.

"Just back up slowly," he said as he pulled her away. "Nice and slow."

She stared at him, then back at the boy, mystified by their reactions. As far as she could tell, the road looked no different than it had a moment ago. The only strange thing she detected was a slightly musky scent in the air.

Abe tightened his grip on her arm and whispered, "Sef uses them to scare the kids. It's how he gets them to be his slaves."

She scanned the alley, still confused, until her eyes landed on a black line slithering across the ground. She had thought it was rope at first, but when she looked closer, she saw it moving. The sleek scales running down its body were blacker than the night sky.

Maye let out a yelp when it slid near her foot. She whimpered and wrapped her arms around her stomach. "I can't do this, Abe," she muttered under her breath. "Cobras? This is too much for me."

Imara gulped and took a slow step away from the cobra. The snake seemed to sense her movement, its head following her until its black eyes glinted in the moonlight. The yellow on its belly shone bright against its black scales. She locked her eyes on it, hoping eye contact would distract it from the boy. But only a second later, the cobra turned to him.

In a snap, the cobra flared out the hood around its face and flashed its teeth. In almost the same moment, she realized it not only headed for the boy, but also that it would be close enough to strike within seconds. All of their efforts to save the boy could be lost in a single bite.

Every thought slipped from her mind as she imagined the snake sinking its teeth into the boy's leg. She didn't know how, but she knew she couldn't let that happen. Her body moved even before she had a plan. Before she could be afraid.

Her hand shot out from her body and snatched the cobra by its tail. Its head whipped back, ready to strike, but she lifted it and swung it through the air so hard, its head whiplashed. She swung it around until its head smacked against the ground. Before the cobra could coil, she swung it again and smacked it even harder on the ground. Three more times she swung it, and the third time, she heard a small crack. She dropped the cobra, hoping enough damage had been done. Just in case, she lunged in front of the boy to keep him from harm.

Ignoring the knife in his hands, she wrapped her arms around his shoulders, desperate to keep him safe. She glanced back to see the cobra lying still on the ground.

Abe's mouth hung open, his eyes wide. "You just..." He blinked. "I don't know how..." he shook his head. "You just killed a cobra. With your bare hands!"

The pride coming from his eyes lifted her spirits considerably. Before she could react to his words, Maye flinched and said, "If there's a cobra, gangsters can't be far behind."

"Right," Abe said. He turned as if looking for someone, then shook his head. He tapped his ring to check the time, then said, "We only have a few minutes. Time to run."

Imara grabbed the boy by the wrist, which he allowed without protest. Again, their feet pounded the ground as they passed building after building. After three blocks, they rounded a corner, and a short, tan building came into view.

"That's headquarters," Abe said as he pointed.

Before she could let out a breath in relief, six people appeared on the street before them. They all wore a red armband and held their fists up, ready for a fight.

15

TWO

IMARA WRAPPED AN ARM AROUND THE BOY'S shoulders and pulled him to her body. He moved in close enough that she could feel the shivering in his limbs.

"Ignore them," Abe whispered. "Just keep walking."

Six gangsters looking for a fight didn't seem like the sort of thing she should ignore. But Abe knew Cairo better, so she tried to heed his advice. The best she could do was step forward and pierce the gangsters with the meanest glare she could muster.

"Out past curfew, I see," came a voice from behind.

It took only a tiny glance back to see the speaker. He was a portly man with a constellation of freckles spread over his light brown cheeks. The freckles might have been endearing on their own, but the eyes above them were worse than the cobra's. He stared at the boy with a fury that didn't make any sense. How could a boy so young incite so much fear and anger in a grown man?

The man tucked a hand into the pocket of his pinstripe suit. "Give me the boy and I'll leave."

The boy gripped Imara's free hand with fingers as hard as iron. Her grip on his shoulders was no softer. What kind of person could go after a mere boy with such vengeance?

Whatever kind of people they were, she didn't have time to figure it out.

With a tiny gulp, she moved toward Abe's headquarters with steps so small, she hoped they would be imperceptible. She made eye contact with each of the gangsters, hoping to distract them.

The freckled man stood in a staring match with Abe when one of the gangsters decided to act. He jumped toward Imara, and the boy at her side screamed.

Another gangster closed in on her other side, giving her no choice but to fight. She peeled the boy's fingers off her hand and pushed him forward. "Run inside that building. I'll keep the gangsters busy," she said.

A gangster reached for the boy as he started to run, but Imara barreled toward the man with the red armband until her head slammed into his gut. While he teetered backward, she rammed a heel into the other gangster's shin and slapped the hand reaching for her hair.

Only distracted for a moment, both gangsters reeled back, ready for new attacks. In the chaos, Imara noticed a female gangster with eyes on the boy. Still running, the boy only needed a few seconds to get inside. She just needed a brief distraction.

She crouched to the ground to avoid a swinging fist. While low, she spread her fingers across the ground until they found a heavy wooden board. Clutching the board, she rolled to the side to avoid a boot.

Soon, she was back on her feet and used the board to whack the woman's leg with as much force as she could. By then, the boy had been stopped from his goal. His feet kicked through the air as a gangster held him up by the shoulders.

The boy flashed his teeth and bit down on the gangster's hand. Even though he yelped, the gangster didn't release the boy.

Shouts rang through the air, including ones from Abe, but Imara was too engrossed in the fight to register his words.

All she cared about now was getting the boy safe. Abe had been so insistent about getting the boy inside. It didn't seem like that would be enough with all these gangsters around, but it would be a start. She had no training in fighting, but for some reason, the gangsters mostly ignored her and focused on the boy. If they decided to ignore her, she would take advantage of it.

She eyed the gangster holding the boy, waiting until he stepped close enough to her. Then, she whacked the wooden board against his head. A crack sounded out, and her gut clenched. Hopefully she hadn't done more harm than she meant.

The gangster shook his head, recovering too quickly. Still, he had dropped the boy when the board hit his head.

"Run inside!" Imara shouted, pointing at the building.

Again, the gangsters ignored her and focused only on the boy. Desperate to stop them, she lunged for the nearest gangster's legs. As he toppled to the ground, the other gangsters tripped over him. Only one was still on the boy's tail.

The boy was up the steps, a hair's breadth away from the entrance. He slammed a fist against the door opener. The female gangster stood at the bottom of the stairs and reached for the boy's ankle, but she missed by a centimeter.

The boy crossed through the doorway, and the door closed behind him. The nearest gangster let out a growl, and Imara raised her fists, ready to fight even with no knowledge of hand-to-hand combat. But, apparently the gangster had given up. She frowned again at the doorway but didn't attempt to go inside. With narrowed eyes, Imara turned and noticed the rest of the gangsters wearing the same dejected expression. Would they really let the boy go just because he was inside?

For the first time since the fight broke out, she heard Abe's voice well enough to comprehend his words. "As I've been trying to say, we have three minutes until curfew." His face turned red as he curled his hands into fists. "If you're going to break your promises, you can bet I will too."

The portly man nodded at one of his gangsters, but it was so fast, she almost didn't notice. A split second later, the gangster jammed an elbow into Imara's side. She clutched her stomach as she gasped for air.

"HEY!" Abe yelled as he marched up to the portly man.

The man scratched his freckled nose and said casually, "Is she one of yours?"

Abe stomped forward until his nose was centimeters from the man's. At this distance, Abe towered at least a head over him. Abe jabbed a finger into the man's sternum and said, "If she gets hurt because of you, I swear you will regret it."

The freckled man swallowed and stepped out from Abe's shadow. Once he backed up, he lifted his chin. "Don't cut it so close to curfew next time."

Abe scowled as the man turned his back and started walking away from them. The gangsters followed without question. As they left, she noticed the wooden board just a meter away. Bits of concrete and broken glass littered the rest of the street. She'd never seen such debris except in the worst parts of Nairobi. What kind of a city was Cairo if this was one of the better roads? Why would Abe choose to stay when things were so bad?

The gangsters disappeared down an alley, and she noticed the road was now empty but for her and Abe. "Where's Maye?" she asked.

"She already went inside." He shook his head while letting out a long, slow breath.

"Who was that man?" she asked. "And what promises were you talking about? Why didn't they try to get the boy once he was inside?"

He grimaced at each of her questions, then screwed up his face as if trying to decide which to answer first. Finally, he said, "That was Sef and a few of his most delightful gangsters."

"Why didn't they try to get the boy once he went inside?"

"It's against the rules."

Her eye twitched at his words. "What rules? It's illegal? I thought Sef broke rules all the time. He's the leader of a child slave cartel. And you said he deals drugs worse than death. What does he care about rules?"

Abe shook his head and let out another long breath. "It's hard to explain. He breaks rules, but he doesn't break his own rules. He must have been really desperate to attack before curfew. And right outside our headquarters too. We have security cameras but he might have disabled them. A couple of his gangsters have electricity-based hilas. I'm sorry that guy elbowed you in the stomach. They're not supposed to do that."

"What do you mean *supposed* to?"

He rubbed a hand down the side of his face with a pained expression. Rather than answer, he reached for her until his fingers rested in a gentle squeeze above her elbow. "Are you okay?" he asked.

The warmth of his fingers turned her brain to mush and suddenly staring into his eyes seemed like the only important thing in the world. She nodded without considering his question.

When a teasing chuckle erupted from his mouth, it brought her back to reality. "Are you sure?" he asked.

This time, she actually considered the state of her body. She'd only escaped the catacombs a few hours ago and now a new adventure had gripped her by the shoulders and shook wildly. Tingles of anxiety danced under her skin, and her heart pounded in her chest. Although, at least a little of the heart pounding had something to do with Abe and the way he was looking at her now.

"I'm fine," she said as she leaned into him. Everything with Abe was so new, but nothing had ever felt so natural.

"You were amazing," he said, wrapping his arms around her. "Better than I expected. Much better. That cobra…" He chuckled and nuzzled his chin into the curls on her head. "I loved that."

Just when she had almost pinpointed the smell of his t-shirt, something spicy, he pulled away and said, "Come on. Let's go meet everyone."

He took her hand, but quickly tore it away and grabbed his forehead. "Oh," he said. "There's just one thing. We have this employee, Husani. You'll see what I mean when we get in there, but he flirts a lot, and we had to make rules about employees dating each other."

She started to open her mouth, but Abe waved a hand through the air. "No, we can still date each other if you start working here, that's not a problem. We just have to be professional when we're at headquarters and on missions and stuff. No holding hands or flirting or fluttering our eyelashes at each other. That kind of thing."

"That makes sense," she said. "But I haven't taken the job yet. I want to make sure I spend plenty of time with my family over the next couple months. I have a lot of making up to do. Especially with Naki."

Her head hung as the memories gripped her. For eight years she had ignored and mistrusted her sister. The memory of those eight years sat like a bitter taste in her mouth. But things would be different now because Imara was determined to be better.

Abe ran his fingers over her cheek with a smile that warmed her up. "You don't have to decide tonight; just come meet everyone. They're going to die when they see the video I took of you and that cobra."

She cocked her head to the side. "You got video?"

"Yeah, you didn't notice?"

She shrugged. "I guess I was a little distracted." Now that imminent danger had passed, she had a new concern. Meeting new people. After years of mistrusting everyone she met, was she even capable of making friends?

Imara stepped through the office doorway, expecting to see a roomful of people. Instead, there were only four. The

22

boy, Maye, a teenage boy, and a young woman with a lilac ribbon in her hair.

The teenage boy stared out the window and said, "Did you see how hot that gangster woman was? When did Sef get attractive gangsters? I might need to cause some trouble just so she has to come and take care of me."

The young woman with the lilac ribbon rolled her eyes. "Please don't start flirting with the enemy, Husani, or we'll all be in trouble."

Abe cleared his throat, and all of them turned to face him at once. Imara started to smile, trying to make a good first impression. Before her lips could curve up, Maye marched toward them with a glare.

"I quit, Abe. I QUIT. This job is insane! I never thought it would be this dangerous."

"Come on, Maye," the young woman said as she tucked a stray hair under her lilac ribbon. "It was just a bad day. You can't give up yet."

Maye turned and jabbed a finger toward the young woman. "Don't patronize me, Edrice. You're afraid to go on missions too. Do you know how many times I almost died today? Eleven. Eleven times! I might as well start preparing canopic jars because I'm going to die if I go on another mission, I know it."

Her voice was rising with each syllable. Before she could continue, Abe raised his hand as if to calm her. "Maye," he said. "You're allowed to quit. I'd never ask you to do something you're uncomfortable with."

"She can't quit," the girl with the lilac ribbon—apparently Edrice—said. "Without her we'll just have you, me, and Husani."

Ignoring her, Abe looked back to Maye with a gentle expression. "You know how much we need you right now, but it's up to you."

Maye seemed to consider his words, but it didn't last long. "I can't do this anymore," she said.

Edrice rolled her eyes. "Really, Maye? It can't be that bad."

Maye turned on her, hunching her shoulders forward. "How would you know? You don't do anything but sit in this office all day."

Abe stepped between them, facing Maye. "There's no shame in quitting. Edrice can send you the paperwork by tomorrow night. It will take a few days before you get your last paycheck. Is that okay? I can loan you money if you need it earlier."

Maye huffed and turned her back on them. "That's fine. Just send me the paperwork, and I'll you see around."

With that, Maye stormed out of headquarters, her hijab billowing behind her. The air went still for a few moments as everyone sat, afraid to react.

Finally, the teenage boy let out a low whistle. He turned to Imara with a smirk. "How was that for an introduction to our team, huh?"

"Uh," she said, toeing the line between saying something nice and saying something truthful.

The boy chuckled and saved her from having to answer. "I'm Husani. And you must be the lovely—" He stopped when Abe shot him a glare. "I mean, the completely normal-looking Imara. Welcome to headquarters."

Husani's copper brown skin matched Abe's making them both look traditionally Egyptian. With a name like Edrice,

Imara had been expecting Abe's business partner to look similar. Instead, her fair skin and hazel eyes almost made her look European. But since air travel had become so fast and cheap in the last fifty years, the world culture was more global than ever. Race was pointless to assume based on name, home country, or even family members.

Edrice stepped forward and took Imara's hand in a warm handshake. The judgmental expression she wore when talking to Maye had disappeared. Now, she wore a smile that made her eyes twinkle. "Welcome," she said, as she dropped her hand and turned back to the others.

When Abe mentioned the name of his business partner back at Nazari Academy of Hila, Imara wasn't sure how to picture her. Edrice was definitely prettier than she expected. And younger. Probably only nineteen or twenty.

A surge of jealousy stung through her and then an accusatory thought.

Coward.

That's what Edrice was. She sat in her office putting other people in danger, all while she did nothing but paperwork. She'd been quick to dismiss Maye's fears. Definitely a coward. And an immature one at that.

The thoughts flew through her mind so fast, Imara didn't have a chance to stop them. More thoughts raced in, but she slammed a door on them.

No. She wasn't this person anymore.

No more judging people before she knew them. No more assuming the worst. Even if it took every bit of brain power she had, she would find something nice about Edrice.

She was young, maybe slightly immature, but still, she co-owned a business. That was impressive. And apparently she was in charge of the paperwork. Also impressive since, to Imara, wrestling a cobra seemed less of a burden than doing paperwork day in and day out. What else? There had to be something else.

Just as she was searching, Edrice pulled an orange from her pocket and handed it to the young boy with a smile. He snatched it away without a thank you, but Edrice didn't seem to mind. She smiled at him and patted him on the head.

There. Edrice could do nice things too.

Edrice turned back to her and said, "It's good to meet you, Imara. Abe said enough about you in a message to know we'd love to have you work here. You probably noticed, we're a little desperate for employees. I'm coordinating a job for tomorrow if you're interested."

"Edrice is our scheduler," Husani said, dropping into a chair. "And the brains. Her hila is photographic memory so she helps us through buildings and stuff by memorizing the blueprints."

Imara attempted another smile as she nodded at Husani. *See?* Edrice was smart and organized. She also figured out a way to use her hila to help the business. All very impressive things.

"I'm a time feeler myself," Husani said. "I act as a stopwatch, timer, alarm clock, and more. I know exactly what time it is down to the nanosecond. It's not a very exciting hila, but you'd be surprised how often it comes in handy."

"What about you?" Imara asked the boy. He stood in the farthest corner of the room, dipping his head down, trying to appear smaller.

When she addressed him, he looked up with wide eyes and said, "What?"

"Do you know your hila?"

He frowned. "I'm only eleven."

She nodded in understanding. "Still too young then? Do you have any guesses? Some children can tell even before their hila manifests."

The boy puffed up his chest. "Twitch finder. They can tell when someone is trying to hide something. Just like Sef was hiding…" His eyes went wide, and he clapped a hand over his mouth. "Never mind," he said as he dropped his attention back to the orange in his hand.

"Good thing we stopped them from kidnapping you," Abe said. "Twitch finders can be useful, and Sef never would have let you go."

"They weren't going to kidnap me, they were going to kill me!" the boy shouted.

Abe narrowed his eyes, then softened his expression to a smile. "Sef doesn't kill children."

"He does if they find evidence that can get him arrested," the boy muttered under his breath.

Abe's eyes went wide, and he stepped toward the boy with a curious hunger in his eyes. "What do you mean? You actually found evidence? Real evidence?"

The boy's jaw flexed, and he took a step back. Before he could retreat anymore, Imara stepped forward and used the most soothing voice she could manage. "What would happen if Sef gets arrested?" she asked.

The boy peeled his orange as he stared at the floor. "There would be less stealing and less fighting. It would be better."

Imara nodded and gave a knowing look to the boy. "Telling us doesn't change what you know, but it might help us stop him. Wouldn't you like that?"

He nodded reluctantly and slipped an orange section into his mouth. "Sef has a list. It names everyone in the city who works for him, including some police. There's a record of what his men did and how much they got paid. If the Egyptian Council had that list, they could arrest Sef *and* everyone working for him."

"Where is it?" Imara asked. "Why hasn't anyone tried to steal it?"

"It's saved on his ring in an un-shareable file," the boy said. "He can sync to a wall hologram and access the list from there, but once he un-syncs, the list automatically deletes itself from the wall hologram. He protects the list carefully, but if anyone downloaded it, Sef would be finished."

Abe let out a short laugh in disbelief. "No wonder he attacked us even before curfew. And here I thought he was going senile."

"Are you tired?" Imara asked the boy. When he nodded, she turned to Abe. "You said there was a place for him to sleep, right?"

Abe nodded and pointed down the hall to a door on the right. "Just down there. There's a little bed and some food as well."

She took the boy's hand to lead him out of the office. She relaxed more than she had in days until Husani asked, "Hey, Imara, what's your hila?"

⟵⟶⟵⟶

Abe slammed the door behind Imara so she wouldn't have to answer. "Don't ask about her hila again," he said to Husani.

"Why? Is it a weird one?"

He clenched his jaw and settled into the chair behind his desk. "She's... mashimo." That seemed like the easiest answer, even if it wasn't technically true.

"I like her," Edrice said suddenly.

Husani sat up wearing a half smile. "Maye said she killed a cobra with her bare hands."

"No, she didn't," Edrice rolled her eyes. "Obviously Maye was exaggerating."

Abe felt his face melt into a smile. "She did, and I got video of it. Do you want to watch?"

They both hurried to his side and gaped at the screen projecting from his hologram ring. When the video finished, Edrice punched a fist in the air. "This is exactly the kind of person we've been missing on our team. Where did you find her?"

Husani waggled his eyebrows up and down with a grin. "Not to mention she's extremely hot. I know I can't flirt with her at work, but after hours I might steal her away..."

"Stop," Abe said, clenching his teeth together. "She's not single, so don't even go there."

Husani's face wilted, but he recovered with a shrug only a moment later.

"Also," Abe said as he sunk into his chair. "I am the *best* at hiring people. You already know this. Besides..."

His thoughts drifted back to the catacombs. The Judge, the leader of a fanatic group called the taggers, had kidnapped Abe's dad, Imara's sister, and a few others. They spent days in the catacombs, braving traps and illusions in order to rescue those kidnapped. Abe's dad, the owner of the best hila school in the entire world, was an obvious target for the kidnapping. Imara's sister had seemed like a random victim, until they found out the Judge was after Imara all along.

Abe could still taste the relief he felt at seeing his dad alive after being taken hostage. His dad even had good things to say about Imara, including how he thought about hiring her. Of course, his dad's excitement faded when he realized Abe had feelings for her, but he'd get used to it. Eventually.

Abe let out a quiet chuckle. "Besides, my dad said he's thought about hiring Imara, so obviously I had to poach her before he got the chance."

Edrice snickered. "You and your dad have the strangest competitions. Can I draw up the hiring paperwork and make it official?"

He ran a thumb along his chin as he replied. "Not yet, but hopefully I can convince Imara in the next couple of days. This job is perfect for her personality. She protects people without any thought for herself."

"I like her too," Husani said. "Not like that. Calm down, Abe, I know she's not single. I just think she's going to do well with us."

Abe sat back in his chair and smiled. Yes, Imara was perfect for this job. And now that they knew about Sef's list, he might actually be able to save his business.

THREE

CLIMBING OUT OF A BUBBLE CAR, IMARA SAID to her sister, "Things in Cairo are not great. But we helped rescue this boy, and he told us about this list, and apparently it's the first time in a long time they think they can actually beat the guy. Sef is his name. Although, we did a job the other night, and I had to punch a guy in the face, and that was really scary."

Naki gave Imara a sideways glance as she joined her on the sidewalk. "Since when do you know how to punch a guy in the face?"

"Abe's teaching me hand-to-hand combat. He says I have a knack for it, but I think he may be flattering me. He does have a massive crush on me, after all." She ended with a snicker. Naki forced a smile on her face and let out a strained laugh.

"What about you?" Imara asked. "What are you doing this week?"

She pinched her tangerine-colored shirt between her fingers in order to keep herself from tugging the hair on the back of her neck. If she did that, it would be a dead giveaway.

Naki rattled off her plans for the week in her usual glittery voice. Every few sentences, her words would stumble, and they'd both be reminded how strange this was.

They were about to have lunch at Naki's apartment. Just the two of them. Imara hadn't been close with her older sister since they were kids. Then the catacombs happened and it changed everything. Imara would have risked her life to save Naki any day of the week, even with their strained relationship.

While in the catacombs, Imara spent days with Abe, her friend Siluk, and eventually, the hostages. In that time, she learned more about herself than she ever wanted to know.

As a truth seer, she could see when someone was lying or telling the truth. She saw emotions as brilliant colors and shapes coming off the skin. As a child, it seemed like a gift, but it quickly became more of a curse.

She learned to see the worst in everybody, herself most of all. But then, Abe came along and convinced her that seeing the worst was not only unnecessary, but also damaging. The idea had changed her life.

The Judge, leader of the taggers, believed that people should be judged and tagged with their crimes. In order to stop the Judge, Imara was forced to do the unthinkable and jump through an eraserfall, forever losing her truth-seeing abilities.

The thought still sent a shiver through her spine, but she recovered when she realized Naki was using her hologram ring to unlock the door to her apartment. As Naki stepped inside, she said, "Sorry it's a mess. Ever since my old roommate moved out, things have been piling up all over the place."

Imara snickered as she headed for the kitchen. "Because you're a slob, and your roommate was the one who did all the cleaning?"

Naki gasped and put her hand over her heart, but then she shrugged and let out a grunt. "Okay yes, I loathe cleaning, but that's not the only reason I miss having a roommate. It's so quiet without her here. I have to bring boys over all the time just so the silence doesn't kill me."

Imara's eyes drifted up into an eye roll as she pulled a loaf of bread from the cupboard. "There are other ways to get rid of silence, you know? You don't have to get a new boyfriend every week."

After retrieving a block of cheese and a package of beef brawn from the fridge, Naki folded her arms over her chest and pouted. "I'm hurt by that. I don't get a new boyfriend *every* week. Are you suggesting I don't really care about them?"

Immediately stopping her search for the honey, Imara dropped her hands to the side, heavy as lead. "I'm so sorry. I was just teasing. I didn't mean—"

Naki giggled and set a fresh onion on a cutting board. "I know, and I was teasing back. Or I was trying to, anyway." Her giggles slowed until a thick silence rested between them. Naki looked back with a different expression, one closer to regret. "It's going to take us some time to learn how to be friends again, isn't it?"

Not knowing how to respond, Imara settled on a nod. Apparently becoming a better person wasn't an instantaneous process—an obvious truth, but no less frustrating. She regretted a lot of things through the years, but shutting Naki out was the one she regretted most of all. Whatever else happened in her life, she was going to fix things with Naki. No matter what it took.

Naki started chopping the onion, and Imara continued her search for the honey. When she found it, she retrieved a pan and put it on the stove.

"Maybe I'll just get a new roommate," Naki said. "Then it won't be so quiet, and I can split the rent. Win-win."

"What if I move in?" The words came out of her mouth before she had a chance to think what it would mean.

Naki jumped into the air, nearly dropping her knife as she clapped her hands together. She grimaced, threw the knife onto the counter, then clapped her hands together several times. "Yes! Oh, Imara, that's perfect. We'll see each other all the time. It's the perfect way for us to…" Her words trickled off into silence, and the bouncing in her knees slowed to stop.

"For us to learn how to be friends again."

Naki pasted on a smile and did a short nod. The reservation in her face didn't last long, and a moment later, Imara's hands were sandwiched between Naki's. "It's perfect, Imara. We can go to movies and rugby games together. Oh, and concerts. There's this band that plays in that park down the street every Friday night. The instruments are all electric, but their songs blend modern and ancient music styles. You'll love them!"

When Imara's hands were released, she set about spreading honey on four slices of bread. Naki threw the chopped onions into the heated pan and sautéed them with oil. "We can go watch the band tonight if you like. They aren't as good as the Shida band, but no one is, so it's not really a drawback."

The glitter in Naki's voice had returned, and this time it wasn't punctuated by awkward pauses. A smile crept onto Imara's lips as she threw the chopped beef brawn in with the onions while Naki continued sautéing them.

"They usually start playing at eight." Naki's face fell as she smacked her lips together and ran her tongue along her bottom lip. As a weather taster, Naki could taste the air and predict the weather. "Never mind," she said. "It's going to rain tonight, but we can go next week, if you like."

Setting two slices of bread each onto plates, Imara held them out to Naki, while she evenly distributed the beef brawn and onion mixture onto the bread.

Imara bit her lip as she watched. Letting the words out slowly, Imara said, "If I live here instead of at home I need a permanent job. I've just been doing contract jobs with Abe's company so far, and it has been going well."

Now that the words had started, they started spilling out faster and faster. "I was nervous about taking the job because it's in Egypt, and I still want to live here in Kenya. But it's only an eighteen-minute flight from Nairobi to Cairo. And it's only twenty points with my airport pass. I think I can handle the commute."

Naki raised an eyebrow as she shredded cheese over the bread slices. "That's not the only thing you were worried about though, is it?"

This time, a grin spread onto Imara's face before she could stop it. "Yes, I was worried about working for my boyfriend. What if things don't work out? What if things get weird because he's my boss? What if we aren't as perfect for each other as I thought we were?" She shrugged, and the smile spread further across her face. "But so far, it's been amazing." A prickly heat rose into her cheeks, forcing her to bite her lip and turn away. "I know we haven't been dating long, but I think things are going to work out."

Imara finally braved a look into her sister's eyes. Naki, however, was busy pressing the bread slices together to make sandwiches. When she finally looked up, she was wearing a smile. Imara could see the smile lines at the corners of her eyes, proving the smile was genuine. But she could also see the smallest hint of disappointment.

Naki let out an exaggerated huff and then a small laugh. "Oh fine. I guess you do need a job, and that one is pretty good. And I do like Abe—he seems to care about you a lot. But promise me you won't spend *all* your time in Cairo. I…" She plopped her plate on the table before sinking into her chair. In a tiny voice, she said, "I want to be friends again."

Imara reached out for Naki's hand and squeezed it, hoping her feelings would somehow seep through the skin and into her sister's heart. "Me too, Naki." She stared down at her sandwich with a gulp. "I promise we can fix things."

FOUR

ABE TRIED NOT TO STARE AT IMARA AS THEY
ambled down the street, but how could he resist? Her eyes
looked like the night sky. The flecks of gold in her black irises
completed the illusion by looking like starlight. Her ebony
skin was soft and lush, which accounted for only some of the
thrill that passed through him every time they touched. But
best of all was the sweet smile she wore, even brighter than
anything he had seen in the catacombs.

It had been three full weeks since the catacombs, and
each day Imara seemed a little brighter, a little happier. A little
better.

She squinted, probably trying to pick out the bubble car
they were supposed to take back to the airport. He didn't
have one himself, since he had dumped all of his savings into
getting his jet. So, they were forced to order one of the self-
moving cars every time she came to Cairo.

She didn't mind. The only thing she seemed to hate was
the same thing he hated. When it was time to say goodbye.

He touched her arm, and she stopped in her tracks. She
turned toward him and seemed to wish he had an excuse for
her to stay, even for a few more minutes. At least, he hoped

that's what she was thinking because that's what he was thinking.

As he brushed his thumb over her ebony skin, he stared into her eyes trying to think of some excuse. Any excuse. But when he looked at her eyes this time, he noticed a thin film of something in the corner of her right eye.

Again.

He'd cleaned it earlier today, but now the tiny yellowish film was back as if it had never gone. With a frown, he said, "You have something in your eyes again."

He lifted his hand toward her face without a thought, but just before his finger reached her eye, he pulled back. "Do you mind if I get it?"

She shook her head and tilted her chin up. At the same time, she leaned into him. When her shoulder brushed against his chest, a feeling dropped through him landing somewhere around his navel.

He wrapped his free arm around her back. Not strictly necessary, but it definitely made the task more enjoyable. And then, he gently cleaned the corner of her eye with his pinky. When finished, he wiped the tiny bit of goop onto his pants and pulled Imara closer. With both arms.

She nuzzled her head into his chest until the curls on her head tickled his chin. How had he ever lived without this?

Lanterns lit up the street with an orange glow. Not a single light was burnt out or broken, marking this as one of the safest streets in Cairo. The road was busy with bubble cars, but so far, no pedestrians had bothered them.

He ran his hand over her back when his eyes fell on a familiar building just across the street. A building where his life had changed.

Imara pulled her head up to look at him, but then quickly shifted and followed his gaze to the building.

"What is it?" she asked.

"I don't think you should go home yet."

She snickered and pulled away from him, using her head to point at the building. "What is that building? It's important to you."

"It's…" he said, starting to deny it, but her surety caught him off guard. He cocked his head to the side and asked, "How did you know?"

"Your muscles twitched," she said. "And then I looked up and saw your face." She shrugged. "I could tell."

"That's not fair," he said shaking his head. "Even without your hila, you know exactly what I'm feeling."

Her eyes grew wide before she dropped her head away to look at the ground. "Sorry," she said under her breath.

He understood why she reacted that way. At least sort of. She had explained to him how guilty she felt knowing people's emotions even when they wanted them secret. But this was different. He wasn't afraid of her knowing things about him. Not anymore. In fact, the more time went on, the more he wanted to share. Needed to.

Something about her made his secrets jump to the surface, begging to be let out. "It's fine," he said. "I don't mind that you can tell how I feel. I actually kind of like it."

She glanced up, and a glimmer of the brightness returned to her expression. He traced his fingers down her spine, and she seemed to take courage in his touch.

"What is it?" she asked again. "Why is the building important to you?"

The air around them stilled as he formulated his response. At last, he squished up his mouth and pointed to a nearby bench. This close to the Egyptian Council chambers should be safe, even this late at night.

After sitting, he ran his thumb along his chin, still not ready to explain. Imara stared into his eyes, and he could see the conflict inside of her. She wanted to know, but she didn't want to pry. Apparently that was all he needed to get the words out. Knowing she cared that much made him open his mouth.

"The first time I saw that building, I was twenty-one. I had just graduated from college and was supposed to start working for my dad. Except I didn't want to work for my dad. Owning the best hila school in the world was his dream, not mine."

Although, he *was* extremely grateful his dad had started Nazari Academy of Hila. Without it, he might never have met one of the top students. Imara.

Abe slipped an arm around her waist and pointed at a window near the top of the building. "Right up there is where a lawyer named Aida worked. She's about the same age as my dad, and she was his lawyer for about seven years. My dad sent me here to get some things from her for the school. I'd met her a few times, but that was the first time I'd ever been to her office here in Cairo."

He chuckled to himself. "The moment I walked in her door, Aida knew I was smitten with the city." He shrugged. "So, she did the only logical thing after that and offered me a job."

"What?" Imara said as her eyes widened. She started to chuckle. "While you were in the middle of running an errand for your dad?"

"Yep. And I took it. Aida and my dad had a habit of poaching employees from each other. It was a friendly competition between them."

Her eyebrow rose as a mischievous glint appeared in her eyes. "Friendly?" she asked. "In a romantic way?"

He snorted and gave her a sideways glance. "Romantic?"

"Yeah, I figured that wasn't likely," she said with a shrug. "He's not into romance of any kind, is he?"

"Not anymore," Abe said before he clamped his mouth shut. Not that secret. Not yet. He gulped, hoping his reaction hadn't been too obvious and then continued. "Definitely not a romantic thing, but still friendly."

"So, how angry was he when you took the job?"

"Not angry at all," he said with a shrug. "My dad is extremely supportive of everything I've ever done. I sort of wished he'd been mad because I felt guilty about quitting the school, but he never was. He just wanted me to be happy. I think he always knew his school wasn't where I wanted to be."

"How long did you work for Aida?"

"Uh," he said as he tugged at his collar. "Not very long. It got complicated." So many secrets, he didn't know if he wanted to share them all.

She flashed him a smile, coaxing the story out. "Tell me," she said, reaching for his hand.

When their fingers touched, he intertwined them and leaned into her. Even with her this close, it wasn't close enough. But it was enough to get him to talk.

A moment later, he looked down and sighed. "Aida had this neighbor. They weren't close friends or anything, but they saw each other on their way to and from work, that sort of thing. And the neighbor had a daughter. Edrice."

Imara cocked her head in surprise.

"Yes, *that* Edrice." He frowned. "A few months before I started working for Aida, the neighbor, Edrice's mom, died."

Imara clapped a hand over her mouth.

"Yeah, I know," he said looking down. "I didn't know Edrice at the time. Aida didn't know her either, not really. She just knew her name and that she was put into the care of the Egyptian Council after her mom died. I'd only been working for Aida for about two months when she suddenly decided to get a birthday present for her dead neighbor's daughter. I don't know how she knew Edrice's birthday, but she did, and she was determined to get her a present. She contacted the Egyptian Council to find out in which care home Edrice was living."

Imara nodded along with the story until her nose wrinkled. Her lips fell into a frown and every muscle in her face seemed to slacken. "But the Egyptian Council couldn't find Edrice. There was no record of her?" she asked.

"Exactly," he said. "The Egyptian Council insisted they had never had a child named Edrice in their care. They did, they just didn't remember. With Edrice's records deleted they had no way of remembering her or finding her or anything. Aida was furious and spent weeks trying to figure out what happened. She uncovered Sef's slave cartel and how he was kidnapping orphans and then deleting their records. Eventually, she found Edrice and helped free her. The only problem was she didn't do it legally."

He shrugged. "Sef has a ton of power here. The Egyptian Council isn't corrupted… yet. But the police are completely useless because Sef has about half of them in his pocket. When Aida discovered his slave cartel, he made sure Aida got caught *and* received the highest possible punishment. She's in prison and will be for another two months."

"Abe, that's…"

"I know. It's terrible. I only worked with her for a few months before she was sent to prison, and Edrice barely knew her at all, but she helped us start our business. We told her what we wanted to do, and she helped us do it. She insisted we do everything legally to make sure we never got into trouble like she did. Oh, and that's how Edrice and Husani met. When Edrice was first put into a care home, she lived with Husani for a couple months. He got taken by the slave cartel first, and then she was a little while later. Once we started our business, Husani was the first orphan we rescued."

"No wonder Husani is still working for you then. Even after all this time."

Abe cocked his head to the side as he shrugged. "Well, he just turned eighteen a year ago so he's only been working since then. Global working age laws and all. Edrice is the one who figured out how to make money though. I just wanted to rescue orphans. She convinced the Egyptian Council to pay us for every orphan we find. And, you already know, we also do contract jobs as a security firm, which pays a lot better than the Egyptian Council does."

She squeezed his hand. "You're pretty fresh, you know that?"

He tried to laugh off the compliment, but he sat up a little taller. If he had impressed the most impressive person in the world, then he must have done something right. With a smile, he said, "Aida is also the reason I hate the taggers so much."

His lips curled up as he mentioned the taggers, and so did Imara's. Not only had the leader of the taggers tried to kill them all, she had also hurt Imara immensely. The Judge had turned out to be Imara's favorite teacher at his dad's hila school. Since Carlotta Santini was dead, he probably still shouldn't hate her, but that didn't stop him from doing it.

Besides, his hatred of the taggers began long before he met Imara. The taggers wanted to add a tag to the end of people's names, branding them with their crimes.

He shook his head as his teeth clenched together. "Aida is in jail, and she *did* break the law, but she did it to save an innocent girl from a slave cartel. If the taggers had their way, Aida would be tagged as a thief for the rest of her life. But she's the farthest thing from a bad person."

"That makes sense," Imara said, tucking her head under Abe's chin.

He lifted a hand to brush his fingers through the shaved hair on the side and back of her hair. When he reached the curls on top of her head, he wrapped his finger around one of the coils. "That's why I'm glad you're here," he said.

He rested his head amidst her curls and let out a sigh. "Things are… they're a little rough right now. The conflict with Sef is escalating, and the security jobs we do are getting more and more dangerous. We've had a lot of employees quit, and we're having a difficult time doing enough jobs to cover our expenses."

Imara pulled away, and he saw a gulp trail down her throat. She opened her mouth, but he waved away her concern.

"I have money in savings. So does Edrice. We have a lot of assets and equipment, so the business is still worth a lot of money."

He pulled his hand away from Imara, and immediately cold seeped into the spots her skin had been a moment ago. He wrung his hands together and said, "I just want to save my business. If we can find Sef's list and get him arrested, then Cairo won't be so dangerous. We'll still get security jobs, but they won't be life threatening, and our employees won't quit all the time. We use to have twenty-five people working for us, and now we just have three: me, Edrice, and Husani."

"Four," Imara said, forcing her hand in between his to stop him from wringing them.

He looked up with a smile, and something swirled around inside of him. His endless hope never left, but for the first time in a long time, he felt like it had a foundation. Wrapping both of his arms around her, he said, "I'm really glad you're here."

FIVE

IMARA RUBBED HER SHOULDER AS SHE rounded the corner to the bubble car. Why did Abe always request the bubble car so far from headquarters? Maybe it would better avoid Sef's men that way. Abe did know Cairo much better than her.

She squeezed her shoulder between her fingers, grateful the pain was dissipating. This time, the pain didn't come from a fight. She merely tripped over a cardboard box in the street and landed on her shoulder. Even after a month, she wasn't used to the amount of debris in the streets.

Just as she waved her thin, gold ring over the bubble car lock screen, she remembered that Abe had ordered the car, and only his ring would open it. Why wasn't he here yet?

A moment later, he appeared around the corner, tapping at the hologram screen projecting from the black ring on his finger. He glanced up with a frown. "Do you care if we take a small detour?"

She took a small step back from the bubble car so he could wave his ring over the lock screen. "What kind of a detour?" she asked.

As she spoke, the door to the bubble car slid open, allowing them to climb inside. The car was made with two-inch-thick plastic. Flat on the bottom where the wheels attached, but dome-like on top, giving it the appearance of a bubble. The bottom half of the car was black, but at the middle of the car, the black faded to transparent so riders could see outside the car.

Abe tapped the hologram screen of the bubble car while the door slid closed again. He typed in a new location, and the bubble car immediately brought up an updated map. He tapped the OK button, and soon the bubble car was off.

Abe scooted on the plush, upholstered seat, until his shoulder settled against hers. Just as close as they both liked him to be.

"So, we're going to a prison?" Imara asked as she watched the hologram screen in the bubble car.

"To see Aida," Abe said. "Edrice has a legal question about one of our security contracts. They don't allow prisoners to message except on certain days, and we need an answer by tomorrow. I said I'd go to the prison and get an answer tonight, but we'll have to hurry. Visiting hours close in fifteen minutes." He sat up suddenly and tilted an eyebrow down while his mouth quirked into a frown. "You don't mind, do you?"

"No," she said barely managing to suppress a chuckle. Abe knew full well that she didn't mind. They both liked to drag out their goodbyes as long as possible. She pressed her shoulder into him, enjoying the warmth his skin radiated.

He smiled at her, but then his eyes narrowed. "You have that stuff in your eye again."

"Can you get it for me?" While he picked the goop out of her eye, she asked. "Do you visit Aida often?"

A look of guilt fell over Abe's face as he wiped his pinky on his shirt. "Not as much as I should."

"Does Edrice?"

A muscle near Abe's nose twitched, but his face quickly hardened to an inexplicable expression that made her ache for her hila all over again. He wrapped his arm around her and started massaging the sore spot on her shoulder. "Edrice visits less than I do. I know I should visit more. We owe everything to her, but things are always busy. And anyway, she'll be released in two months, and then we can see her more often. She's excited to see our headquarters in person."

"What does she look like?" Imara asked, but her thoughts were more focused on her shoulder. Abe's fingers found a spot that caused a tingle to spread through the muscle until the pain was nothing but a whisper fading away.

He pulled his arm away to tap his ring and said, "I'll show you."

A moment later, an image of Aida blinked from his hologram screen. She wore an emerald green hijab that matched her emerald green eye shadow. A tiny, oval-shaped mole sat underneath her left eyebrow. Her black eyes were confident but not fierce.

She had a nice face, but Imara's favorite part was the smirk under her light pink lipstick. Aida wore a smile that suggested she knew much more about the world than she let on.

"She looks a lot older now," Abe said. "I guess being in prison can do that."

"Oh," Imara said as she sat up straight. "I just remembered." She trailed her fingers down her leg until they gripped her knee. She tried to smile and said, "Can you come to dinner at my apartment on Monday night? Naki wants to cook for us." She bit her lip and peeked through her eyelashes at Abe. "And my parents want to come also. If that's okay with you," she added hastily.

"Of course," he said with a wide smile. "We can take my jet after work and then..." His tone shifted as he looked down. "I forgot I already have a meeting scheduled that night. It's kind of a crazy week. Maybe next week. Will they forgive me if it's next week?"

A laugh escaped as relief washed through her. All that worry over nothing. She should have known Abe wouldn't mind. "Next week will be fine," she said as the bubble car rolled to a stop.

"It's just around the corner," Abe said, climbing out of the bubble car. "They like it when you approach on foot because it's better for security."

She nodded as they walked toward the corner he had indicated. Before she'd gone a few steps, a short yelp followed by a grunt pulled her eyes away. She scanned the street noticing glass missing from several of the nearby windows. A door to one of the houses shuddered as if someone was trying to open it but didn't know the unlock code. The door shuddered again, and then a window next to it shattered.

A moment later, a large man jumped out the window with a small girl in his arms. Her legs were crumpled up to her chest. The man held his hand tight over her mouth while she clawed at it, trying to free herself. Imara didn't recognize the man, but she knew from the red armband he wore that he was one of Sef's gangsters.

Without thinking, she pounded a foot against the ground, ready to run. But her body jerked back a moment later when Abe caught hold of her elbow.

"Don't," he said breathlessly.

"That girl is being kidnapped." She tried to jerk her arm out of his grip, but he only held tighter.

Tugging her closer still, he turned his head away from her and whispered, "We can't do anything right now."

She searched his eyes for an explanation, but everything she could imagine came up short. She tightened her mouth into a knot. "Stop pulling me back. We have to rescue that girl."

"We can't," he said, softening his grip but not letting go. He glared at a tarnished ring lying forgotten in the street while a trace of shame twitched at his lips. "It's complicated."

Complicated? That wasn't an explanation at all, and they had no time to be standing around. She finally wrested her elbow from his grip and said, "I'm going after her."

She turned on her heel and promptly ran straight into Abe's chest. How he managed to get there so fast, she didn't know, but it wouldn't change her decision. She lifted her hands, ready to push him out of the way, when his voice cut through the air.

"You can't rescue her right now. We're not allowed to when it's after curfew."

Her eyes narrowed to tiny slits. "Allowed to? What does that even—" Her voice cut short as another question filled her mind. "Who allows it?"

As Abe gulped, he looked away, unable to meet her eyes. He kicked the tarnished ring away and said in a whisper. "Sef."

"Sef? The leader of the slave cartel *Sef*?"

"What other Sef is there?"

She hissed and dug her heel into the nearest patch of broken glass. "What power does he have over you?" Did he—" Her voice cut off, and suddenly her first night in Cairo started to make a lot more sense. She pointed an accusing finger at him and asked, "Did he threaten you with something?" She narrowed her eyes. "Or did you make a deal with him?"

"It's complicated," he said again as he relaxed his position in front of her. He could tell she wasn't about to run, but that didn't mean she was subdued. He seemed to wilt under her glare, and finally raked both hands through his hair with a grunt. He opened his mouth to speak, but then tapped his ring instead.

"Explain," she said through her teeth.

"We'll have to visit Aida another night. Visiting hours are over now."

Imara scoffed and turned away from him. "That's not what I meant."

He pressed his palms against his face and let out a sigh. "There are rules we have to follow," he said. "We aren't allowed to rescue children when it's past curfew." He tugged at the collar of his shirt. "That's the deal."

"So you *did* make a deal with a cartel leader." She hoped the tone of accusation in her voice stung him as much as this secret stung her.

But when she looked closer, she could see signs of anger bubbling under his shame. A clenched jaw, a lowered brow, a balled-up fist. Maybe she had been too quick to accuse him.

But maybe not.

"*I* didn't make a deal," he said. His fist drew tighter until she could see his knuckles going white. Then, nearly spitting the words out, he said, "Edrice made the deal."

At once, each of his body language signs pointing to anger intensified. Even though it was anger, it was a passionate anger. And that bothered her. Sometimes passion was passion, and anger could quickly turn to something else given the right circumstances. She didn't like that it was all directed toward a young, single, and *attractive* young woman. One he owned a business with, no less.

Abe started pacing but stopped a second later. The movement seemed to snap her out of it. Was she really doing this again? Assuming the worst? She'd already been through this same thing in the catacombs when she thought Abe had feelings for Naki. But she had been wrong about that.

Abe had earned her trust. He deserved a chance to explain. Even though the idea of making a deal with a slave cartel leader made her want to throw up.

She waited three whole seconds until her face was relaxed and then said, "What happened?"

"Sef offered us a deal a few months ago. He promised he would never attack our headquarters as long as we agreed to never rescue children who were out after curfew. I told Edrice we wouldn't sign that deal even if the apocalypse came."

"But?"

He dug his fingers into his hair and grimaced again. "She went over my head and signed the deal anyway. She insisted we needed the protection or the landlord for our headquarters would kick us out."

His nose twitched again, but then his shoulders fell, and all the anger in his expression seemed to drift away. He let out a sigh, which dropped his shoulders another centimeter. "Whatever. It's done now, and there's nothing I can do about it. But trust me, I hate the deal as much as you do."

She nodded, but nausea bubbled in her stomach. Nothing he could do? She didn't like the sound of that.

"Well," Abe said. For a moment, a flash of hope flitted through his eyes so strong she could almost see the turquoise blue swirls coming off his skin. Almost. "There is one thing we can do," he said with a half smile. Looking at him now, the hope burned as bright as if it had never left. "We need more employees, *and* we need to get rid of Sef."

She raised an eyebrow. "And you know a way to accomplish both?"

He chuckled. "Yes. See, that's what I love about you, you're quick. There's a small business fair in a couple of weeks. We have a booth and so do a bunch of other small businesses, including a few of the shell companies Sef uses as a front for his slave cartel. He never comes to fair, but a bunch of his gangsters do.

"I don't understand how that helps us," she said as a strange buzzing rang through the air. Her eyes wandered until she noticed a security camera tilting until it directly faced her. In the exact moment it stopped moving, the buzzing also stopped.

"The business fair gives us the perfect opportunity to talk to his gangsters without him there to stop us."

She peeled her eyes away from the security camera while the feeling of being watched tingled up her spine. "So?" she asked. "What are we supposed to say to them?"

Abe clapped his hands together, grinning. "Each booth has a chance to give a presentation if they choose. That gives us ten minutes where we can talk to all of the other businesses. We'll give a speech that will convince some of Sef's gang members to join us. If we can get even a few of his men on our side, we have a much better shot at getting Sef's list."

"That's…" She blinked and pursed her lips to keep from laughing out loud. With a strained smile she asked, "Who exactly is supposed to write this magical speech?"

"You."

She almost laughed again. And then she almost cried when she realized he wasn't joking. "But," she said. "I can't do that."

He took her hand and squeezed it gently. "Yes, you can."

She reached up until her fingers found the back of her neck. Short, shaved hair graced the back and sides of her hair while a mess of curls tumbled on top of it. For some reason, grabbing the short hairs at the nape of her neck always provided her with a sense of comfort. She brushed her thumb along the hairs, feeling each hair as it fluttered past. "I'm not that good at persuading people," she said with a frown.

This time, *he* laughed. "Yeah," he said, shaking his head. "That's why you led a group of people down to the trap-filled catacombs, rescued hostages, and then took down the Judge. Your old teacher, I might add, who you would have given anything to protect. Plus, every time we have to rescue a kid, it takes you less than five minutes to gain their trust."

No, Abe," she said. Maybe it should have felt good to know he believed in her like that, but all it did was flood her veins with anxiety.

He chuckled again and shook his head. "You really have no idea how amazing you are, do you?"

She tugged harder on her hair while biting too hard on her lip. "You're putting way too much trust in me. I know a few tricks to persuade, but what you're asking is completely different. I've only ever written speeches for school."

"Well," he said, glancing up at the same security camera she had noticed earlier. "I'm positive you can do it. But even if you can't, it's not like we have anything to lose if it doesn't work."

Her fingers stopped tugging as she looked at the camera. A full second passed before she realized Abe had stopped talking. Looking back at him she tried not to cry. She loved that he believed in her, but did he have to believe in her so much?

She bit her lip again. "I'll try, but it might not work. It probably won't work."

"You'll do great," Abe said with every confidence in the world. He laced his fingers in hers, and soon they were heading back for the bubble car.

As much as it hurt to admit, Abe was right. If they could get some of Sef's gangsters on their side, those gangsters might know more about the list. Maybe they could even help download it. With the list, they could take Sef down and more importantly, save Abe's business.

SIX

IMARA TAPPED HER GOLD RING AS SHE RAN down a street in Cairo. She scrolled through her hologram screen, rushing to call Abe. "Sorry," she said when his face appeared on the screen. "There was a delay at the airport."

"How close are you?" he asked. The business fair had started over an hour ago and it was almost time for her speech.

Checking her surroundings, she said, "I don't know. A couple of blocks. Am I going to be late?"

"You'll be fine," he said with a smile. He glanced over his shoulder just as Husani gave a flirtatious grin to a passerby from behind him. Abe shook his head as he turned back to face Imara. "You'll be great. Your speech will get tons of gangsters to join us, I know it."

"It's not that good," she said, though her frown was stifled by her need to jump over a broken delivery drone. The circular, industrial drone came up to her knees. The long arms coming out from the bottom were meant to carry large packages, but now they were sprawled over the pavement in a crumpled mess.

She took a quick glance back at the drone as she jumped over it. The Egyptian Council owned delivery drones and usually kept them in perfect repair. As far as she knew, Sef and his gangsters had never used them or attempted to destroy them. But that drone didn't land broken on the street by accident.

"Your speech is perfect," Abe said pulling her out of her thoughts. "I know that for a fact since you practiced it on me last night."

"We'll find out soon, I guess," she said, trying to ignore the drone. Cairo had so many problems, it didn't need another one.

She said goodbye and tapped off her ring. Just as she prepared to round a corner into an alley, a small drone flew right into her face. Without thinking, she slammed a hand against it and swatted it to the ground. With her mind already on a drone, this seemed like more than a coincidence.

When the drone hit the ground, one of its propellers bent into a crooked angle, rendering it useless. She grimaced and searched for the owner of the drone who, luckily, wasn't far.

A tall woman with thin eyes and silky, black hair stared back at her.

She looked familiar.

Imara shook the thought away. There was no time to worry about that now. "I'm sorry about your drone," she said.

The woman bent over and cradled the drone in her hands before turning to Imara with a sneer. "Look what you've done! My drone is ruined."

Imara curled her fist into a ball while heat flooded her veins. This wasn't her fault. The drone flew right in her face. What was she supposed to do? Before she could say anything she would regret, she sucked in a deep breath and tried to relax her jaw.

She had to stop seeing the worst in people. There had to be something good. The woman seemed selfish for blaming Imara for the broken drone, but there had to be more to her than that.

While the silky-haired woman bent down to retrieve the drone, Imara forced herself to look for the best instead of the worst.

"I demand you pay for the damages," the woman said as flecks of spit flew from her mouth. Her lips curled up to show her teeth as she glared. She took a step forward, brushing the toes of her shoes against Imara's. "Open your hologram and sync with me. Then, you can transfer the money to me immediately."

Imara took a step back attempting to regain her personal space. Aggressive, selfish, *and* accusatory. How could one person be all three? She jiggled her head to erase those thoughts. No, there had to be something good as well. If Abe had found something good in her, then she could find something good in this stranger. She tried to smile and tapped her hologram ring. "I'm happy to pay damages. You just need a new propeller, right? How much should I transfer to your account?"

The woman tapped her own ring and selected Imara's photo from her syncing app. While they synced, the woman tapped her hologram screen so fast Imara couldn't see what she was doing. As the woman worked, a smile seemed to hide under her lips. "Four hundred points," she said.

Imara bit her tongue, but she couldn't stop her eyes from widening. Greedy too? How was she supposed to see something good when there was so much bad? She forced herself to smile as she stared. There had to be something good. There *had* to be.

Once the syncing finished, the woman's name appeared on her hologram. Takara. As she read the name, a hidden thought in the back of her mind sprang to life. But the thought died as soon as it had appeared. Why did her name seem familiar?

Before Imara could forage through her memories, her hologram flashed, blacked out, and then flickered with a sputter. She let out a gasp and pulled her hand up until the hologram screen shined right in front of her nose. She shook her hand, hoping it would jolt the ring back to life. Instead, the hologram blacked out again before a golden stream of numbers covered the screen. Her mouth dropped, but a moment later the screen went back to normal as if nothing had ever changed. She narrowed her eyes at the hologram, searching for a trace of the golden numbers.

"What happened to your ring?" Takara asked.

"I don't know. I've never seen that happen before." She shook her hand again, but the hologram continued to shine just the same as it always did.

Takara folded her arms over her chest. "Then send me the money."

Rude, but also tenacious. Tenacious could be considered a good thing in the right circumstances. It wasn't great at this particular moment, but it was as close to a good quality as she'd get. She'd take it.

Selecting the banking app, Imara transferred four hundred points to Takara's account. While the money transferred, Imara admired the black hair Takara was brushing over her shoulder. Long, thick, and silky smooth. That was another good thing. Takara was beautiful. Of course outward beauty wasn't as important as the things inside, but she was finding it more difficult than usual to find something good about this woman. Tenacious and beautiful would have to cut it. She still needed practice seeing the best in people, but at least she was trying.

Takara smirked when the money arrived in her account. She wrapped her fingers around the drone so tight, her nails clicked against the metal. Then she walked off without a word.

‘‘‘•‘‘

Imara found the booth just as Edrice was shaking hands with a man in a business suit. Once the man walked off, Imara asked, "Am I late?"

"No," Husani said. "They'll announce our group in two minutes and eight seconds. Or they would if anyone working here was a time feeler. It will probably be more like four minutes and thirty nine seconds, which is a little ridiculous if you ask me."

Abe hid his smirk so only she could see it before he gestured to the stage. "That's where you'll stand."

She gulped as needles seemed to prick into her toes. "Why is it so big?" she asked.

The announcer came onto the stage three minutes and fifty seven seconds later, which Husani felt necessary to point out. Imara might have thanked him for the information if her insides weren't busy doing flips. She wanted to grab Abe's hand to help with her nerves. But this was a work thing, which meant they had to be professional. Stupid rule.

A clear, plastic podium sat in the middle of the stage. Bright yellow and red lights shone from light bulbs embedded inside the plastic. It gave off an eerie orange glow that made her stomach flip even harder.

Just as the announcer found his microphone app, his ring chimed with a notification.

At the exact same moment, every person in the area got a similar notification. For a moment, Imara's anxiety was staved off by curiosity. What were the odds that every person would get a notification at the exact same moment?

About a billion to one.

The announcer stared at his ring, but shook his head and looked out at the crowd. "Our next business presentation will—"

Another notification rippled through the crowd as everyone's rings chimed once again. And then it happened a third time. Unable to stave off her curiosity, Imara tapped her ring. The announcer, and almost everyone else in the room, did the same thing.

"It's a news alert," the announcer said. He narrowed his eyes at his hologram screen as an audible gulp rang through his microphone. "I'll bring it up on the wall hologram," he said.

He marched to the back wall and pressed a button, causing a large hologram to cover the entire back wall. After syncing his ring with the wall hologram, a news feed suddenly appeared. It matched the news feed that was now playing on Imara's own hologram screen.

Four separate news stations displayed simultaneously on the screen. In each of the videos, government-issued delivery drones zoomed through the air.

A news reporter's voice sounded muffled over the sound of the drones, but her words were written in subtitles on her news station's feed. "Delivery drones are being hacked. The Egyptian Council has been notified, but they don't know how it happened."

In the news feed in the top right corner, a building appeared that Imara recognized from just the other night.

The prison with Aida inside.

She narrowed her eyes at the screen and tried to relax her jaw. In each of the other three feeds, a prison loomed in the background.

"Abe," she said.

But he was already nodding, apparently having noticed the same thing. "All the drones are flying inside."

Her eyes latched onto the news feed that focused on Aida's prison. The news reporter jogged inside while the camera followed after her. She burst through the doors of the prison and gasped as she pointed to two bodies lying still on the ground.

"The drones," the news reporter said. But then she stopped and swallowed because her explanation was unnecessary. At that moment, everyone saw one of the delivery drones reach its arms out until they were wrapped around one of the prisoners. As the prisoner struggled to free himself, the drone sent out an electric shock with bright blue sparks.

The prisoner's body jolted for several seconds and then he fell to the ground. Imara clapped a hand over her mouth and whispered, "How?" She shook her head. "Who designed those drones?"

"They shouldn't be able to do that," Edrice said, surprisingly well composed. "There are safeguards in place to keep electricity from running through drone arms. Someone must have modified them."

Imara's breath shuddered as she watched the screen. The news reporter opened and closed her mouth, trying to find her words.

"They're killing the prisoners," the news reporter said. "There are already," she gulped, "four dead in this room. I don't know if they're targeting specific prisoners or if the attacks are random." She closed her eyes and muttered, "Let's get the camera out of here."

"Help!" another woman screamed from somewhere beyond the camera's reach.

The news reporter grabbed a handful of her skirt and rushed around a corner until she stood outside a prison cell. The drone had wrapped its arms around another prisoner. The moment the prisoner appeared on the screen, Abe pulled Imara's hand into a death grip.

"Aida," he said as his face hardened.

Imara's throat contracted as she tried to hold back her gasps. Abe looked ready to kill, but there was nothing he could do. Nothing any of them could do. Aida pushed against the drone arms, trying to free herself. Blue shocks flew through the arms, and soon the woman was dead on the ground.

"No!" Edrice said as she let out a strangled cry.

Husani wrapped his arm around her shoulders as she covered first her mouth and then her eyes.

Abe pulled his hand away from Imara to wipe a trail his tears had left. His breaths came out in short and heavy puffs as he stared at screen. As if staring at it would change what had happened.

Imara clutched her elbows as she forced herself to watch the news feed. Prison guards appeared, trying to shoot the delivery drone out of the air. The bullets seemed to have no effect on the drones, and soon the drone reached its arms toward the prison guard.

The news reporter started running from the building the moment the drone headed for the guard. She clutched her hot pink hijab in a death grip as she ran.

In the middle of the screen, a new feed popped up showing a tiny and very old woman from the Egyptian Council. "Someone hacked the delivery drones," she said. "Not all the drones, just a few. We tracked down the location of the hacking and should be able to stop this attack soon." She paused to whisper with another Egyptian Council member and then said, "We just bypassed the hacking on one drone. We should have the others down in a few minutes. Rest assured, we'll put security protocols in place to prevent this from ever happening again."

A third Egyptian Council member rushed to the woman's side. "We got him," the man said. "The drones are down."

The Egyptian Council members spoke quietly with each other for a few moments and then the old woman said, "There were five drones total." A quiet silence filled the air as the Egyptian Council members hung their heads. "Twenty eight deaths in all."

A shiver ran up Imara's spine. So much death in such a short amount of time. Who could possibly do something like this? And who had the hacking skills necessary to infiltrate government-issued drones? With hacking involved, her mind automatically went to one person. Someone who wouldn't mind targeting prisoners either.

Professor Santini.

She shook the thought out before she could run away with it. Professor Santini was dead. She had run deep into the catacombs knowing the oncoming boiling water would kill her. The rest of them barely escaped the same boiling water. They all agreed there was no possible way for her to survive. Besides, Professor Santini had excellent hacking skills, but not *that* excellent.

Before she could consider it any longer, the screen cut out both on the wall hologram on the stage and on her personal hologram ring. The red and yellow lights in the plastic podium shined brighter, making the stage look like it was engulfed in flames. A tall woman with silky, black hair stepped up to the podium.

Takara.

Abe seized Imara's forearm as he took in a sharp breath. She turned to him with a start. Through his teeth he said, "That woman was in the catacombs."

"What?" she asked, looking back up at the stage.

"She led that group of taggers who attacked us. The ones who left, but never came back."

Her mouth dropped as she finally remembered why the name Takara seemed so familiar. Professor Santini had said it. Now that the connection was made, she could hear the words in her head as clearly as when Professor Santini had spoken them. *A former student helped me make the helmet. Takara said everyone would assume I was a telepath, but I didn't believe it.*

Imara reached up and tugged the hair on the back of her neck so hard, a few strands came out. Not only was Takara a tagger, she was the next in line after Professor Santini. Maybe the only one capable of continuing Professor Santini's work.

The taggers were back, but this time Imara wouldn't sit back and do nothing.

She jumped forward, ready to storm the stage. Abe caught her hand and said, "Not here. We need more information. Let's listen to her first."

She folded her arms in front of her chest, knowing he was right. She gritted her teeth with a frown. Maybe she would listen, but she didn't have to do it happily.

Takara stood at the podium with a sickly sweet smile. "Hello," she said. "You may have heard of the taggers in Alexandria. Well, now we're here, and we're taking over."

A murmur went through the crowd, but Takara ignored it and tapped her ring. She scrolled through her screen and then began reading words off the hologram. "Cairo is a beautiful city, but also flawed. What once was great, is now crumbling under the oppression of those too powerful to overcome. Like each of us, Cairo is beautiful, but flawed. And like each of us, Cairo is in need of help."

Imara gasped at the words. Her mind went back to those golden numbers on her hologram screen that appeared after her encounter with Takara. Now she understood why.

"Can Cairo be saved?" Takara asked. "Does Cairo deserve a chance? The answer is yes. Let me tell you how."

"She stole my speech," Imara whispered as her teeth gritted together. "She synced with me, and my ring went crazy. She must have heard us talking about it. She must have…"

Too busy gaping at Takara, Abe didn't react to her words until she grabbed his arm.

"The other night," she said. "A security camera watched us. She must have hacked it and heard our conversation. She knew I wrote a speech, and then she found me and stole it. She's going to get new followers, and it will be my fault."

Takara stood at the podium, promising change and hope. Even after murdering so many people, the words instilled courage and action.

"Let's go," Abe said, turning toward the exit. They all followed him without a second glance at the stage. They didn't need another reminder of all they had lost.

SEVEN

IMARA MARCHED DOWN THE ROAD WHILE A gut-wrenching fury filled her body. The only footsteps heavier than hers were Abe's.

"This is why I wanted to stop Santini while we were in the catacombs," he said through his teeth. "I thought the taggers would stop after she was gone. But your friend Siluk was right. They're continuing the work without her."

Husani picked up a shard of glass from the street and chucked it into a wall. "We already have Sef to deal with. How are we supposed to deal with another power-hungry murderer?"

"Who cares about that?" Edrice shouted as she plunged forward. "Aida is dead." Edrice lowered her head. "She never even got to see our headquarters."

Abe turned away with a sniff. Imara reached out to comfort him, but before her hand raised more than a few centimeters, a shock buzzed through her ring. She instinctively flicked her hand at the gentle flutter. She tapped her ring on, and the gold numbers flooded her hologram screen once again. "My ring is glitching," she said.

Another shock buzzed through her ring, but this time it felt much stronger than a flutter. Her heart raced as she remembered the drones. Could Takara have done something more to her ring than just steal the speech?

She scrolled through her hologram screen, searching for a way to stop the golden numbers. They rounded a corner, and Husani nearly toppled over a girl with long, silky black hair. He reached for her forearm to steady himself, but she shoved him away and aimed a gun.

Edrice gasped and curled herself into a ball at the edge of the alley.

"Stay back!" the girl shouted.

"Hey," Abe said, not staring at the girl, but at the gun. A stun gun.

She jabbed the gun toward him, but he simply plucked it from her hand. "This is *my* stun gun. Where did you get this?"

Without waiting for an order, Husani grabbed the girl and held her hands behind her back. She struggled against him, but Husani held tight.

Forgetting her ring for a moment, Imara looked at the girl's face. The long, silky black hair reminded her of Takara, but soon, the memory of another face filled her mind.

"This is the stun gun we lost in the catacombs," Abe said as he ran his finger over the serial number.

"Keiko?" Imara asked, staring at the girl. This was the very same girl Imara met only minutes before Naki and the others were kidnapped by the Judge. Keiko had been bullying a boy and would have pushed him with a hover cart if Imara hadn't stepped in. Keiko had been jealous then, but watching her body language now, she only looked afraid and far from dangerous. Imara shook her head and said, "Husani, let her go."

Husani and Edrice seemed to relax at Imara's words, but Abe only glared.

"No," Abe said, holding the stun gun in front of her. "This is the gun the *taggers* stole from us inside the catacombs. They were the last ones to have it."

Imara blinked at the gun but then looked at Keiko with an expression she hoped was comforting. "Where did you get this?" Just as she asked, another zing of electricity shot through her hand.

Keiko's gaze immediately fell on Imara's hologram screen, which still showed nothing but a stream of golden numbers.

"Hey," Abe said. "Answer the question."

Keiko glared at Husani as she pulled away from him. "It's a long story."

Husani let her go, but reached for her hair. "You kind of look like this murderous tagger we saw on the news."

You mean Takara?" Keiko said as she slapped Husani's hand away. "Are you just saying that because I'm Japanese like her? We all look alike to you?"

"No," Husani said, waving his hands through the air. "I didn't mean it like that. I love the global culture we have now."

Keiko nudged an empty take-out container on the ground with her toe. With her eyes on the ground she muttered, "I'm kidding. Takara is my mother, and we do look alike."

"WHAT?" Husani yelled as he stepped back.

"Abe, stun her," Edrice said, cowering against the alley wall.

The black-haired girl hissed and sent the take-out container soaring. "It's not like I *want* her to be my mother.

70

I'm even half Egyptian, but apparently my genes thought it would be hilarious to make me look exactly like my mother, who I hate. And nothing like my father, who is literally the best."

Before anyone could respond, another shock shot out of Imara's ring. This one was powerful enough that it tightened all the muscles in her hand and forearm.

"My ring," she said looking at Abe. "It's shocking me. I think Takara did something when she synced with me earlier."

Abe's eyes flitted between Imara and Keiko, trying to decide which one needed more attention. But then, another jolt ran up her arm so strong, she gasped.

"I can fix it," Keiko said.

"No," Abe said glaring at her.

Keiko glared back. "My mother made the virus that's doing that. I spent a lot of my childhood trying to stop viruses like that. My mother forced me to do it so she could learn how to make the viruses even more unstoppable. But I know her style."

Abe gave Keiko a long sideways glance before he turned to Imara. "How do you know this girl? Can we trust her?"

Keiko stood up on her toes and pushed her chin out. "How do I know I can trust *you*?" she asked. "I don't like your face very much."

"Feisty, huh?" Husani said with a chuckle. "I've always liked a feisty girl."

Edrice rolled her eyes, still curled into a corner of the alley. "You like *any* girl."

Another jolt went through Imara's arm, and she threw her hand toward Keiko. "Fix it," she said. "And while you're doing it, tell us how you got this stun gun."

Keiko started tapping on the hologram screen and said, "Basically, my dad and I ran into the taggers when they were on their way back to the catacombs to kill you guys. And..." She shrugged. "We stopped them. After the fight, I stole the gun. I didn't know it was yours. I thought it belonged to the taggers."

"But why are you in Cairo?" Imara asked again.

Keiko sighed. "We were trying to get away from my mother."

Another shock came out from Imara's ring, this one sending a jolt up to her shoulder.

Keiko's eyebrows flew up her forehead. "Hang on. I almost got it." A moment later, she hissed at the screen. "She wrote this in Japanese."

"Don't you know Japanese?" Husani asked.

"No."

Imara shuddered, and Keiko quickly said, "Don't worry, I can still fix it. I'm almost there."

"Why don't you know Japanese?" Husani asked.

"Because," Keiko said. "They only teach English, the global language, in schools now, and unfortunately, my mother only taught me things that would help her, not things that would help me."

Just then, another shock started, but Keiko tapped the screen, and it died, stopping the shock before it went up Imara's arm. "Better?" Keiko asked.

Imara shook out her hand and looked at her hologram screen, which was back to normal. "Much better."

Husani took the opportunity to step closer to Keiko. "You said your dad is Egyptian though, so do you know Arabic?"

Keiko rolled her eyes. "My *dear* mother said Arabic is inferior to Japanese and wouldn't let my dad teach it to me. But she wouldn't teach me Japanese either because she never *had time*. So now I know nothing about my heritage on either side, but at *least* I know English. Who cares if we all forget our native languages, right?"

"You think it's stupid that we have a global language? You don't like the global culture?" Edrice asked, finally braving to leave her spot in the corner of the alley.

"No, it's not that," Keiko said. "I love the global culture. Travel has never been faster or cheaper. But I guess with any change, there are good and bad things about it. I'm just sad I don't know anything about my heritage."

Husani took another step toward Keiko until there was less than a footstep between them. With a smirk he asked, "You don't know *anything* about Egypt?"

Keiko raised an eyebrow, but didn't step away from him, even though his shoulder had brushed up against her. "Do you always ask this many questions?"

He hooked his arm around her elbow and said, "Only when I'm talking to someone as beautiful as you. If you need a tutor, I'd be happy to teach you a few things about Egypt."

Edrice snorted and rolled her eyes.

"Can we trust her?" Abe asked, focused more on Keiko now that Imara's ring was working properly.

"Yes," Imara said. She thought it best not to explain, but based on the body language Keiko exhibited when talking

73

about her mom, it was obvious she'd been hurt in much more than the normal ways by her mother.

"Well then," Husani said, running his fingers over Keiko's hair. "Welcome to the club. If you need a job, we're hiring." He tilted his head. "On second thought, if you work with us I won't be able to flirt with you, and that would be a tragedy."

Keiko grimaced. "I'm only sixteen, and the global working age is eighteen."

"Even better," Husani said as he took in a not-so-subtle sniff of her hair. "Just promise you'll come to our headquarters every once in awhile for those lessons on Egyptian culture. What's your hila?"

"Let's go back to headquarters," Abe said. "We need to figure out what we're going to do about the taggers, if anything. Maybe Sef will get rid of them for us."

Imara fell into step beside Abe, itching to take his hand, but figured this wasn't the time.

"I'm a sound seer," Keiko said after Husani poked her.

"Fresh," he replied. "I'm a time feeler, and Edrice has photographic memory. Abe and Imara are both mashimo."

"Mashimo?" Keiko asked, giving Imara a sideways glance.

Luckily, Imara was spared from having to explain when Husani asked, "You got any weird hobbies because of your hila?"

"I play the violin," Keiko said with a shrug. "Which is *not* weird, but I do have perfect pitch because I can see sound waves."

Husani wolf whistled. "I've always loved a lady who plays music."

Edrice smacked Husani so hard his shoulder reeled back. "You love anyone with two eyes and a mouth. And maybe you'd compromise a little bit on the eye thing." She turned to Keiko with a much gentler expression. "That is interesting about the violin. Are you in an orchestra at school?"

Keiko's body wilted. She looked down at the ground, sticking her thumbs into her pockets. "No. My violin is stuck at my old hila school. I'm not a student there anymore, so I can't get in and get my stuff. The owner is being a jerk about it."

"Abe can help with that," Imara said.

"Can I?" Abe asked.

She let out a soft chuckle. "Unfortunately, your dad is the jerk owner Keiko is talking about. Keiko was the one at the graduation party who pushed the cart at that tagger boy."

Abe stopped in the middle of the road and his jaw dropped. He stood still for several seconds, and then looked at Keiko with all new eyes. "You're the reason Imara and I met," he said. He rubbed his chin in thought. "My dad is coming to visit in a few days. I'll ask him to bring your stuff with him. But before that, why don't you tell us everything you know about Takara."

ಬಬಙಓಙಓ

Abe sat at his desk, trying not to stare at the door where Imara had left mere minutes ago. He was supposed to be on his way to Kenya with her right now, but that plan died with the drone attack. A million and one problems had just arisen thanks to Takara. There were already rumors about groups of

75

Sef's gangsters who had joined the taggers. He knew Imara understood, but he still felt guilty.

"Is Imara really mashimo?" Keiko asked suddenly. "I thought she was a truth seer."

He clenched his jaw and stared at his desk, not sure if he could explain without punching something. Luckily, Edrice saved him.

"Do you ever watch the news?" Edrice asked.

"I hate the news," Keiko said with a glare. "My mother is on it way too much."

Edrice raised an eyebrow, but let it fall a moment later. "Do either of you know what happened in the catacombs? Keiko, I understand, but Husani? Didn't you bother checking the news feeds to see what Abe was doing that whole time? Didn't you ever wonder what could possibly be so important to him that he would leave us for five days without any warning?"

Husani shrugged. "Oh come on, it was for his dad. Abe would drop anything for his dad, no matter what the cost."

"What happened?" Keiko asked. "I mean, I know a little. I saw this one recap where they said Imara was a talented truth seer, and she killed the Judge. But then the music got all depressing, and I stopped watching."

Husani cocked his head to the side. "But she's not a truth seer. She's mashimo."

"She didn't kill the Judge," Abe said, jumping to his feet.

They all started as if they had forgotten he was there. He curled his hands into fists and glared. "The Judge killed herself, even after Imara tried to save her. And Imara's not technically mashimo. She..." His fist curled tighter, but they

76

were all staring at him now. No matter how much it hurt, he had to finish. At least Imara wasn't here to say it herself.

Abe gulped. "Imara jumped through an eraserfall in order to save us. She sacrificed everything to stop the Judge from tagging."

Husani looked mystified, but it was nothing to the expression of pure horror that covered Keiko's face.

"Eraserfall?" she whispered.

Abe nodded, trying to regain his composure. "Imara gave up her hila to fight against the taggers. We owe it to her to stop them once and for all."

EIGHT

A FEW DAYS LATER, SEF'S GANGSTERS STILL terrorized Cairo, the taggers now added their own tricks, and all Imara could think about were her dinner plans. Dinner with Abe.

And his dad.

She slumped onto the couch in Abe's apartment fidgeting with her powder blue wrap dress. She tried forcing her fingers to stop tugging at the fabric, but they wouldn't be stilled. She reached up for the hair on the back of her neck instead.

Abe's head popped around the corner. "My dad is on his way. He just dropped Keiko's stuff off at headquarters."

She tried to smile, but bit her lip instead.

Abe chuckled and went back into the kitchen. "He's excited about this, by the way," Abe called from the other room. "For all three of us to have dinner together."

She jumped to her feet and scurried into the kitchen. "Can I please help? I'm going to go crazy if I don't do something with my hands."

He set down his whisk and dropped a hand onto her shoulder. "Don't be nervous. It's going to be fine."

She reached for the short hairs on the back of her head again. She tugged each tuft until her neck burned. "When are you coming to Kenya to have dinner with Naki and my parents?" she asked.

"Agh," he said as he jumped back, a splash of juice barely missing his pants. He reached for a towel. "I'm sorry it's been so crazy lately, but I promise we'll do it soon. When things calm down a little. Before my dad gets here, I wanted to ask you about Keiko."

Imara clasped her fingers together, forcing them to stay still. "What about her?"

Abe went back to whisking his sauce and said, "You trust her, which is the only reason I trust her. But her mom is the leader of the taggers. Are we sure she isn't going to..."

"Spy on us to help her mom?" Imara finished.

"Yeah."

"No."

Abe poured the finished sauce over a plate of chicken. "You don't think she would?"

Imara leaned against the wall, tapping her teeth together as she tried to decide how to explain. Finally, she said, "You remember the other day when she flinched like you were going to hit her?"

Abe grimaced so hard, his shoulders jerked. "I don't know why she assumed I'm that kind of person. I never would have hit her."

"Abe." Imara waited until he looked her right in the eyes. "She didn't assume that about you. It was a reflex. She did that because she's used to..."

In an instant, his face fell. "She's used to someone else hitting her?" He shook his head. "Takara."

Imara nodded, grateful that the conversation had provided her a moment of distraction. But a second later, someone knocked on the door, and her heart seemed to stop. She clutched the wall behind her, and Abe chuckled.

He put his hands on her shoulders, and the warmth from them spread down through her arms. "Relax," he said. "And remember, no talking about work. This is supposed to be fun."

She stood behind Abe as he answered the door. Mr. Nazari embraced his son while wearing a wide smile. But when Abe stepped back and reached for Imara, Mr. Nazari's smile disappeared.

"Imara," he said with a nod.

"Hi, Mr. Nazari." She twisted a piece of her blue dress around her thumb while she decided whether or not she should shake his hand. That seemed weird. But it seemed weird to do nothing too. Mr. Nazari stared back with no expression at all. Maybe she just needed to adjust the temperature controls on her underclothing because it suddenly seemed about five degrees warmer.

"Let's go eat," Abe said with a smile.

ಜಜುಣೞೞ

Hours later, Imara dropped a pile of dishes into the sink. Abe made her promise she wouldn't wash them, but he was still outside saying goodbye, and she needed to keep herself busy.

"Hey, you promised," he said when he walked in a few minutes later.

She scrubbed the last bowl clean and set it in the QuickDry before speaking. "I don't think your dad likes me very much."

"What?" Abe said and then chuckled. "Of course he does."

Imara dried her hands with a towel until they were rubbed raw. "He's so…" She waved her hand through the air, trying to think of the right word. "Closed. He's hard for me to read. and it drives me nuts, especially without my hila."

"He doesn't hate you," Abe said, leading her out of the kitchen and back to the couch.

He dropped down next to her and leaned in as if to kiss her, but stopped a few centimeters short. Narrowing his eyes, he said, "You have that stuff in your eye again. You must have allergies or something because it gets worse the longer you're in Cairo."

"Did you do this in the catacombs?" she asked, tilting her head up so he could wipe the goop away. She never seemed to notice it herself, and since she was still avoiding mirrors, she appreciated Abe removing it for her. "I've been trying to remember" she said. "It seems like ever since we met, you've been getting stuff out of my eyes, but I can't think of a time it happened in the catacombs."

He wiped the goop onto his shirt and moved his finger toward her other eye. "I can't remember either. Are you sure you're not allergic to anything?"

She snickered. "You're the only one who seems to see it. Are *you* sure you aren't just using it as an excuse to be close to me?"

"Maybe," he said with a sly smile. He leaned in again, this time not stopping until his lips pressed against hers. All the worry about what his dad thought of her seemed to vanish.

When he pulled away, she settled her head on his shoulder and asked, "Who's Onofria?"

She felt the muscles in his shoulder tense as he pulled away from her. "What?" He swallowed. "What do you mean?"

As she stared, a flash of plum erupted from his skin, wriggling out like a worm. Discomfort. A moment later, it was gone. She stared again, barely noticing how her heart seemed to stop. A plum-colored worm coming out from the skin? She used to see things like that all the time with her hila, but her hila was gone. She shouldn't have been able to see things like that now.

But now the moment had passed. No more colors, plum or otherwise, came out from his skin. It must have been a trick of the lights, or it must have been in her head. No healer in the world had been able to heal a hila after an eraserfall. It must have been nothing.

"I saw the name embroidered on your dad's handkerchief at dinner. Onofria Nazari. Does your dad have a sister or something?"

Abe stared with his lips parted. She found herself searching for more colors coming off his skin, but she knew, she *knew* it was hopeless. She went through an eraserfall. Her hila would never come back.

The seconds ticked by, and still Abe stared. His nostrils flared each time he let out a breath. Suddenly, he sucked in a gulp of air and leaned deep into the couch. He glanced at her again, then stared at his lap. "Onofria my mom," he said.

Her back shot up straight as she turned toward him. "Wait, what?" She shook her head. "How do you have a mom?"

He smirked. "Well, you see. I actually thought you would have learned this from school, but that's okay. You see, in

82

order to get a baby, you have to have DNA from both a male and a female."

"Oh, shush," she said, nudging him in the shoulder. "You know what I meant."

He snickered and tugged a curl down over her forehead.

She screwed up her face, trying to remember the details of a conversation they'd had weeks ago. "I thought your dad wasn't into romance," she said.

"Yeah, he's not. Not anymore. My mom was the only one he loved like that." He looked down while he tugged at the bottom of his shirt. "She died when I was three."

"Abe." She covered her eyes with one hand and simultaneously used her other hand to grab his forearm. "I had no idea."

"I know," he said, each word dropping heavy like rocks. "I don't usually talk about it. Well, that's not true. My dad and I talk about it all the time. He's open with me, but with everyone else, he's basically learned to turn off all emotion."

"That explains a lot," she said, reaching for his hand. He took it willingly, and she noticed at once how much warmer than usual it felt. She wrapped her spare hand around the back of his and traced his knuckles with her fingers. What could she say? What could anyone say in the face of such tragedy?

He ran his other hand through his hair before letting out a sigh. "I don't remember her. My dad tells me about her all the time, which is good, I guess. I know what kind of a person she was and how much she loved me and everything." He squeezed her hand and swallowed. "Sometimes I wish I had just one actual memory of her. She was really amazing apparently."

"I'm so sorry," she whispered.

He shrugged and said, "It's okay. It's horrible, obviously, but I've adjusted well. My dad, on the other hand, has never gotten over it."

She doubted anyone could be completely adjusted after a tragedy like that, but she decided not to voice that particular thought. She dropped her head onto his shoulder, feeling the need to be close. She wanted to support him, but all she could really do was be there for him. At least she would be there in every way she could.

Touching him so he could feel that she was there for him. Talking so he could hear it. "How did she die?" she asked.

She looked up just in time to see him bite the inside of his cheek. "A freak accident. She had a filtered water bottle, but it was mostly empty. She flicked the straw to suck up the last little bit of water. When she did that, part of the filter shot up and lodged in her throat. The chemicals seeped into her esophagus and poisoned her. It was in there for a week, and she didn't know anything was wrong because she couldn't feel it. By the time she noticed, it was already too late."

Imara drew her finger along the inside of Abe's forearm. His jaw worked as if he had more to say, but the words stayed inside his throat. She looked into his eyes and gave his hand a little squeeze, hoping to coax the words out of him. After a moment, he continued.

"My dad is mashimo, and my mom only had a vague knowledge of her hila. Apparently, if she had known how to use her hila, she would have known the filter piece was in her throat, and she could have gotten it removed before the poison killed her." He paused. "She died because she didn't know how to use her hila."

84

"What was her hila?"

"She was a healer."

Imara dropped his hand and sat up straight.

"No," he said. "I know what you're going to say, and no. Just because she was a healer doesn't mean I am."

She pursed her lips, forcing back the words she wanted to say. Finally, some words burst free despite her restraint. "Hilas *can* run in the family like that."

"But they don't always," he said, clenching his jaw. "Besides, my dad is mashimo. That runs in the family too."

She sat up, still wanting to argue, but eventually chose to relax back in her seat. She was still ninety percent certain he was a healer, but this probably wasn't the best moment to argue about it.

"That's why my dad started his hila school," Abe said almost as an afterthought. "My mom died because she didn't know how to use her hila, and my dad had survivor's guilt to the extreme. He made it his mission in life to help people learn how to use their hilas as best as possible. It's a good mission and everything, but at some point he has to accept it wasn't his fault she died."

Imara nodded, slowly letting it all wash over her. "Is that why you're so reckless?" she asked.

Abe jerked his head toward her with one eyebrow raised.

"So your dad won't blame himself if you get hurt?"

Abe laughed and said, "No." He shook his head and laughed again. "Maybe I just like being irresponsible."

"Abe."

"No," he said with more insistence. "I said I'm well adjusted, remember? I'm happy. I miss my mom every day, but I'm fine. Why does everyone think I have some mysterious unresolved issues just because my mom died when I was three?"

"Your brain isn't mature enough to deal with every issue at three, so it stores issues in the back of your mind until you *are* old enough to deal with them."

He raised an eyebrow at her. "You're a psychologist now?"

Her shoulders fell as she dropped her eyes to stare at her lap. "Professor Santini taught me that." She looked up again, nodding as she spoke. "Yes, I know she was the Judge, and I know she taught me some messed up stuff, but you have to admit it does seem logical. How could you be sad about your mom missing your school graduation when you're only three and don't even know school exists?"

He reached for his chin and started rubbing his thumb back and forth along its bottom edge. "I guess that sort of makes sense, but I promise I'm fine. You should be more worried about that goop in your eyes."

She thought back to the goop while simultaneously thinking if Abe's mom was a healer, he had to be too. And then the two thoughts connected. No one except Abe ever saw it. And earlier, when he got the stuff out of her eyes, she saw plum worms of discomfort coming off his skin. Maybe it was just a trick of the lights, but what if the goop had something to do with the eraserfall? What if Abe was healing her without realizing it?

It was impossible. *Impossible.* But what if it wasn't?

NINE

THE NEXT FEW NIGHTS, NAKI WAS ALREADY in bed by the time Imara made it home to their apartment. When she finally got there early enough to see her sister, Naki assaulted her with a hug the moment she stepped through the door.

"I'm so glad you're here, Imara. My favorite sister."

Imara laughed and locked the door behind her. "I'm your only sister."

Naki shrugged. "Still my favorite. Mom and Dad were here an hour ago to see you, but you were late, as usual, and they went home."

"It was important," Imara said biting her lip. "We had to figure out how to send a message to some of Sef's gangsters. A bunch of them joined the taggers, but Abe thinks we can still get at least some of them to join us."

Naki rolled her eyes and skipped down the hall. "I know, I know. Something important came up. It always does."

Imara shuffled into her room and pulled her shoes off slowly. She hadn't seen any more emotions since the night at Abe's apartment, but that didn't change her Abe-is-a-healer theory. She was more convinced than ever now that she knew his mom was a healer. Then again, she was still getting used to the idea that he even had a mom.

It wasn't until both of her shoes sat on the ground that she noticed Naki staring at her from the doorway.

"What's with you?" Naki asked. "Why are you so quiet?"

"Um." She tapped her teeth together before reaching for the hair on her neck. "It's a long story."

Naki jumped onto Imara's bed and propped her chin onto her hands. "I love long stories. Especially if they involve a bit of drama."

Imara chuckled and pulled her knees up to her chin. The story belonged to Abe, not her. But he was her boyfriend, which made his stories her stories. In a way.

Naki blinked furiously and propped her chin up further. "Tell me, tell me," she said.

Imara chuckled again. Abe never said she couldn't tell anyone. And Naki was her sister. Sisters were supposed to bond.

She took in a deep breath. "Abe has a mom."

"Yeah, right," Naki said with a snort. "You mean the woman who donated her DNA so he could be born?" She chuckled to herself until her eyes met Imara's. Her jaw dropped, and she sat up straight. "Seriously?"

"She died when Abe was three."

Naki clapped a hand over her mouth. "I always thought Mr. Nazari bought donor DNA and used a surrogate to have Abe."

"So did I," Imara said. "Apparently she died from flicking her water bottle." As soon as the words left her mouth, a strange sensation swept through her. A flood of memories entered her mind, causing a ripple of guilt that compounded each second. "Oh, no," she said.

"What is it?" Naki asked worried.

Imara dropped her head into her palms and shook it back and forth. "In the catacombs." She shook her head again. "I was flicking my water bottle, and Abe told me to stop. I could see he was scared, even though I had no idea why. But then…"

She hit the palm of her hand to her forehead over and over. "Immediately after that, I told Abe his dad started the hila school because of greed." She looked down while the guilt settled into every corner of her body. "His dad started the school so no one would die like his wife did, and I told Abe it was because he wanted money."

"That's awkward," Naki said, failing to conceal a smile.

"I have to call him and apologize."

"Oh," Naki said, sitting up straight. "Before I forget. Sorry, I know this is terrible timing, but I'll forget otherwise. Guess who Basara and I ran into today?"

Imara jerked her head toward her sister. "Who's Basara?"

"My boyfriend."

Imara cocked one eyebrow up. "Since when do you have a boyfriend?"

Naki laughed and flipped her hand through the air. "Since yesterday. Don't worry about it. It won't last. He's way too clingy. It'll be a solid two-week romance, and then I'll have to let him go."

Imara rolled her eyes. "That sounds like a really fulfilling relationship."

"I'm bored," Naki said. "You keep running off to Egypt when we're supposed to go to the movies, and I was getting lonely. I'll break up with him once you start spending time here. Aren't we supposed to be friends now?"

Her gut twisted at these words. They *were* supposed to be friends now. Apparently it would take more than just being roommates. She did want to make things up to Naki. She wanted it more than anything. But she didn't know where to start, and things had been so busy with the taggers and Sef to deal with.

"Can I meet him at least?" she asked.

"Forget about Basara. I have to tell you who we saw. It was that police lady who loves you. Serafina or something."

"Safiya?" Imara asked, remembering the woman who interviewed her before she went into the catacombs.

"Yes, Safiya. She said she needs your help."

Imara tapped her ring to check if Safiya had messaged her, but Naki grabbed her hand and shook her head. "No, she said she couldn't send a message. She wants to meet you tonight outside the Nairobi Gallery. I have a note for you."

Naki tapped her own ring and sent the note to Imara's phone. Imara tapped her ring back on, but tilted her head to the side as she pulled up the note. "Why didn't she just message me?" Imara asked.

Naki shrugged and jumped toward the door. "No idea. I'm going to the park with Basara to listen to that band I keep telling you about. Will you please come hang out with Basara and me when you're done talking to Safiya?"

"Sure," Imara said, staring at the note. But then she jerked her head up. "Oh, but after I call Abe. I have to apologize about the water bottle thing."

Naki rolled her eyes, but a frown tugged at her lips. "That will take you all night. You two never run out of things to talk about. Forget it, we can hang out another time."

Imara's gut twisted again as Naki left the room, but there was nothing she could do about it right then. Safiya's note said she needed to meet, and Imara had to leave immediately to get there in time.

Only a minute later, she was out the door.

TEN

WHEN IMARA ARRIVED AT THE NAIROBI Gallery, Safiya called to her from behind a column. The woman's afro bobbed as she greeted Imara with a warm smile.

"Imara," she said. "I'm so glad you could find time to discuss Imamu's case again. Your insight was invaluable. I'm excited to work with you more."

"Uh," Imara said. The message didn't mention anything about Imamu. In truth, she didn't even remember who Imamu was. She opened her mouth to explain but stopped when she noticed Safiya's pursed lips.

Safiya covered her mouth as if she was coughing. In a voice lower than a whisper, she said, "We're being watched. Follow me, and I'll explain everything."

With a gulp, Imara arranged her face into a look she hoped wasn't too suspicious. Safiya started chattering about the expertise of the Kenyan police force and how they were receiving another global award.

Soon, they ducked into an alley and rushed past abandoned buildings. The whole thing felt like one of the missions with Abe, and she didn't know what to make of it.

At the end of the alley, Imara panted trying to keep up. Safiya glanced back and stopped with a start. "Sorry," she said. "My hila is speed. I forget that's too fast for most people."

They rounded the corner and jogged through a few more alleys. Finally, they arrived at the back of an abandoned building. Safiya looked both ways before she used a digital key on her hologram ring to open the door. Once inside, Imara saw pictures plastered all over the walls, a few chairs positioned about the room, and several food wrappers littering the floor.

She sat in the chair Safiya pointed out until they directly faced one another. "I'm sorry for all the secrecy," Safiya said. "I wouldn't have come to you, but I'm extremely desperate."

Imara scanned the room again, but it didn't help her anymore than it had the first time. "You need my help?" she asked.

Safiya's afro bobbed as she nodded. "I need someone who can read lies."

Imara frowned before she dropped her chin to her chest. "I still don't have my hila. They say eraserfalls can't be healed."

Safiya nodded and bit her lip. "I know, but I was hoping…" She stopped and looked to the side for a moment. "I know you don't have your hila, but in her recommendation, your professor was highly complimentary of your skills. She suggested you might know enough simply about body language to tell when people are lying. Even without your hila."

"That's…" Imara trailed off, unable to continue. The reminder of Professor Santini sent a familiar shock through her. She tried to ignore it as she swallowed over the lump in her throat. "I don't know. I can try, but I relied a lot on my hila." She looked down. "More than I realized."

Safiya's eyebrows lowered as she tilted her head to the side. "I'm so sorry. I can't imagine the pain you're going through. I know each day must still be a challenge, and I promise I wouldn't have come to you at all. Except... like I said before, I'm desperate. Extremely desperate."

Imara gulped and reached up to tug the hair on the back of her neck. She looked at Safiya, considering her words, but didn't promise anything yet.

Safiya went on undeterred. "Here's the thing. Funny things started happening a few weeks ago. Criminals have been getting away while innocent citizens are framed. Half the people I arrest these days don't feel like the right guy. I used to be one of the most efficient detectives, and now I don't know if we're catching the right people."

Safiya looked into Imara's eyes. "I think there's someone in our department who's being bribed or blackmailed to give out bad information."

Imara's mouth dropped. She couldn't help it. The Kenyan police force hadn't always been efficient or trustworthy. But one hundred years ago, when Nairobi became home to the first hila, everything changed. Almost overnight, Kenya became the most important place in the world. Everyone wanted to move there.

Things changed, and for the most part, Kenya got better. A lot better. Now it was home to one of the most efficient, trustworthy, and well-respected police forces in all the world. But if what Safiya said was true, that could be gone in a matter of months.

Imara yanked a small tuft of hair on the back of her neck. "I'll try to help," she said. "I don't know how much I can do without my hila, but I'll try."

Safiya smiled. "That's fine. I want you to watch some videos. I already have a guess about who is involved. I just need someone who is unbiased to watch the videos and form an opinion. If it's the same as I what I think, I'll move forward to step two of my plan."

Imara nodded.

Safiya tapped her ring and used her fingers to enlarge the screen. Then, she moved it so Imara could have a clear view.

Imara leaned forward to watch, every muscle in her body attentive. The video showed a press conference for some big police case that had just been closed.

Four members of the Kenyan police force took turns answering questions about the case. Imara watched, still looking for glowy or dulling skin, even though she knew she would never see it. But then, something caught her eye. One of the policemen scratched his nose and deflected his eyes as he answered a question.

Imara narrowed her eyes and watched more carefully. She couldn't see his skin dull, but it felt like he was lying. She felt it in her gut, just like she had before her hila manifested when she was young. She watched for a few more minutes and noticed his breathing kept changing. And every time he had to answer a question, he would turn his head to look the other way.

No one else exhibited deceptive behavior until the very end. A policewoman covered her mouth while she explained that they didn't have help solving the case. It wasn't necessarily incriminating, but Imara could tell it was a lie.

The video ended and Safiya held up her pointer finger before Imara could speak. "Don't say anything yet. I have two more videos. I want to know if you see a pattern."

Imara nodded as Safiya started the next video. In this one, the woman from the other video was lying left and right. But her body language demonstrating the lies was almost too pronounced. Almost as if she wanted to look like she was lying. The man who had lied before looked more truthful in this video, but Imara knew in her gut he also lied.

The last video was similar to the first. At the end, Safiya looked at her expectantly. Imara pointed to the man and said, "He's lying. In all three videos."

Safiya quirked an eyebrow up with a satisfied grin. "Thought so."

Imara then pointed to the woman. "I don't know for sure about her, but something funny is definitely going on."

Safiya's eyebrows rose before she looked carefully at her hologram screen. "Interesting," she said.

Imara continued. "She only lied a little, but it was really strange. In the second video she acted like she was lying, but her body language seemed deliberate. It was like someone had instructed her to do those things, not like they were happening naturally."

"That's very interesting." Safiya as she tapped her chin in thought. Without warning, she turned off her ring. "That is tremendously helpful. You have no idea."

Imara sat up straighter with a growing smile.

"I hear the taggers are back," Safiya said. "I saw a few news feeds about it, and Naki told me you've been working in Egypt where they are."

All the pride, Imara felt a moment earlier came crashing down. "Yes," she said, glowering at the ground. "We're trying to recruit new employees so we can hopefully get rid of the taggers."

Safiya patted her on the shoulder. "If anyone can convince people of something, it's you. I wish you the best of luck."

"Thanks," she said with a tiny smile.

Safiya strolled to the door to let them both out. At the last second, she turned and said, "Oh, and Imara? Don't tell anyone about what happened here today."

ELEVEN

IMARA RUSHED INTO HER BEDROOM, A month later, and grabbed the first shoes she could find. She, Abe, and the others had been sitting around making plans since Takara gave her speech at the business fair, but today they finally had the chance to *do* something.

"You promised we would go to the rugby game together," Naki said.

"I know, but something came up," Imara said as she stuffed her foot into a shoe.

Naki glared and kicked over an empty trash bin. "What is it this time?"

"Abe is trying to get new employees. He just got a message from some gangsters saying they want to join us. We have to go meet with them and see if they're genuine."

"Can't someone else go?"

"Husani and Keiko are already on a different job."

Naki grumbled and followed after Imara as she ran into the kitchen. "Can we hang out tomorrow then? And will you please bring your boyfriend because Mom and Dad are getting mad that he hasn't come to Kenya yet."

Imara froze in her place and turned on her heel. "It's not his fault," she said. "Please tell them it's not his fault. He's trying to save his business. Cairo is being overrun by taggers *and* gangsters. It's just crazy right now, but things will calm down soon."

"I'll believe that when I see it," Naki said under her breath.

Imara jumped toward her sister and tried to topple her over with a hug until Naki started laughing. "I promise, Naki," she said. "I promise things will be different soon." She looked down with a swallow. "We have a lot of lost time to catch up on."

Naki pulled away with a tiny shake of the head. "Oh, go on and save the world. Or Cairo, whichever one you're working on at the moment. And tell Abe if he doesn't come to visit soon, I'm going to start talking bad about him to Mom and Dad."

Imara rolled her eyes as she threw her purse over her shoulder. "It's going to be different soon. Just wait and see."

ဆဝဆဝ၆၃၆၃

Imara settled into the seat the waiter had offered. The restaurant seemed suspiciously empty, but it was late afternoon. Not exactly a normal meal-time. She scanned the empty tables again while a thrum of anxiety danced through her.

Abe didn't seem to share any of her concerns. He grinned at her before glancing around the room. "This is great, isn't it? Finally some of the gangsters are going to join *us* instead of Takara."

She bit her lip, eyeing the nearest exit. Before she could spend too much time thinking about running away, a group of three gangsters sat down at the table with them. Two

99

young men and a young woman, each with scars covering their knuckles and a red armband above their elbows. All three looked to be about Imara's age.

A rich, earthy smell accompanied them, reminding her of both leather and wet earth after rain. She breathed in deeply, almost forgetting why they were there.

The first one leaned forward. "We want to join you," she said.

Imara's teeth set on edge the moment the young woman started speaking. The way her eyes shifted around the room felt strange. Dishonest. The gangster sitting next to her wore an unconvincing smile.

"Me too," he said. A lie. It had to be.

She clenched her jaw as her fingers reached under the table for Abe. She didn't know how, but she needed to communicate to him that they had to get out of here. This felt like a trap. Just before her fingers reached him, the last gangster looked up at her.

Her hand dropped to her lap as she noticed his chestnut brown eyes. The expression in them looked completely different than the other gangsters. He sucked in a breath that seemed to tremble through him. Was he afraid, yes? But was he dishonest?

"I *do* want to join you," the third gangster said. The emphasis in his words put a different feeling in the air. She didn't trust the other two, but that didn't change the truthfulness of his words. This gangster didn't want to work for Sef anymore. She was sure of it.

She'd gotten so distracted by the gangster that she didn't notice a new crowd of people arriving. All gangsters and all angry. Abe grabbed her hand from under the table and jumped to his feet. "Time to go," he said.

Apparently, he hadn't been as oblivious as she assumed. He ignored the front door and went for the back one instead. Unfortunately, the gangsters seemed to have expected that.

When Imara and Abe stepped out the back door, a fire blazed in front of them, blocking the alley. They were trapped.

She whirled around to look at the door with a frown. "What do we do when the gangsters get out here? Fight?"

"They won't come out here."

She tilted her head to the side, but as she did, a flame from the fire burst toward her. Abe pulled her back just in time to keep her safe from the flames. Even as he pulled her away, they both stopped and leaned toward the fire. The musky smell of smoke, not only seemed inviting, but intoxicating. As stupid as it sounded in her head, she found herself wanting to jump into the fire and let the fragrance engulf her.

Luckily, she'd known a smell master since her first day of hila school. Siluk. They didn't have the most pleasant history, but she remembered one thing he taught her.

Never trust a smell that tries to control you.

"Stop!" she shouted as Abe stepped toward the flames. "That will burn you." She yanked him back, which seemed to help him snap out of it.

He joggled his head until the glazed look came out of his eyes. "Right," he said, narrowing his eyes at the fire. "The gangsters won't come after us out here, but if we go back inside, they'll probably beat us until we pass out. But we can't go through the fire either. No matter how good it smells," he added under his breath. "So, which one's worse? Fire or gangsters?"

She drummed her fingers against her thigh, considering his question. A moment later, she grinned at the wall on her right side. Smirking, she said, "When faced with two choices, one bad, the other worse, I like to ignore them both and choose a third option."

Abe's lips curved into a half smile. "Such as?"

She pointed out a rickety ladder attached to the side of the building. It was half hidden by a stack of boxes, but still easily within reach.

He grinned and waited for her to grab the ladder first. Her fear of heights did not make the climb easy, but she felt safer knowing Abe was right behind her. The ladder led all the way up to a covered roof.

Once at the top, she braved a glance over the edge and down at the fire. Her heart nearly stopped at the sight of such a distance. She had to take several steps away from the ledge to calm her pounding heart. "Do you think there's another way down?" she asked. "Another ladder or something."

Abe walked around the roof, looking over the edge as he went. When he got back, he said, "Nope. We'll have to wait until the gangsters leave the restaurant or until that fire burns out."

She let out a huff and sneered at nothing in particular.

"You have stuff in your eye again," Abe said.

She tilted her chin up without thinking. But as he started cleaning her eye, she remembered the last time he'd done this. After the dinner with his dad, she saw a flash of an emotion coming off his skin. Or she thought she did. It could have been a trick of the lights. But this time, she was anxious to find out if the mysterious goop was related to seeing her hila again.

Abe wiped the goop on his pants and tapped his ring. "Do you want to check the news feeds while we wait?"

After she nodded, he sat down cross-legged, and she settled next to him. Their hands instinctively moved until they found each other. He pulled her fingers up to his lips and then held on tight as he chose a video.

With his eyes on the screen, hopefully he wouldn't notice her staring. She bit her lip as she stared. Watching his copper skin and hardly taking a breath. Waiting.

And then she saw it.

Just a wisp. The ghost of a color, not even the color itself. But she saw it.

A raven black rash of anxiety wafted away from him as he narrowed his eyes at the video. The rash disappeared a moment later, but she definitely saw it.

Now she knew for certain that the stuff in her eyes did have something to do with her hila. When Abe cleared it away, she could see emotion again. Not like she could before, but more than she had since the eraserfall.

Should she tell him? He didn't even believe he was a healer, yet. Maybe it was better to wait until he accepted his hila before she tried to convince him he could heal hers.

With her mind on hilas, another question bounced forward. "What is Sef's hila?" she asked.

"I don't know. Nobody knows. He keeps it a secret." He pulled his eyes away from the screen for a split second. "Why? Do you think you know what it is?"

She bit her lip, trying to decide if it was all in her head. "No. It's probably not what I think. But the smell of that fire reminded me of—"

"You've got to be kidding me," Abe said, staring at his screen.

"What?"

He shook his head as his lip curled up. "Sef's latest antics. Watch this video."

He restarted the video, which showed Sef standing behind a short podium. The spattering of freckles over Sef's nose didn't look sinister at all in the daylight. He wore a gray pinstripe suit and looked out at the crowd with an air of authority. "My proposed plan has the potential to make Cairo even better than the revered Alexandria. I propose we do away with prisons completely. We will replace all of them with reform institutions."

"Good idea," Abe said to the screen. "Except if you're the one implementing it, then those reform institutions might as well be named Slave Cartel 2.0."

With a grunt, he jumped to his feet and kicked an empty flower pot. "I'm so sick of Sef ruining my city." He kicked another flower pot, which soared off the roof until it broke against the building nearest them.

When the pot shattered, Abe stared at the building across from them with narrowed eyes. She tried to imagine what he was thinking especially with his sudden outburst toward Sef. Even with all her guesses, she never could have imagined the words that came out of his mouth next.

"Do you think I can jump across to the other roof?"

"No," she said, trying to laugh off the suggestion. When he kept staring, her stomach dropped. "Abe, no. It's way too far. You'll never make it."

"I'm going to try it," he said.

"No," she shouted.

But he was already running. He leapt up and pushed his feet off the ledge, causing his body to soar through the air.

Her breath had been sucked entirely from her lungs as she watched him fly. For one terrifying moment, she thought he would fall when he was only halfway across. But his body kept soaring, and his feet arched ready to touch down on the roof ledge across from them.

His toe made contact with the ledge. He swung his other foot forward so it could touch down. But as his foot moved, the momentum swung his body back. The toe that had touched down first got pulled away from the ledge. He gasped as his entire body swung back. Falling.

He had *almost* made it.

"ABE!" she screamed out. She ran to the edge of the roof, ignoring the fear that bubbled in her chest. She lifted her leg, ready to jump after him, but knew it would do no good. Her heart froze for three breaths. But where his feet had failed, his hand succeeded. He gripped, not the roof edge, but a window ledge. His body jolted to a stop as his fingers found the wood jutting out from the building side.

"Reckless!" she screamed at him.

He tried to respond, but his grip started failing, and he had to focus on gripping the wood.

"Just hold on. I'll find something to help you. Don't let go," she said. *And don't die.* She scanned the roof, looking at it for what seemed like the first time.

More empty flower pots sat in one corner. A broken chair was tipped on its side next to the flower pots. A long wooden board was propped up against it. She scowled at the worthless items until she found a yellowing rope draped over a flower pot.

She snatched it from the ground and her excitement quickly faded. The rope was barely a meter long, which meant she'd have to be much closer to Abe in order to use it.

Her eyes flitted up to the wooden board propped against the chair. It looked sturdy and pretty long. Maybe long enough to...

She lifted it and set it up straight to check the length. With how high it towered over her, it had to be long enough to bridge the gap between the two buildings. She scuttled to the edge of the building and lowered the board, holding her breath as it fell to the edge of the roof across from her. It landed with a thud, which confirmed what she had already guessed. It fit perfectly as a bridge between the two buildings, but that meant she'd have to cross it in order to help Abe.

She gripped the wooden board while images of her tripping off it and falling to her death played over and over in her mind. She tried to take deep breaths, but each one felt shallower than the last. Blinking rapidly, she willed her feet to climb onto the roof ledge, but they stayed rooted to their spot, heavy as lead.

"You don't have to walk across it," Abe called out. "Maybe I can climb up on my own." He jammed a toe against the building and tried to push his body up. He raised himself a head length up before his toe slipped, and he was falling once again. He gripped the window ledge, but held on with even fewer fingers than before.

A bead of sweat slid down Imara's forehead as she finally convinced her feet to move. Abe's fingers wouldn't last much longer, which meant she had to act. Now.

She climbed onto the wooden board, trying to decide if the journey would be better with her eyes open or closed. She stuffed the yellowing rope into her pocket, then shuffled across with her belly against the board.

Eyes closed. That was better.

She peeked out after several seconds only to grimace. Not even halfway across yet, and Abe was losing his grip with every second that passed. Squeezing her eyes shut, she shuffled across the board at a speed she hoped was faster than before.

After peeking three more times, she finally made it close enough. She dug her nails into the board with one hand as she pulled the rope from her pocket. Her body shivered as she lowered the rope down to him.

The rope pulled taut as he took hold of it. But she knew right away that she'd have to grip the rope with both hands in order for Abe to climb. Long beads of sweat trickled down her cheeks as she extracted her nails from the wooden board. She sucked in a gasp, but managed to wrap both hands around the rope.

Soon, Abe was climbing. The grip required to keep him from falling was enough to keep her mind off her fear of heights. But then he made it safely to the wooden board, and her fear was back in full force. He led her the rest of the way across the board until they both jumped onto the safety of the second roof.

Her body shook as she clutched him, burying her face in his chest. He moved along the roof but kept one hand firmly on her back, providing a small measure of much needed comfort.

"There's a ladder here," he said. "It's far enough from the fire that we should be safe."

She nodded and let him lead her as long as possible so she wouldn't have to open her eyes. He ordered a bubble car as they climbed down, and by the time they reached the bottom, it had arrived.

TWELVE

EVERY MUSCLE IN IMARA'S BODY SEIZED AS she fell into the seat of the bubble car. Abe's limbs seemed to be shaking too, but not as bad as hers. He tried to paste on a smile and said, "Thanks for saving my—"

She punched him in the shoulder before he could finish. "Do you have a death wish?" she asked.

"No," he said. "And, *ow.*"

She smacked him again. "Are you sure? Because…" Her chin trembled. She tried to breathe, but the air came in as a shudder. "That was so stupid. And reckless." Her chin trembled again, and her shoulders started shaking. She folded her arms over her stomach and dug her nails into the fleshy part of her elbows.

Her lips parted as she tried to speak, but then she lost control, and everything inside her shivered so hard it hurt. Abe pulled her head to his chest, and she buried her face without question. She tried to take deep breaths, but each one felt too shallow or so deep it made her head spin. All the while, her muscles seized so hard they ached.

Abe held her the entire car ride. When they arrived at his apartment a few minutes later, her muscles burned, but no longer trembled. Once inside, she turned on him again. "You thought you could jump across the roof? What were you thinking?"

He stared at his feet while tucking his elbows into his sides.

She wagged a finger at him with her eyebrows lowering more every second. "Sometimes you're reckless to help people, and it's very brave. But sometimes you're reckless for no reason at all, and you needlessly put your life on the line. *Why* do you do that?"

He looked up, and a hint of guilt lingered in his eyes, though not nearly enough. He shrugged. "I don't have a death wish. Sometimes I just do stuff without thinking it through."

"No," she said, plopping down onto his couch. "You know that isn't the only reason." She reached for the hair on the back of her neck and gave it a tug. "I think it's because of your mom."

"No," he said with a flinch. "It has nothing to do with her."

She crossed her arms over her chest. "Are you sure? Because sometimes the things you do border on insanity."

He huffed and dropped himself onto the couch next to her. "Who cares? It all worked out in the end, didn't it?"

"Are you serious?" she said through her teeth.

"What?"

"I care!" she said, jabbing a thumb toward her chest. "Your dad cares. Lots of people care. Aren't you the least bit concerned with how devastated your dad would be if something happened to you?"

"My dad is strong. He'd survive."

She let out a growl and punched the nearest pillow. "Out with it," she said. "There's more to this whether you realize it or not. So, dig deep. What is it?"

He rolled his eyes and waved a hand through the air.

"Oh, no you don't," she said as she crossed her arms in front of her chest for a second time. "I'm not leaving until you figure this out. I don't care if it takes all night." She glared at him until he turned away from her stare.

Soon he was crossing his arms over his chest and huffing through his nostrils. He tried to stand, but she raised one eyebrow at him, and he slunk back into the couch. She wasn't sure exactly how long they sat like that, but it was long enough for a cramp to form in her leg.

Little by little, the muscles in his shoulders started to relax. Soon, his face wasn't glaring, so much as staring off into space. At one point, his thumb found his chin, and he began stroking his jaw line.

He took a careful glance toward her but quickly turned away. "It…" he swallowed. "Maybe it does have something to do with my mom."

She wanted to roll her eyes since that was, by far, the least surprising revelation of her life. But somehow, she managed to keep her eyes in place. "Go on," she said.

He shrugged as he stared at the ground. "It's not what you said the other day, about not wanting my dad to take responsibility. It's because… my mom died because of a freak accident. She had no control over it." He lifted one hand to rub the back of his neck. "I don't know. I just…" He shrugged again. "When I die, I want it to be on my own terms."

She blinked at him and had to clench her jaw shut to keep from saying something she'd regret. When she finally spoke, it took all her energy to keep the sarcasm out of her voice. "I guess I can see how you mildly used logic to come to that conclusion." Her face softened with a sigh and she reached for his hand. "But don't you think you should take responsibility for your life instead of your death?"

He turned to look in her eyes before breathing out a long sigh. "Well, when you put it like that."

He let out a tiny chuckle, and she joined in a second later. He squeezed her hand and said, "I do see what you're saying, but I can't just undo this compulsion I've had for years."

"Yeah, I know what you mean," she said, thinking how easy it still was for her to see the worst in people instead of the best. She dropped her head onto his shoulder, and he wrapped his arms around her. She sighed. "Next time you get an impulsive urge, can you at least try to remember people care about you? And that you shouldn't be so reckless with your life, for their sake."

He gulped loud enough for her to hear and then pulled her closer.

"Why didn't the gangsters come after us?" she asked after they sat in silence for a few minutes.

"There were security cameras in the alley," he said. "The gangsters would have been caught and arrested if they tried to attack us."

She nodded, wondering how they started the fire in the first place. She shook her head. "What was the point of that trap? Has Sef ever tried attacking you like that before?"

Abe snorted. "Sef has been trying to get rid of me for at least a year. He has to be extra careful though because I work for the Egyptian Council, and they'd personally investigate if anything happened to me." He narrowed his eyes and slid his thumb across his chin. "He's never done anything that direct before. Maybe the taggers are making him desperate."

Her nose curled, and she said, "I thought we'd have a way to stop the taggers by now, but it's been months, and they're just as powerful as the day they got here."

Abe shrugged. "Yeah, but the only people they hurt are Sef's men. Maybe we should be more concerned about Sef than the taggers."

"Four people have died since the business fair," she said with a scoff. "The police think Takara did it herself. How can we stand by and let that happen, even if they're just Sef's men?"

"I know, I know," Abe said as his head bobbed up and down. "We definitely need to stop the taggers. The problem is, I have no idea what to do. But Sef has that list. If we can get even one of his men to join us, we can find out more about the list and might have a way to stop him."

Imara grinned, remembering the gangster with the chestnut brown eyes. "I think I might know just the gangster."

THIRTEEN

THE NEXT DAY, ABE SAT IN A BUBBLE CAR reciting his plans for the day. Go to headquarters. Do the security job. Find the gangster.

They didn't know much about the gangster except he had brown eyes and wanted to join them. But they'd find him. They had to.

While his thoughts consumed him, he barely noticed when his ring buzzed with a phone call. He pulled up his hologram screen and saw a familiar face staring back at him.

"Hey, Siluk," he said. "It's been awhile." It was strange seeing Siluk in Alaska. His wild black hair was tucked under a thick coat hood, and his pale cheeks had turned pink with wind burn. He looked much different from when they'd become friends during their time in the catacombs.

"You'll never believe what I just caught," Siluk said as he lifted a huge fish up for Abe to see. Siluk looked down at the fish and sighed. "This is why subsistence living is the best. Food tastes a thousand times better when it's fresh. My dinner tonight is going to be amazing."

Abe laughed. "Is this why you called me? To brag about your dinner?"

Siluk dropped the fish onto a tarp and chuckled. "No." He stood up and faced the hologram screen with a more serious face. "I called to ask about the taggers. I've been watching the news feeds, but I wanted to hear it from you. How bad is it?"

"It's..." Abe trailed off while his face settled into a frown. "It's pretty bad. The new tagger leader, Takara, is completely insane. Plus, Cairo already has Sef to deal with. He runs a slave cartel. Things are getting more and more dangerous every day."

"How's Imara?" Siluk asked.

He felt the worry fall from his face as a smile replaced it. "Good," he said. "Really, really good." He knew the grin growing on his face would look ridiculous, but he didn't care.

Siluk chuckled and leaned back onto the hover mobile behind him. "Is she still nagging you about being a healer?"

"What?" Abe shook his head. "How did you know about that?"

"How could I not know about that?" Siluk asked through a laugh. "She kept talking about it every other second in the catacombs. Frankly, I think she's right. You are really good at fixing up wounds."

Abe waved his hand through the air. "As I've told Imara a hundred times, I have medical training. Sometimes I get a gut feeling about where a person's pain is, but that doesn't mean anything."

Siluk nodded slowly and tapped his chin. "Oh, yeah, that kind of sounds like a natural talent that's better than most people. Like a mundane ability that could be honed to be incredible. Sort of like..." He started snapping his fingers as if he was trying to remember something. "What's it called

114

again?" He kept snapping. "Oh yeah!" His face fell and he deadpanned, "A hila."

Abe rolled his eyes but decided not to argue because a new idea suddenly hit him. "Hey, can you use your hila to make some cologne for me? So I smell enticing to Imara? Like, can't you smell pheromones or something? I'll be honest, I don't know much about pheromones, but isn't there some connection between pheromones and attraction, and aren't pheromones a smell?"

Siluk laughed. "You want me to create a spray that complements Imara's exact pheromones so you're literally irresistible to her?"

"Yes?"

"That's illegal."

This time Abe laughed. "Why? Smells can't be that powerful."

Siluk raised an eyebrow. "Yes, they can." He shrugged. "I think the law is a bit excessive because the pheromones can't force you to do anything. But they *can* make you highly suggestible. Lower inhibitions, that kind of thing. People don't like having their inhibitions removed without deciding to remove them themselves."

Abe ran his thumb across his chin as he nodded. "Yeah, that makes sense, I guess. I still doubt smells could be that powerful, but yeah, I guess it makes sense."

Siluk bent down to wrap a tarp around his huge fish and another small pile of fish. He tied a rope around them and secured the bundle in a basket on the back of his hover mobile. He said, "I can still make you a cologne that's complementary to Imara's natural scent though. It will smell amazing to her. And I can even put pheromones in it, but they have to be diluted to a specific percentage."

"Uh," Abe said. "But you're in Alaska. Wouldn't you have to smell her to know what her complementary scents are? Wait, are you going to come visit us?"

Siluk swung a leg over the hover mobile and sat down. "I've been thinking about it. I know the taggers don't really affect me here in Alaska, but after the catacombs I sort of feel a duty to fight them. Maybe that's weird. But yeah, I'll definitely make you some cologne, and trust me, Imara will think you smell heavenly."

He cocked an eyebrow up. "But how are you going to make it without smelling her?"

Siluk laughed. "I already have a formula written out that's specific to Imara. I've had it for awhile."

Abe blinked four times before he narrowed his eyes and leaned toward his hologram screen. "I knew you had a thing for her." He closed his eyes and shook his head. "I knew it! You wrote out the formula and used it on yourself, didn't you?"

Siluk laughed again, which only caused Abe's insides to writhe. "Yeah, I've made the formula before, but who said it was for me?"

"Was it?"

Siluk gave a frustratingly non-committal glance. "Imara is twenty-one. Did you think you were the first guy to ever have a crush on her?"

Abe huffed and crossed his arms over his chest. "Well, whoever it was, I hate him. And if it was you, don't tell me because I don't want to know."

116

Siluk let out a throaty laugh, and the sound grated on Abe's nerves. "Do you still want me to make it?" Siluk asked.

Abe tried to be suspicious of Siluk, but all he could think about were those gold flecks in Imara's eyes, her soft curls, and how she had faced her fear of heights to save his life. "Yeah, make it," he said.

"You got it," Siluk said with a snap of his fingers. "And let me know if things with the taggers get worse."

FOURTEEN

IMARA REARRANGED THE STUN GUNS FOR the fifth time in a row. Abe and Edrice were still in the office making plans for their next mission, and she was beyond bored waiting for them. At least she could enjoy an entertaining conversation between Husani and Keiko while she waited.

"Your hair is extra shiny today," Husani said to Keiko. "Did you do it special just for me?"

Keiko snorted as she picked at a hole in her shoe, but a smile twitched at her lips. "You flirt mercilessly with anyone within ten feet of you, which makes your compliments a little less significant."

He put a hand to his heart and dropped his mouth in a pout. "But, Keiko, you are truly the most magnificent young woman I have laid eyes on in the entirety of my life. I can assure you of that."

Keiko flipped her silky, black hair behind her shoulder casually. "Oh, I believe it. I *am* gorgeous."

He laughed and brushed a stray hair out of her face. "Your hair is perfect, but how can I forget your eyes. I would stare at them all day—"

Edrice suddenly smacked Husani in the shoulder. "Do you ever stop?" she said.

Imara turned with a start. She didn't realize Edrice and Abe had left the office already.

Husani grinned. "You know I never stop. Besides, how can I hold my compliments back when I have such perfection in front of me?"

Keiko giggled, but quickly twisted her mouth into a knot to hide the smile.

Edrice stepped back until she stood so close to Abe, their elbows collided. He glared at his arm and took a step away, which made Edrice roll her eyes.

A surge of jealousy swept through Imara. She wanted to squeeze into the spot between the two of them, keeping Edrice away from Abe. It was times like this she hated the no flirting rule. Husani only got away with flirting with Keiko since she wasn't technically an employee.

Abe flashed a quick smile at Imara, and she let the jealousy float away. Edrice had never *really* done anything that warranted jealousy, and neither had Abe. She had no reason to get so carried away.

"We have a job at the rehabilitation center a couple blocks away," Abe announced. "Apparently the taggers are there giving a 'join us or die' speech to everyone inside. Our job is to get the taggers out."

"I'll coordinate from here," Edrice said. "If you haven't gotten rid of the taggers in twenty minutes, I'll have to contact the police. Husani, that twenty minutes starts now." Husani nodded, and she continued. "Imara, as usual, you use your irresistible convincing skills as well as your fighting prowess. Keiko, since you're sixteen and under the global working age, we can't hire you."

"What?" Keiko said, stomping her foot on the ground. "Stupid global working age," she muttered under her breath.

"Of course," Abe said tilting his head to the side. "If you happen to follow us and decide to help us just for fun, we can't do anything about that. And if I happen to give you some money as a gift at a later date, that's perfectly legal. It definitely wouldn't be payment for doing this job or anything like that."

"Excellent," Keiko said with a grin.

Soon, they were off. Husani hung back with Abe. He spoke so quietly, Imara just barely heard his words. "Why are you avoiding Edrice?" Husani asked.

"What?" Abe said, loud enough for everyone to hear. "You mean because I was late this morning? I told you, I was talking to my friend from the catacombs. Siluk. He's a smell master."

"You know what I meant," Husani said.

Abe jogged forward to Imara's side and said, "No, I don't."

Husani opened his mouth to speak again, but Abe huffed at him. "We have a mission right now. Can you please focus?" Abe handed out the stun guns, giving each person a pair. He gave them strict instructions to draw the taggers out, but hopefully without getting hurt.

When they arrived, they rushed in through the doors, and Imara immediately went to the left to hide behind a pillar. Husani did the same thing on the other side of the room. Keiko slipped up the stairs next to Imara's pillar. When they were all in place, Abe marched into the building wearing a hardened glare.

"If you're a tagger, then get out," he said through his teeth.

All at once, four taggers rushed toward Abe with fists raised. Imara aimed her stun gun and dropped the tagger nearest her. By the time her tagger fell to the ground, Abe, Keiko, and Husani had taken out the others.

Abe raised his voice. "As I said before, if you're a tagger, get out."

Imara heard shuffling from behind a nearby wall, but apparently the taggers were smart enough to not jump out again. She saw a rustle of curtain fabric at one point, but it had stopped before she could aim at it.

Suddenly, Abe ducked, barely missing a golden canopic jar that flew through the air. Before she could jump out to offer help, six more people entered the rehab center. Imara recognized one of them at once. The gangster with chestnut brown eyes.

Before the gangsters could stop him, Abe rushed to Imara's side and ducked behind her pillar. "What are they doing here?" she asked.

"I don't know for sure, but Sef has a bunch of people living here at the rehab center, which is probably who the taggers are after. My guess is the gangsters are trying to take out the taggers before Sef's men get hurt."

"What should we do now?"

Abe shrugged and glanced across the room at Husani.

After Abe tapped his wrist where a watch might have been, Husani held up ten fingers and then two more. Twelve more minutes.

Before either of them could theorize a plan, fighting broke out. A group of four taggers had appeared and went straight into a fist fight with the gangsters. Abe watched them for a moment, then shrugged. "I guess maybe we should let them fight."

But then, one of the taggers pulled a knife and jammed it into a gangster's thigh. The gangster rushed from the building, grabbing his leg. They couldn't stand by now that weapons were involved. She wasn't about to sit around and watch someone get killed, even if it was a gangster.

Luckily, Abe seemed to have the same thought as her. He shot his stun gun, dropping the tagger with the knife. Then, he jumped out to join the fight. Before Imara could jump out, Keiko came down from the stairs and ducked behind the pillar next to her.

"I can see the footsteps of at least two people behind that curtain," Keiko said.

Imara raised an eyebrow. "You can *see* the footsteps?"

"With my hila," Keiko said. "I'm a sound seer, remember? I see sound waves."

"Oh yeah," Imara said with a nod.

"One of the people is my mother. Takara."

Imara's eyes widened as she looked back at the curtain. "Are you sure?"

Keiko nodded.

"Stay here." Imara joined the fight, hoping Keiko would follow her advice, especially because her mother was here.

In the midst of the fighting, Imara shot her stun gun twice before someone tripped her from behind. Before she fell to the ground, she shot the tagger who had tripped her.

She got back to her feet and aimed at a gangster when someone wrested the stun gun from her hands. She ducked, but someone kicked her on the thigh. The kick caused her to trip over her feet. That effectively saved her from the stun gun blast, but not from the shooting pain in her thigh.

Just when she regained her balance, a knife sliced across her shoulder. A scream erupted from her throat, but she didn't waste any time crying over it.

She lunged for a stun gun lying on the ground. A gangster got there a split-second before her, and she fell on top of him before she could stop herself.

She was back on her feet a second later, ready to pry the stun gun from the gangster's hands. But then, someone punched her in her lower back before she got the chance. While clutching her back in pain, she stood up straight to face the gangster.

Except now, his stun gun was facing her. Point blank. She had no time to react. Her arms flew toward her face as she imagined what it would feel like to pass out. Would the others be okay without her?

Another second later, she hadn't fallen, and she peeked out from behind her arms. The gangster lay on the ground in front of her in a heap. Abe stood behind him, stun gun pointed out. He gave her a wink then turned to rejoin the fight.

Despite being in the middle of chaos, a happy grin spread all across her face. She plucked the stun gun from the gangster on the ground and shot a tagger with it as she twirled around in a circle.

Without warning, she received a punch along the side of her face, but she simply turned and shot the gangster, still wearing her grin.

As she went to aim again, she noticed all the gangsters and taggers were down. The only people still standing were her, Abe, Husani, and Keiko.

She screwed up her face, preparing to drop a scolding look on Keiko for joining the fight. That's when she noticed Takara's body missing from the pile of stunned people.

"We did it with seven minutes to spare," Husani said, smirking. "That's got to be some kind of record."

Keiko gulped as her eyes locked onto the ground right under the curtain. Assuming she was looking at sound waves from footsteps, Imara grabbed Abe and pulled him behind a pillar.

Takara appeared from behind the curtain, just as they slipped out of her view. They both peeked around the side of the pillar, watching as the woman approached her daughter. She wore a menacing glare so intense it could have been comical if it weren't so terrifying. Once she stepped close enough, she and Abe moved past the pillar to come up behind her unseen.

Keiko fumbled with her stun gun, trying to aim it with trembling fingers. Takara knocked the gun from Keiko's hands. Then, she slapped Keiko across the cheek so hard, she fell to the ground.

Before Takara could move again, both Abe and Imara held their stun guns directly on the temples on either side of her head.

Takara cleaned under her fingernail with a look of pure boredom. "If you stun me and try to take me with you, my taggers will find you and kill you within the hour."

Imara glanced at Abe, but he looked as unsure as she did. Maybe Takara was bluffing, but this probably wasn't the best moment to find out. Imara gritted her teeth together and said, "Then get out."

Abe nudged his stun gun into her head until Takara started moving. Knowing she'd been beat, she left without argument. They locked the door behind her and turned to see Husani helping Keiko to her feet.

Husani gulped as he held Keiko by the elbow. "I know you said you don't like your mom, but I had no idea—"

She turned away from him and wrapped her arms around her stomach. "I know," she said. "I don't need any reminders." Her lips trembled as she brushed the dirt off her knees. She scowled. "Why are people always having to rescue me from Takara? Why can't I rescue myself just once?"

Imara rested her hand on Keiko's shoulder, waiting until the girl looked at her before she spoke again. "You aren't weak for being afraid of your mother. You're brave for fighting against her anyway."

Keiko squished up her mouth and swiped her wrist across her nose. "Thanks," she said.

"Husani, go find the owner and let him know we finished the job," Abe said. "Then grab a couple hover carts so we can get these stunned people out of here before they wake up."

As Husani turned to leave, Abe clapped his hands and rubbed them together. "Now it's time to clean up injuries. Imara, I'm taking care of that cut on your shoulder first."

FIFTEEN

IMARA TILTED HER HEAD AS ABE CLEANED her wound. "How did you know I cut my shoulder?" she asked.

"How mad was Naki when you had to postpone your picnic because of this mission?" he countered.

She shrugged off his question, trying to forget that she delayed plans with her sister. Again. Naki hadn't been mad. She'd been disappointed, and that hurt worse. All this talk about being better friends, and, so far, they'd barely spent a few hours together. Even being roommates.

She frowned and pushed the thought away. "You're trying to change the subject. How did you know I cut my shoulder?"

He gave her a look, apparently knowing exactly where this conversation was headed. "You're never going to let this go, are you?"

She waited until Keiko and Husani were busy lifting people onto the hover carts before she continued. Even then, she lowered her voice. "I won't let it go until you accept you're a healer."

He swept a cleansing wipe across her skin. "I'm not, and you're wasting your breath.

"How did you know about my shoulder?" she asked, raising an eyebrow.

He shrugged. "I saw the blood on your shirt and…"

"You had a gut feeling?"

"Yeah," he said with a nod. His fingers froze, and he shifted focus to her eyes. "Wait. Is that how you first started noticing your hila? With a gut feeling?"

She nodded, not trying to hide the grin on her face.

He shook his head. "I'm just a random guy with medical training. My gut feeling isn't the same as yours."

"Why not?"

He dug through his bag and let out a huff. "Why won't you let it go?"

"Why won't you just accept it?"

He narrowed his eyes at her, clearly trying to look angry, but failing miserably. He put a bandage over her cut. "I'd be very upset with you right now if… If I didn't love cleaning your wounds so much."

She snickered and gave him a quick stare that was decidedly unprofessional. She wiped the look away a moment later. "You never told me why you got medical training. Was it because of your mom? So you'd always be prepared if something happened to someone you love?"

"No," he said, shaking his head. "It was because of this job." He stopped shaking his head, and let out a quick sigh. "Okay, yes, and because of my mom, but it doesn't mean I'm a healer. You're reading too much into it."

He glanced back at Keiko as she and Husani lifted the last person onto the hover cart.

"Are you thinking about your mom?" Imara whispered.

"Yeah," he said before he gulped. "And Keiko's mom."

She reached for his hand and gave it a quick squeeze before Husani or Keiko could see. Abe looked back with a little smile, but it fell a moment later. He shook his head slightly. "Takara is insane. If she hates Keiko so much, why doesn't she just ignore her?"

"And why did she slap her for no reason?"

"Exactly," Abe said with a nod. He let out a sigh and stuffed the rest of his supplies into his bag. "It's weird. I know what I went through with my mom was horrible. It was. But what's worse, losing a parent who loves you or having one who doesn't?"

ಐಐೞೞ

They left the rehab center, only to be met with a gangster gripping his bleeding thigh. Imara gasped, but Abe was on his knees stopping the blood before the gangster could say a word.

"You were at the restaurant," Imara said. "You wanted to join us."

The gangster let out a yelp as Abe pressed against his wound. Only a moment later, he seemed to feel some relief. "Yeah," the gangster said.

Husani and Keiko looked at each other, and Abe seemed too distracted by the wound to be aware of the conversation.

Imara swallowed and spoke in her soothing voice, which she hoped would make him feel more at ease. "What's your name?" she asked.

The gangster stared at her for a few seconds before he responded. He seemed more surprised by this question than unwilling to answer. He shook his head as if trying to shake away the shock, then said, "Rajesh."

"How long have you been with Sef?" Abe asked.

Again, Rajesh stared. He narrowed his eyes at Abe, then at Imara, clearly puzzled by both of them. He shook his head again and said, "I started working for Sef when I was thirteen years old."

He stopped, and Imara gave him a little nod, urging him to continue.

He blinked at her, but then the words came spilling out. "Before that, I didn't even live in Egypt. I'm from India. I came here with my parents on a vacation." He sucked in a breath and held it while he stared at the ground. After holding it, he let out the breath slowly. "My parents died in a sand-storm by the pyramids. Sef had me captured before anyone could realize I was missing. I've been *working* for him ever since."

His story twisted her gut into a jumbled mess. She tried to smile and said in her soothing voice, "Why do you want to join us?"

"I want food," he answered. "And freedom. Sef is controlling, but... not. When I'm with him, I want to help him. It seems like the most important thing in the world. But then sometimes it hits me all the terrible things I've done and I cringe that this is who I've become. I just want him out of my head. I don't want to hurt people anymore."

She nodded, hoping to encourage him. "It feels good to do the right thing instead of the wrong thing."

He looked down at his hands and swallowed. "I don't have money. Or a job. Or a place to live. I have nothing. Can I even join you if I have nothing?"

"Guess what?" Abe said as he finished applying a bandage over Rajesh's wound. "You're hired. We have a place you can sleep, and I'll make sure you get plenty of food."

Rajesh blinked again, but not so much from surprise. This time, it was because tears formed in his eyes.

Imara felt like crying too. Not only could they help him, but they also finally had one of Sef's men on their side.

SIXTEEN

A WEEK LATER, IMARA ARRIVED AT headquarters with a plate full of baba ganoosh and pita triangles. Everyone was there. Even Rajesh. When they saw her, their faces went from haggard to delighted in a matter of seconds. Just as she'd hoped, her arrival had been expertly timed.

Before she sat down, Rajesh inhaled almost half the food on his own. She cocked up an eyebrow. "Have you eaten today?"

She glanced at Abe who averted his eyes. He tugged at his shirt collar with a frown. Rajesh didn't always tell them when he needed more food.

"Sorry," Rajesh said. "With Sef, we only got food every once in awhile so I learned to eat as much as possible when it was offered."

"But have you eaten today?" she asked again.

He looked away as soon as she caught his eye. "I had a little. Enough. I had enough."

She looked at Abe again, and he met her eyes this time, but only for a moment. Just last night he'd been saying how he wished they could to do more for Rajesh. He came to them expecting a better life. So far, they'd only given him a tiny bed and some food.

And a better cause, she reminded herself. It felt good doing the right thing, and he hadn't been able to do that with Sef.

"Are you sure you don't know anything about Sef's list?" Edrice asked, picking at the peach ribbon in her hair.

Rajesh frowned as he traced the scars on the back of his hand. "I already told you everything I know. He has the list, but I've never seen it." He lowered his voice a notch. "I'm sorry I can't help. Please don't take my food away."

"You don't have to apologize," Imara nearly shouted.

At the same exact moment, Abe said, "We'd never do that."

They shared a look, and Imara sat down next to Rajesh. "It's not your fault you don't know more about the list. We were hoping you would, but we'd never take your food away."

"Not for anything," Abe said. He looked to the side for a moment, and then looked back to Imara. "Maybe it's time we go after the taggers."

She nodded. "We should try to get Takara arrested. There have now been six deaths since the business fair. There must be some of kind proof incriminating her after that many grotesque murders."

Keiko bit her lip as she twisted a strand of silky, black hair around her finger. "I don't know if arresting her will be enough. If she goes to prison, she might go on a killing spree on the inside. Then, once she's done, she'll break out and move on to her next plan."

Husani gave Keiko a sideways glance. "Break out of prison? Excuse me, but the prisons in Cairo are basically impossible to break out of. Why do you think Sef thought it would be easier to get rid of prisons than to try and release his gangsters?"

"Excuse *me*, but have you ever met my mother?" Keiko asked. "She can hack into anything. Plus, she's gaining more followers by the day. She could probably get the prison wardens on her side in a few hours."

Rajesh choked on his pita triangle. "Did you say mother? As in…"

Keiko rolled her eyes with a growl. "It's not my fault who my mother is! Yes, she's a complete psycho, but she hates me, always has. So, don't worry, I'm not in any danger of turning out like her."

As she finished, Imara noted how she scratched her nose and looked away. Keiko was lying.

Before the catacombs, Imara would have assumed all of Keiko's words were lies. Now she knew lies weren't so easy to interpret.

Was it a lie that Takara was psychotic? Definitely not. Was it a lie that Takara hated her daughter? Not likely. That meant the last sentence was a lie. That Keiko wasn't in danger of turning out like her mother. But even then, it didn't mean Keiko *wanted* to turn out like her mother. In fact, it probably meant the complete opposite. That Keiko was *afraid* of turning out like her.

Husani cleared his throat. "All right, we can't get Takara arrested because she'll kill everyone in the prison and then break out anyway. Any other ideas to stop her?"

Imara tugged the hair on the back of her neck. She let the strands slip between her thumb and forefinger as she tugged and released. As she thought deeper, she pulled harder. Just when an idea moved to the front of her mind, it would slip back again. Then another thought would take its place, even better than the last. When the strongest idea stayed firmly at the front of her mind, she opened her mouth. But as soon as it opened, she snapped it shut again.

"What is it?" Abe asked. She didn't realize his eyes were on her. She gave him a little smile, hating that he sat all the way across the room.

It was for the best since her hand would have found his a long time ago if they'd been sitting closer. And he probably would have played with her curls. Both of which were definitely against the rule of acting professional.

She tugged another hair strand on the back of her neck and finally said, "I have an idea, but I don't know if it will work."

Only Edrice looked as excited as Abe. She sat on the edge of her chair with a gleam in her eyes. The more time Imara spent with her, the more she liked Edrice. They'd all been spending more time at work the last few weeks, and a bond was forming between them that strengthened every day. It reminded Imara how rare it was for her to have a friend. Something she hadn't had in years.

If only she'd had such time to spend with Naki.

"What's your idea?" Edrice asked.

Imara took a little breath to prepare herself. She soaked in Edrice's enthusiasm because she was pretty sure Abe would hate her idea. "If Takara attacks or injures a Kenyan citizen badly enough, the Kenyan police could be persuaded to intervene. Especially if the citizen happens to have done a few favors for the Kenyan police department lately."

"No," Abe said with a stone cold face. Every bit of light had sucked out of his eyes as he glared.

"You can't say no yet," Edrice said. "You don't even know her plan. You don't even know who the Kenyan citizen is."

He hissed at Edrice, but turned his full attention away from her. "It's her. She's the citizen." He looked into Imara's eyes, making no attempt to hide the clenching of his jaw. "And you can't sacrifice yourself like that; it's too dangerous."

She folded her arms over her chest and scoffed. "Yeah, and going into catacombs with deadly illusions wasn't dangerous either. I decided to work in Egypt, which means I'm going to do something useful while I'm here. Now, listen to my plan."

He glared back at her, but, surprisingly, didn't protest.

She continued. "The Kenyan police force is the best in the world and has been for twenty-five years. Getting them involved is the only chance we have. I think we should try to get Takara to kidnap me. We'll do it in a way that gives us proof Takara is involved. Then, Abe and my sister can go to the Kenyan police department for help, and the police will come and get rid of Takara for us."

Keiko's mouth dropped, and she raised her pointer finger. After blinking several times, she smiled. "Imara, you're the freshest, but just so you know, this is a terrible idea."

Husani laughed and put his arm around the silky-haired girl. "Telling it like it is; that's my girl."

Keiko immediately gave him a sideways glance and removed his arm from her shoulder. "You have a long way to go before I'd be *your girl*, but you can keep the compliments flowing any time you like."

He gave the biggest mock frown before he said, "You are absolute perfection, my dearest Keiko. I will win you over yet."

She laughed. "Yeah, just as soon as you stop flirting with everything on two legs. Oh wait, I just realized, that's never going to happen."

"Why is it a terrible idea?" Imara asked.

Keiko gave a snide smile to Husani, then her face grew serious again. "It all comes down to one thing. If you get kidnapped, what do you think Takara will to do with you? Do you think she's going to put you in a nice room and give you food every couple hours? You'd be lucky to have a room at all. It's more likely that she'll keep you in a cage, not feed you anything, and when she's feeling extra saucy, she'll take you out and torture you."

Abe nearly hit his chin to his chest from nodding so hard. "Agreed. This is a terrible plan. Let's think of something else."

Imara opened her mouth to protest but Edrice spoke before she could say anything. "I think you have a good plan, Imara, but maybe there's a way to do it without you getting hurt."

"I can help with that," Rajesh said, his voice rising barely above a whisper. He'd been so busy eating, Imara almost forgot he was there. He wrung his hands together as he spoke. "Sometimes Sef made us get captured by rival leaders. While there, someone else would come bring food or medicine to make the capture more tolerable. The extra person would loosen shackles or take them off so the prisoner could walk around and stretch their muscles. It makes the kidnapping easier to endure. I've been the captured and the helper lots of times. I can do it no problem. All we really need is a reason for Takara to kidnap you."

"That's easy," Imara said with a smile. "I'll pretend I got Sef's list."

SEVENTEEN

EVEN AFTER TWO WEEKS OF PLANNING, THEY still hadn't come up with a better idea than letting Imara get captured. Over the past few days, their planning had shifted to consider the logistics of the kidnapping. Despite Abe's protests.

Imara stepped out of the airport. Abe was there to greet her with a bubble car, just like he promised. As always, as long as she was in Egypt, he was there for her completely. She shook that thought away and scolded herself. Of course he was always in Egypt. He was trying to save his business.

Either way, he did not look happy. He typed the location into the bubble car's hologram screen as she climbed inside. Once the car started moving he said, "I don't like this kidnapping plan."

"I know," she said as she reached for his hand. "But I'm still doing it."

He ground his teeth and let out a burst of air through his nostrils. "Why?"

She cocked an eyebrow up at him, and the fury in his eyes melted away in an instant. She looked down and said, "This plan will stop the taggers for good. And once we get the Kenyan police involved, they'll probably find a way to stop

Sef too. We'll save your business and—maybe more importantly—all of Egypt."

He pressed his lips against the back of her hand, then rested his chin on top of her head. "You don't have to save everyone, you know?"

She let out a soft laugh just as she picked up a spicy smell. "I thought you liked that. In the catacombs you specifically said *that's what I love about you.*"

"I do love it," he said. He pulled his hand from hers and used it to prop up his forehead. The veins in the back of his hand popped out as he gathered up a fistful of his hair. He sat that way for several seconds without saying a word. Finally, he said, "Maybe I'm starting to understand what you were saying about how people care about me and I shouldn't be so reckless with my life. For their sake."

"Good," she said through pursed lips. It came out harsher than she meant it. Even still, she was grateful for his realization.

There was the spicy smell again. Strong, but with a sweet undertone.

She pulled his hand away from the death grip it had on his hair. Squeezing it lightly, she said, "I love you. And I'll be careful."

He popped a curl down over her forehead. "You better be because I love these curls too much, and I don't think I could ever find the perfect replacement."

She gave him a gentle jab with her elbow. "Just my curls, huh?" She said *I love you* and he said he loved her curls. It probably meant nothing, but for some reason it stung anyway.

139

He ignored her question and slid his fingers through the short hair on the back of her head. "Just promise you'll be extra, extra careful."

She nodded and rested her head on his chest. Now she had pinpointed the source of the smell. Abe. He smelled like spicy cinnamon and cardamom wrapped in a rich milky scent and layered with a hint of musk. The milk and musk brought back memories of hila school, but the spice was all Abe. The combination of them made her certain she'd never smelled anything so exquisite.

"Are you sniffing me?" Abe asked.

"No," she said as she sat up with start.

He snickered. "Hurry and kiss me because we're almost to headquarters, and then we'll have to be—" he stuck his tongue out and grimaced— "professional."

As he leaned toward her, he screwed his face into a knot. "Hang on. You have stuff in your eyes. Tons of it."

She leaned into his touch as he cleaned her eyes. When he wiped the goop onto his pants, she saw faint scarlet red threads of desire dancing out of his copper skin.

"Abe," she said, watching the threads disappear as quickly as they had appeared. "There's something I need to say."

He smiled and stroked his thumb across her cheek. She hated to ruin the moment, but she'd made up her mind. She turned back to him and said, "I'm only going to say this once, and then, I promise I won't ever bring it up again."

He cocked an eyebrow up in question, but didn't stop smiling.

"You're a healer."

Just like that, his smile fell. He rolled his eyes and pulled his hand away from her. "Not this again."

She plowed on, knowing he'd react like this. The one thing that changed was the tone in her voice. She didn't turn to the soothing voice Professor Santini had taught her. Instead, she turned to a softer voice. One that hopefully demonstrated how much she recognized his pain.

"It took me forever to realize why you wouldn't believe it, but I finally figured it out." She clasped her hands together and closed her eyes. This next part wouldn't come easily.

"It's because of your mom," she said quietly. "She died because she didn't know how to use her hila, and now you're afraid to have the responsibility of a hila. It's not just your hila either. You fear any responsibility except when it comes to your dad or your business." She opened her eyes to see the effect of her words.

Abe folded his arms over his chest and clenched his jaw tight in a scowl. "What do you mean I fear responsibility?"

She bit her lip, trying to think how to explain. She didn't want to offend him, but he needed to know. "Any time someone starts expecting something from you, like you being able to provide medical care, you insist you have limited skills, and no one should rely on you. You only ever save people when they aren't expecting it."

His jaw clenched again, and her stomach sank as they arrived on the last block before headquarters. She knew he'd be frustrated, but she also knew she'd regret it if she never said anything. He kept bugging her in the catacombs about seeing the worst in people. If anything, she had a duty to keep bugging him about this. She just wished she had kissed him first because they'd be at headquarters soon, and her next chance wouldn't be until late into the evening.

"What about with you?" he asked in a frosty tone. "A relationship takes responsibility, doesn't it? Haven't I accepted that responsibility?"

"Only when I'm in Egypt." She immediately regretted her words. His scowl turned darker, and he jerked his head away. If only she could take the words back. She was frustrated that he still hadn't come to Kenya, but he was busy with his business. He couldn't help that it took so much time.

When this recon mission ended, she'd just apologize over and over and keep her promise to never bring up the healer thing again. They'd be fine if they could just get through the next few hours.

EIGHTEEN

ABE THREW A BAG OVER HIS SHOULDER WITH
a scowl on his face. He glared at Imara and said, "I want to
remind everyone this is the worst plan in the world."

Edrice flicked the edge of her hair ribbon, almost rolling
her eyes. "You aren't putting yourself at risk, Abe, so why do
you care? Quit sulking."

His frown dove deeper as he gave her what he hoped was
a mutinous stare. All too soon, they were out the door. He
had to take a deep breath every few seconds to keep himself
from going crazy.

This was strictly recon. They just had to decide on the
best spot for Imara to get kidnapped. He still had an entire
week to convince everyone to try a different plan. There had
to be another way they could get the Kenyan police involved
that didn't include Imara being kidnapped by the world's
most psychotic woman.

The only good thing about this mission was it gave Rajesh
something important to do. Abe hated that the only thing
they'd been able to offer him was the tiny room they used for
orphans. And he never said when he needed more food. With
so much on his mind, Abe kept forgetting to bring it, and
then Rajesh went hungry. That was the last thing Abe wanted.

"That's the spot," Husani said, pointing across the road to an alley.

Abe had to lean back on his heels to keep from toppling over onto the boy. His mind had been so distracted, he didn't realize Husani had stopped. Abe took a step back and pressed his shoulder into the alley wall. "That's where the taggers keep appearing?" he asked.

Husani nodded. "We think their headquarters must be nearby, but it doesn't matter anyway. As long as the taggers come when we want them to."

Imara stepped forward, narrowing her eyes at the spot. Her smooth ebony skin bunched up around her eyes as she stared. The gold flecks in her eyes caught the light, making his breath hitch. After all these months together, and she still took his breath without even trying.

"How do you know the taggers will come when we need them to?" she asked.

Keiko brushed her hair over her shoulder and stepped out onto the road. "It's easier if I just show you," she said.

She jogged across the street, but tumbled back when she collided with a man wearing a tagger *T* on his chest.

The man ran his eyes over Keiko from her head to her toe. Without warning, he slid his fingers into her hair. It took less than a second for her to respond by punching him in the jaw. The man had to step back to regain his balance after the hit.

Husani let out a low whistle, quiet enough only they could hear. "Did you see that right hook? That girl has got some moves."

"Quiet," Abe said. He glanced back to make sure Imara hadn't leapt from the alley to rescue Keiko already. She stood on her toes, leaning forward, but hadn't leapt yet.

"I love me a girl who can fight," Husani said. "What about you, Imara? Can your boyfriend fight?"

"Yes," she said giving him a sideways glance. "But, you know him better than me so I don't know why you're asking."

"What?" Husani said as he blinked back at her.

"Hey," Abe said. "I think we might have a problem."

At first he was only trying to end their conversation as fast as possible, but by the time he finished talking, they really did have a problem. Not just one, but three more taggers came out of the alley, all headed for Keiko.

One of the taggers nudged Keiko backward. "You may act like you don't know her, but your shiny hair and pretty eyes prove that you're your mother's daughter. Quit acting like you're better, and join us already. You know you will eventually."

"Back off or I'll hit you harder," she said as she planted her feet shoulder-width apart. "I may look like my mom, but I don't act like her. I'd rather stab myself in the eye with an eraserfall icicle than join you fanatics."

"We can arrange that," one of the taggers said with a snicker. "Your mother was disappointed she didn't stab you in the eye back in Alexandria."

Keiko shoved the tagger away from her, but two more closed in around her.

Husani gulped. "We probably have three minutes before more taggers arrive. We need to get Keiko out of there or we'll all be in trouble."

"I have an idea," Imara said. "Rajesh, if we do the plan now, do you have everything you need to follow me?"

Rajesh narrowed his eyes and cocked his head to the side.

"No," Abe said before anyone else could speak. "You aren't supposed to go until next week! What am I supposed to tell Naki?"

"I can do it," Rajesh said.

"No, not now. Not today." He tried to reach for Imara, but she was already going down the alley with Rajesh.

As she left, she said, "Just tell Naki we had to start the plan early."

NINETEEN

IMARA TIPTOED DOWN THE ALLEY BEFORE rushing past a building and back up a new alley. Naki wouldn't be happy about this. They were supposed to go to a concert together that night, and she'd finally get to meet Naki's boyfriend, Basara. It seemed pointless since Naki kept talking about how she was going to break up with him.

But maybe that was Imara's fault, too. Maybe Naki wouldn't have an unnecessary boyfriend if Imara had been there for her like she was supposed to be.

She checked over her shoulder to make sure Rajesh still walked behind her. Seeing his head bobbing as he stepped, she rushed out of the alley and into full view of the taggers. She clomped around for the first few steps to make sure they heard, but then let her entire demeanor change. She hunched her shoulders forward and wrapped her hands over her elbows. She looked quickly from one side to the next. Pretending not to notice the taggers nearby, she tapped her ring and looked at her hologram screen with a grin she hoped would look greedy.

"Do you have it?" Rajesh asked, appearing at her side. He fell into his role more seamlessly than she had. Or maybe it just seemed that way because she couldn't see any underlying emotions with her hila.

"This is it," she said pointing to her screen. "Sef's list. The real, actual list. It has the names of all the police working for him and also a record of other illegal activity."

"How did you get this thing?" Rajesh said loudly.

"*Shhh*," she replied. For show, she glanced over her shoulder and pulled Rajesh to a more secretive corner of the road. She glanced over her shoulder again and took note of the distance between her and the taggers.

She lowered her voice to a much quieter whisper, this time, making sure the taggers couldn't hear. "I think it worked. They're whispering and keep looking at us. They've forgotten Keiko completely. Are you *sure* you'll be able to keep up once they kidnap me?"

He nodded.

"And you're sure you can bring me food and everything without anyone seeing?"

"Trust me," he said. "I've done this more than I'd care to admit. If things ever get too bad for you, just let me know, and I'll help you escape."

She lowered her eyebrows and set her jaw. "I'm not going to do that. This is our only chance to stop Takara. I'll do whatever it takes to get her arrested."

"But will you be safe if Takara tries to kill you or something?" Rajesh asked. "I should help you escape if that happens, right?"

"Just get photos that prove Takara is keeping me hostage, and I'll do what I have to do." She glanced over her shoulder to see the taggers chatting, seemingly uninterested in the pair of them. It was convincing, but hopefully it was nothing more than act. She needed them to want Sef's list badly enough to kidnap her. They all needed it.

Rajesh tapped his ring and shrunk the screen so the taggers couldn't see it. He scrolled through and tapped a few things, but as far as Imara could tell, it was all for show.

After a moment, he reached up and brushed his thumb across her cheek. She was so surprised by the sudden intimacy, she couldn't do anything but blink. "Be careful," he said. He disappeared into another alley before she could say anything.

She shook her head. They'd have to have a talk about appropriate physical contact next time they saw each other. She realized, a little embarrassed, that maybe it was part of his act anyway. Good. Because it seemed a little rude for Rajesh to do something like that when he knew she had a boyfriend. Especially when that boyfriend was watching. But then again, maybe Rajesh didn't know about her and Abe since they had to be professional around everyone else.

She shook her head to erase all those thoughts and then walked down the road with an air of confidence. The street remained empty except for her and the small group of taggers. She approached them after only a few steps.

One of the taggers closed in on her. It would probably look better if she at least pretended to put up a fight. When the tagger grabbed her arm just above the elbow, she sucked in a breath in mock surprise. She tried to wrest her arm away, though not as hard as she would have under normal circumstances. Just enough to make him think she was trying.

He grabbed onto her with both hands while another tagger grabbed onto her other arm. "Let me go!" she said.

Loud enough to sound like she wanted them to stop, but not so loud to attract anyone from nearby streets.

A third tagger grabbed onto her waist from behind. The movement was so unexpected, she couldn't help but react by trying to jerk her body away. The tagger squeezed her stomach fast and hard, knocking the wind out of her. Her instincts kicked in, and she tried to jump away.

When another pair of hands wrapped around her chest and her mouth got smothered by a large palm, she started to worry. Maybe this information wasn't as valuable as she hoped. Maybe they'd just kill her without trying to get the list. The taggers wouldn't have killed a random citizen with Professor Santini in charge, but things were different with Takara.

She thrashed at the arms around her. The palm over her mouth soon covered her nose as well. With each second that passed, she lost more oxygen. She knew getting kidnapped was exactly her plan, but her body fought against it anyway. She pushed and pulled, but all the while her vision narrowed, and a ringing started in her ears.

The earth began to sway underneath her. She felt two sharp jabs to her ribcage, and then there was nothing.

TWENTY

IMARA BECAME AWARE OF HER WRISTS FIRST.
A throbbing pain burned around her wrists making them feel on fire. The same burning pain around her ankles stole her attention next. And then her side. A shooting pain knocked through her side and into her ribs like clockwork gears mangling through her flesh. The underlying bruises were nothing to fire engulfing her ribs.

Just when the pain forced nausea into her stomach, she noticed one last pain in her shoulder. It was nothing more than an ache from lying in a strange position, but it only made her situation worse.

She dared to lift one eyelid, anxious to know if their plan had worked. The other eyelid she kept firmly shut in case she needed to pretend to be asleep. Taking a tiny peek through the one eye, she saw a bare floor and felt she had her back to the wall. The hardwood floors gave her the answer she sought. Since Abe's headquarters had marble floors, she knew she wasn't there. A shot of anxiety flipped through her.

Their plan had worked. All she had to do now was stay kidnapped long enough for Takara to get arrested by the Kenyan police. Easy.

As long as she didn't get killed in the process.

She dared to open her one eye the rest of the way but kept the other closed, just in case. No one else seemed to be in the room. In fact, nothing at all seemed to be in the room except her. She opened her other eye and tried to shift her body to a sitting position.

The pain in her rib cage jarred through her, and she gasped in pain. She took in a sharp breath and attempted to grab her side. It wasn't until then that she realized her arms and legs were bound with strong cords. They wrapped so tight against her wrists and ankles it had caused rope burns. Once Rajesh arrived, the first thing she'd have him do was loosen those cords.

Once again, she tried to sit up, but the gnawing pain in her ribcage made it impossible. Maybe Abe was right all along. Maybe this was a bad idea.

She shook her head and gritted her teeth. Would she rather have Keiko in her place? Those taggers looked ready to kidnap Keiko if Imara hadn't intervened. Takara would have treated her daughter just as badly. Or maybe even worse.

Besides, Imara had a duty to stop these taggers once and for all. She couldn't stop Professor Santini in the catacombs, which meant she had to do everything she could to stop her followers. She wasn't about to let the world see the worst in people like she once had.

She turned her attention back to the room. She needed a backup plan in case things got too crazy. A splash of light streamed in through a curtained window. The window could be an escape route, but there was no way to tell how many stories up she was. Jumping out the window might not be an option, but maybe climbing out, with the curtains as a rope, could be. Maybe she'd keep one curtain in place and tie the other curtain to the bottom of it.

Her fingers itched to tug the hair on the back of her head. That always helped her think. Although, now that she had a contingency escape plan, there wasn't much to think about. When she thought up this kidnapping plan, she never thought about how bored she'd be. Only three minutes in, and she was ready to lose her mind.

She tried to swallow, but her throat was so dry, it felt like sandpaper scraped down her esophagus. Rather than dwell on the feeling, she tried to glean information from it. She'd been here long enough to get dehydrated, which meant at least several hours. Ten maybe.

That wasn't a pleasant thought.

If they'd knocked her out, and it took her that long to wake up, would it cause permanent brain damage? She shook that thought away. *Find something useful not terrifying*, she told herself.

She cocked her head to the side. Where was Rajesh? He was supposed to be here within thirty minutes of being kidnapped. She shook her head again. Maybe he had been here already, but she was still unconscious at the time.

Another burning pain shot through her ribs, prompting her to find a more comfortable position. As she shifted her hips, she winced and squeezed her fists. Even that couldn't stop the groan that erupted from her mouth. She tried to shrug off the fire inside her, which wasn't easy with her ribs screaming at her. Were any of them broken?

She grimaced and clenched her jaw. She was here to save Cairo and Egypt. And Abe's business.

She could take a little pain.

As long as the Kenyan police got there soon.

The minutes dragged on, and the sandpaper sensation kept scraping through her throat every time she tried to swallow. Her shoulder ached from being pressed against the hardwood floor, but every time she tried to move, her ribs shouted in protest. Trying to guess how much time had passed became a burden. Eventually, she heard a noise that froze the blood in her veins.

Someone was screaming.

The muffled sound came from far away, but it was unmistakable. The harrowing scream bit through the air, making her hairs stand on end. It seemed like the screamer had something pressed over their mouth, like a blanket or a wad of fabric. Still, the sound seemed to come from only a few doors down. Definitely from inside the same house. Another tingle of anxiety crawled up her spine.

Where was Rajesh?

Before another thought could enter her mind, something shuffled just outside her door. She slammed her eyes shut and slumped her body against the ground so she would appear unconscious. The door opened a moment later.

"I know you're awake." Takara's chilling voice filled the room before her footsteps even entered. "I have a monitor on you. Get up. I have some questions."

Imara swallowed, and the sandpaper feeling in her throat only got worse. She opened her eyes, but didn't make any attempt to *get up* as Takara had commanded. She did this in part to defy her, but also because it hurt too much every time she tried to move.

Takara recognized the defiance and wrinkled her nose at it. She marched up to Imara and jammed a toe into her ribcage. Imara screeched in pain and immediately did her best to sit up. With a sneer, Takara said, "That's better."

Imara pushed her elbow as close to her ribcage as she could, but nothing seemed to help with the grinding gears of pain now rolling through her.

"You're a truth seer, right?" Takara asked.

Imara shifted her eyes to the ground and held in the sniffle her nose was trying to let out. She had expected more physical pain, but not this addition of an emotional one. Staring at the ground, she said, "Eraserfall."

She looked up in time to see Takara grimace and slam a fist against the side of her leg. "I was hoping the rumors weren't true." Takara ground her teeth together, then she looked back with something that strangely looked like hope. "Can you still tell if someone is lying without your hila?" she asked. "Did Carlotta teach you how?"

Imara blinked at the question. Not just because she didn't know if she should answer, but also because the pain in her side grew to blinding levels. Takara raised her foot to kick again, but before she could do it, Imara blurted out, "I don't know." It wasn't a convincing lie, but it was the best she could do under the circumstances.

Takara bared her teeth as she slapped her across the face. "Don't play stupid with me, girl. I know you were close to Carlotta. She said you were like a daughter to her." Takara spit on the ground. "As if Carlotta knows anything about daughters."

Maybe the pain had affected her mind, but for some reason, most of Takara's words completely slipped through her mind. Instead, she noticed only one thing. "What do you mean *knows*?" Imara asked. "Don't you mean *knew*?" She swallowed, but easily ignored the sandpaper feeling in her throat when a pit the size of the Sahara desert grew in her gut. "Is she still alive?"

A smile laced Takara's lips, the sight of it causing another bout of nausea. "Ah," Takara said. "I forgot to thank you for that. With Carlotta in charge, my goals kept getting pushed to the back burner. Now that she's out of the way, I'm the leader. I can continue things 'in her name,' but I get to do it my way instead of hers."

"So, she is dead?"

Takara rolled her eyes. "You were there, weren't you? Maybe I should be asking you the same question." She scowled and dug her heel into a knot in the hardwood floor. "Normally I'd never bother with someone useless like you, especially because you lied about having Sef's list. Unfortunately, without Carlotta, I can't figure out which member of the Egyptian Council is lying. And I need to know."

Imara leaned back against the wall. She had to bite down on her cheek to distract herself from the pain in her side. The burning sensation wouldn't let up, driving her to think at least one of her ribs was broken. Maybe two. Rajesh wouldn't be able to do anything about that, but maybe she could have him bring some pain killer from Abe.

"You are ignoring me!" Takara said.

Imara shifted on her hips, but it did nothing for the ever mounting pain. "Professor Santini never taught me how to see lies without my hila." She turned her head down. "She didn't care about me as much as I thought." With that, tears welled in her eyes. No matter how much she tried, the guilt over Professor Santini's death still hurt her.

Even more than her death was the fact that Imara hadn't been able to convince her how harmful tagging was. No matter what she said, Professor Santini wouldn't listen. Imara had learned and grown so much in the catacombs, but it wasn't enough to save the one person who had been there for her all those years.

Angry huffs blew out from Takara's nose. Imara glanced up to see her checking a message on her hologram screen. Under her breath, Takara muttered, "So stupid, Connors. Stupid. *Stupid.* Do I have to do everything around here?" She stomped out the door, seeming to forget Imara completely. Once outside the room, she turned on her heel and traipsed back. With a laugh that rattled through the veins, she said, "By the way, I thought you'd like to meet your guard."

She grabbed someone by the elbow and forced him into the room.

Rajesh.

The sinking feeling in the pit of Imara's stomach fell even deeper. Ignoring it, she clenched her jaw and forced herself to see the best instead of the worst. Maybe this was his plan all along. Maybe he pretended to switch sides so he could get things to Imara more easily.

Abe would have been proud of her for considering something so hopeful, but she already knew it was an empty hope. Rajesh tugged at his shirt and kept his eyes glued to the ground. He tried to shift his shoulder behind Takara. To make himself less visible. She couldn't see the mustard yellow drips of guilt, but once again, it was easy to pinpoint his emotion with only the body language cues. The shame seeped out of him, making it clear this wasn't part of any plan.

Takara chuckled. "He snuck in through the window, past my security team and cameras. He would have gotten away with it except I happened to be sitting here when he came in. He was about to go back out through the window, and he would have gotten away." She laughed again. "But then I offered him a deal. I told him I wanted him to work for me. I offered him a pile of money and his own apartment, and guess what? Money is more important than morals. Don't forget that, girl. He tried to do the right thing. But I didn't have to torture him or kidnap him. All I had to do was give him money."

Imara's fist coiled as she watched Rajesh's shoulders hunch down further. The betrayal ripped through her. She trusted him—they all trusted him—and this is where it got them? Now she had no idea if a rescue was coming and no relief in the meantime.

Even as she tried to clench her fist tighter, it began to relax. Despite everything, she couldn't blame Rajesh. He came to them expecting a better life and so far all they gave him was a small bed and some food. Not exactly the better life he wanted.

She wanted to be angry and blame him, but what good would it do? How could he refuse when Takara offered so much? She could only hope Rajesh would learn from this betrayal.

TWENTY-ONE

ABE SLAMMED A FIST AGAINST HIS DESK AS HE got to his feet. He'd been sitting for a few minutes but had to start pacing again. "Where is Rajesh? He was supposed to be here three hours ago!"

Even Edrice wore an anxious look. She pursed her lips and Abe knew exactly what was coming. She was about to tell him not to worry. Well, that wouldn't do any good.

He started talking before she could open her mouth. "We need pictures from Rajesh. We need proof in order to get the Kenyan police involved. If something went wrong, he should have been here by now so we can fix it. He should be here!"

But Rajesh remained absent, and Abe was ready to strangle him.

"He said it might take longer than we expected," Husani said.

Abe felt his lips curl into a sneer. "Not *this* long. Something went wrong; I know it."

Edrice bit her lip and tapped at her hologram screen. "I'm sure he'll be here any minute." She frowned and tapped again. Her unease only made him angrier. None of them cared about Imara like he did. Why did he let them go through with this idiotic plan?

At least Keiko looked sufficiently upset. She had tucked herself into a corner and held her knees up to her chin. The permanent glare she usually wore still graced her face, but it did have more worry etched into it than usual.

Husani stood up with his hand reaching out, as if an idea sat before him, just within reach. "We should track their location. Has anyone allowed location sharing with Rajesh or Imara?"

Keiko laughed, her curled up lips looking smug.

Husani glanced toward her and clenched his jaw. "What?" he asked. "You think it's unrealistic that one of us allowed location sharing with them? Or do you think it's obvious someone has?"

Keiko rolled her eyes. "Neither. I think the first thing Takara did when she chose a spot for her base was block the location. I guarantee it's impossible to track them if they're anywhere near my mother's base. Probably not a kilometer around it either."

Husani blinked before he let out a huff and slumped to the ground.

"She's right," Abe said. "And just so you know, I thought ahead and got Imara *and* Rajesh to allow location sharing with me before we went through with this stupid plan. I've checked it a thousand times already. Their location pins disappeared by the citadel. They've been dark for hours."

Edrice drummed her fingers on the desk and bit her lip yet again. "We could try messaging Rajesh."

"You think I haven't tried that?" Abe said as he glared at the ground. He grabbed a fistful of his hair, but it didn't help him think. Nothing did. He rolled one hand into a fist and cracked his knuckles as he stared at the door. He kept expecting Rajesh to burst through the door and tell them everything was fine.

Another few minutes passed while he finished cracking his knuckles. Rajesh still didn't come. Abe kicked the chair under his desk and folded his arms over his chest. A moment later, he released his arms. "I'm calling Naki," he said.

"Who's Naki?" Husani asked as he tapped his fingers against his knees.

"It's Imara's sister," Keiko said. "Don't you ever pay attention?"

Husani frowned and gave Keiko a sideways glance. "I'm starting to like you a little less."

Keiko glared back. "I'm starting to not care."

Ignoring them, Abe tapped Naki's picture to call her.

Edrice stood up and tugged at her hair ribbon. She was full on chewing her lip now. "Don't call her yet. We can't even prove to the Kenyan police that Imara is in trouble. We have to be reasonable. We have to wait for Rajesh."

Abe turned his back on her. Something had gone wrong, and he knew it. He wouldn't wait around for another second. Soon, Naki appeared on his hologram screen. She sat on a couch millimeters away from a guy who twirled her braids around his fingers. She looked bored. He didn't wait for her to speak before he launched into the conversation. "Imara's been kidnapped," he said.

The guy stopped petting Naki's hair for a split second and glanced mildly interested toward Abe.

"Already?" Naki asked. "I thought you weren't supposed to do it until next week."

The guy leaned closer to Naki and raised an eyebrow. "Supposed to? She was *supposed* to get kidnapped?"

Naki pushed him away as she rolled her eyes.

"We had to do it early." Abe closed his eyes as he took in a deep breath. How could he explain? When he opened his eyes, Naki had leaned closer to her hologram screen. Her eyes bugged out, which didn't make his next words any easier to say. "Something went wrong."

The random guy gasped, and he tried to put a hand on Naki's shoulder. She immediately pushed him away even harder than before and turned back to Abe with a hardened glare. "What do you mean *something went wrong*? You said this plan would work!"

His jaw tightened as he shook his head twice. "*I* never said it would work. Imara said that. I said it was dangerous and stupid, but nobody seemed to care about my opinion." He let out a breath, trying to relax his jaw in the process. "Can you help?" he asked.

Naki brought her eyebrows so close together, they were practically touching. "If anything happens to her, I'm holding you responsible."

"That's a little redundant since I already hold myself responsible, but fine. Can you help? We probably won't get proof, but I'm hoping Imara's police friend will help anyway. Can you contact her?"

Naki's eyes widened as she clapped both hands over her cheeks. She shook her head in hurried jerks. "I don't have her contact information. Imara never left it with me. She and the police woman had a meeting next week. The kidnapping was supposed to coincide with the meeting so I could meet with her in Imara's place. I'll have to call the police department." She stood up and pushed her hands into her cheeks as she shifted her eyes from one side of the room to the next. "I

162

don't know if I should ask for Safiya directly. Something weird happened in their department. The meeting was supposed to be the perfect thing."

She shook her head suddenly and shifted her eyes back toward Abe. He could tell she wasn't looking at him, but at her hologram screen. She started tapping and scrolling through it. She stopped suddenly and plucked a blanket from the ground to look under it for something. When that didn't give the desired result, she snatched a jacket off the ground. Then some pants.

"What can I do to help?" the guy said.

Naki gave out an exasperated groan. "You can leave. You're so clingy, Basara. I'm sick of you hanging on me all the time. Why do we have to be together every free minute of your day? Sometimes I like having space."

The guy, apparently named Basara, frowned. He reached for her shoulder and put his other hand on her cheek. "You don't mean that," he said. "You're just upset about your sister."

"I do mean it!" Naki said. She turned away from him and plucked more articles of clothing from the ground. "Ugh. Where are my shoes?" She turned to grab a purse from off the ground, but Basara grabbed her hand instead. She ripped it out of his grip. "I've been thinking about breaking up with you for awhile. Maybe now is a good time."

Basara's face fell. "Naki, no. *Please*. I'll give you space. I'll do anything."

Naki put her hands onto Basara's shoulders, giving him her complete attention. She sighed. "I don't mean to be rude, but this has gone on long enough. I need a break. Maybe I need more than a break. Maybe I need—"

"Naki, focus!" Abe said through his teeth.

She sneered back at him. "Has Imara ever told you you're very bossy?"

"She's been kidnapped, remember?" Abe rubbed circles into his temple. "Something went wrong. We need to find her as soon as possible. What's the name of the police lady? Imara was supposed to tell me before she got kidnapped, but she left early and now everything is falling apart."

Basara dropped to his knees in front of Naki. He took her hand and buried his face in it. "I love you, Naki. More than anything."

Naki rolled her eyes and looked back at Abe. "Safiya," she said. "I can't remember her last name, but I know it starts with an O. Otten or Otno or something." She glanced back at Basara who was now stroking her arm. "I'll call you back as soon as I get rid of him," she said indicating the guy on the ground. Then she tapped her screen and ended the phone call.

When Abe turned around, everyone stared at him. Edrice had a smile tugging at the corner of her mouth. "That was Imara's sister?" she asked.

"Yeah," Abe said. "Naki's life is a little dramatic. Husani and Keiko, you two get out and scout the area where Imara and Rajesh's location pins went dark. Edrice, get ready to do some P.R. because we might need the entire Nairobi police department on our team, not just Safiya. And I will try to contact Safiya. Let's just hope she agrees to help us."

TWENTY-TWO

IMARA FOUGHT TO REMEMBER THE conversation with Takara, but her consciousness seemed to be playing tricks on her. She felt a spasm in her side and curled into a ball to alleviate the pain. She should have known it was no use. Nothing made any difference for the burning in her ribs.

The room went dark, and for one terrifying moment, she couldn't tell if she had blacked out or merely closed her eyes. While blinking her eyes into focus, Rajesh suddenly appeared in front of her.

His shoulders hunched forward, and his eyebrows furrowed. Still guilty. He crouched down in front of her holding a tiny cup of water filled only a quarter of the way with water. He also held a plate, but that must have been a joke because the only thing on it was a piece of moldy bread.

He cleared his throat as he set the plate down. It looked like he planned to say something, but he let out a sigh instead. With eyes drooping, he lifted the cup to her mouth.

"What's in it?" she asked. Her anger at his betrayal still lingered within her, but not enough to mistrust him completely. Still, even if she trusted him, she didn't trust Takara.

"It's just water," he said.

She cocked one eyebrow up even as her throat scratched for the taste of it. "How sure about that are you?"

In response, he raised the cup to his own lips and took a gulp. She would have appreciated the gesture more if the cup had been all the way full. He tucked his hand behind her head and raised the cup to her lips since her hands were still bound.

She gulped greedily, but the water disappeared all too soon. She ran her tongue along the inside of the cup to search for any stray drops. Rajesh watched in agony. He closed his eyes as he began to speak. "She said she'll kill me if I try to help you. She wants you alive, so I'm supposed to give you water every couple hours to keep you barely hydrated."

When she'd licked up every last water droplet, Imara rested her head on the wall behind her. She let out a sigh, which did nothing for the variety of pains shooting through her.

"Do you want the—" Rajesh indicated the moldy bread, but his face fell, and he turned away before he could finish the sentence.

Ignoring his question, she took a quick glance at the window and asked, "Do you know why I started working for Abe?"

"Why?" he asked as he rubbed a hand over his arm, eyes examining the knots in the hardwood floor.

"Because." She waited until he made eye contact with her, and then she said, "It feels good to do the right thing."

He seemed to hold his breath as he stared back.

She held his gaze for several seconds and then nodded toward the window. "Is there any way I can escape? How high up is that window? Could I jump out of it or would I have to climb?"

Rajesh opened his mouth. Before any words escaped, a look of horror overcame him. He jumped to his feet and stepped away from her. "I'm not helping you," he said. "I have the life I want now. It's not my fault this happened."

She tried to coax him back, but he sprinted out the door before she could utter another word. She looked down, giving in to the frown that pulled her mouth down. Things were pretty bad. The tight cords binding her hands and feet seemed impervious to her attempts at loosening them. Her body needed food and especially water. She had at least one broken rib, maybe two. Even if she did somehow break free of her cords, her muscles would be too sore to move right away.

She licked her lips trying to savor the last of the water still lingering there.

Her head hung as she thought back to the catacombs. When Naki had been kidnapped, Imara had been so worried about how she'd be treated. But then, Naki was given plenty of food and water and she wasn't even bound. The worst problem she faced was boredom.

If only Professor Santini were the one holding Imara hostage now.

But even that thought gave her pause. With Professor Santini, the line between good and evil had been nearly impossible to decipher. Imara had trusted her teacher's advice implicitly even when the advice was twisted. At least with Takara the line was clearly drawn. Even the taggers seemed to question some of her murders.

Imara took a deep breath and let the air fill her lungs. She released the breath slowly as she considered her situation again. If escape was out of the question, then she'd just have to do things the hard way. She'd have to trick Takara into letting her go.

TWENTY-THREE

ABE SCROLLED THROUGH THE NAIROBI police directory while Husani and Keiko bickered over possible locations for the taggers' base. The directory only listed one Safiya with an O last name. That had to be her.

He stared at his hologram screen, ready to call. He blinked and stood up instead. "I'm going to the other room," he announced. "You two are distracting me."

"Keiko's hair is distracting me," Husani said. "It's too shiny; it's making me lose focus."

Keiko flashed her teeth at him. "Don't be stupid, Husani. This is important. Do you have any idea what my mother could be doing to Imara right now?"

Abe curled his hand into a fist as he slammed the door behind him. That was one thought he didn't want running rampant through his mind. He called Safiya and raised his eyebrows when she answered right away.

Before he could open his mouth, she was already speaking. She glanced over her shoulder and said, "They deleted the file, but I have a backup at…" Her head rounded back, and she saw Abe's face for the first time. "Who are you?" she demanded.

"Uh," he asked, "Why did you answer without looking at my picture?"

She grunted and looked over her shoulder again. "I was expecting a call from someone else. It doesn't matter. I have to go."

Before she could turn off her ring, she ducked, and two gray blurs flew over her head. It took a moment before he realized they were bullets.

Safiya's face popped back into view, and she aimed a gun before shooting it twice. She seemed to have completely forgotten about the phone call.

"I'm Imara's boyfriend. Imara Kalu," he said, trying to divert her attention back where he wanted it.

The police woman narrowed her eyes and jumped up to smash a fist across a man's face. Abe noted, with no time to interpret the information, that the man wore the exact same police uniform as Safiya. "Congratulations," she said. "As you can see I'm a little busy." She ignored her hologram screen completely as she threw another fist at the man.

Abe thought it strange she hadn't ended the call already, but with her mind on the fight, she probably didn't have a spare moment to turn off her ring. Once Safiya was a safe distance from the uniformed man, Abe said, "Imara's been kidnapped."

A broken drone hurtled over the woman's head, and a cold fear started crawling up his arms. What if she couldn't help them?

Safiya grabbed a nearby ladder. As she climbed, she said, "Kidnapped? Do those Kalu girls have a thing for being kidnapped, or what?"

"She's in trouble. I know she's been helping you. We hoped you could get the Kenyan police to rescue her and maybe help us with some other issues while you're here. We have a lot of corruption in our police force right now."

She snorted at that. "There's the understatement of the century." She dodged another bullet and pulled herself to the top of a roof. "Unfortunately, my own police department is facing corruption as well. I can't do anything for her at the moment."

"But Imara helped you," Abe said. His words seemed empty considering Safiya had been dodging bullets a moment ago. But they *needed* her help. They were counting on her. "If you don't do something, she might die." The words came out before he could process them, which only made the lump in his throat harden like a rock.

"I would if—" Safiya's words turned into a strangled scream. A large hand had wrapped itself around her neck from behind. After the momentary shock, Safiya grabbed a knife from her pocket and stabbed the hand clutching her throat. The hand retracted, and the woman turned and swung a fist. She fished through her pocket and pulled out a stun gun. A second later, the attacker fell to the ground in a heap. He also wore the same uniform as Safiya.

She stuffed the stun gun into her pocket and ran across the roof to a door. With impossible speed, she raced down a dark set of stairs. "I owe a lot to Imara," the woman said. "And I promise I would help her if I could. Unfortunately, I'm being framed for murder at the moment. My airport pass is frozen, and I can't leave the country in a bubble car either. Who kidnapped her? Please tell me it's not that tagger woman, Takara."

Abe gulped. "How do you know about her?"

Safiya entered a dark alleyway and opened a dirt-stained door. Inside the room, take out containers littered the floor, and photos were plastered onto every inch of the wall. She shook her head. "I've been following the news in Egypt. If Takara doesn't take over Cairo soon, Sef will. I'm sorry, I know you have problems, but I have them too."

Just then, Safiya turned toward a knock at the door. She ended the phone call before Abe could say another word. Letting out an angry growl, he kicked a nearby wall. Maybe the help they needed wouldn't be coming at all. Just when he was ready to throw his ring into a fire, someone started calling him. For a split second, he hoped Safiya had changed her mind. Instead, he stared back at a picture of Siluk.

When the call connected, Siluk had his arms folded in front of his chest. His eyebrows were furrowed into a glare. "Naki said Imara got kidnapped, and it's your fault."

"It *wasn't* my fault," Abe said as he ground he teeth together. "It wasn't even my idea." He let out a huff and relaxed his fingers out of the fist he had formed. "It doesn't matter. We were counting on someone to help us, but she can't. I have no idea what to do now except maybe storm Takara's base and take Imara by force. If we do that, we need more people. Hey—" He looked up with a start. "Do you want to fly to Egypt and help rescue Imara?"

Siluk glanced over his shoulder. For the first time, Abe noticed the commotion going on behind his friend. Wood beams, ladders, and tools lay neatly on a patch of snow. It looked like Siluk was in the middle of building some sort of shelter. Not exactly the best time to drop everything and leave.

Siluk looked back again and stroked his chin in thought. "Yeah, I'll come," he said finally.

"Uh," Abe said. "Aren't you busy?"

"Obviously." Siluk shook his head. "I can get to the airport in half an hour, and then it takes an hour to fly to Cairo. Should I bring anything?"

"Uh," Abe said again. He looked to one side and then to the other. "I don't know. We don't even have a plan yet. Just get here as fast as you can, and we'll figure it out as we go."

Siluk nodded, and soon Abe was staring at his empty hologram screen. He was grateful for Siluk's willingness to help. He was. But then why did his writhing gut seem to think it would be better if Siluk stayed far away?

He shook his head and kicked the wall again. He knew why.

History.

Siluk and Imara had history. Maybe not good history, but enough that Siluk willingly dropped everything for her. It begged a question Abe didn't want to think about. Especially not right now. But the question rolled through him knocking on every nerve as it passed.

Could that much history be overpowered?

TWENTY-FOUR

WHEN TAKARA ENTERED THE ROOM A FEW hours later, Imara was ready for her. She pressed herself up against the wall but wore an expression of boredom. She'd been practicing it and hoped it covered at least some of the pain in her face.

"I'm going to show you a video of the Egyptian Council," Takara said. "And then you're going to tell me who is lying."

"I need water first," Imara said. She had decided this was the best way to start off negotiations. She'd try to get something small first, and then something a little bigger. And then a little bigger and then bigger until she could somehow convince Takara to let her go.

"You'll get water when I decide you need it."

This response didn't faze Imara. She didn't expect an agreement right away. While straightening her back, she took care to keep the pain from seeping onto her face. "The guard drank some of my water," she said. "He wanted to show me it wasn't poisonous. But that means I didn't drink as much water as you planned. In order for me to have enough strength to answer your questions, I need water."

Takara stared at her without blinking for almost thirty seconds. She held her body rigid, making it impossible to read. Imara wished for her hila. Even seeing one tiny wisp of emotion might be helpful. But it was useless to dream about. As usual, she had to rely completely on body language. Takara's was cold and distant.

Suddenly, the dark-haired woman shot her hand out and slammed a fist into Imara's side. A crack sounded through the air, and another burning pain rushed through her. She screamed out and fell to the ground, gripping her side.

Another rib broken.

Takara looked down on her with exactly the same expression she wore a moment ago. Tears streamed down Imara's cheeks as she gasped, trying to gulp in air.

After almost a minute, Takara tilted her head to the side. "You're smart, I'll give you that. I like people who are smart; but don't think you can trick me. Be straight with me, and I might give you what you want."

More tears slid down Imara's cheeks, each one mixed with a drop of sweat. The sweat came from her fever, which had only started in the last hour. Or maybe more. She couldn't keep track of the time with all this pain. The fever gave her chills, which was dehydrating her faster. She needed water, and she needed it soon. Curling into a ball, she said, "I want you to leave Cairo."

Takara's eyebrow twitched up for a split second before it fell back to its usual spot. "Why?" she asked.

Maybe the pain had lowered her inhibitions, but soon Imara found the truth spilling from her mouth. "You're ruining the city."

"Why do you care about Cairo?" Takara asked. She folded her arms in front of herself. Her body language remained cold, but a trace of something else lay beneath it.

Curiosity maybe. "I thought you were from Kenya," Takara said. "I didn't even recognize you at first; one of the other taggers did. She said you were the truth seer girl from the catacombs, and I had to check the news feeds to be sure." She shook her head as if trying to dispel a nagging thought. "Carlotta said you wanted to save Kenya. She said you cared about that more than anything else. That's why she planned to take control of Kenya as soon as she had control of Egypt. Egypt first, Kenya second."

The words had barely started to sink in before a fresh burning sensation in her side caused Imara to gag. She took in a shallow breath, and then let it out slowly. "You're going to Kenya next?" she asked. The words tasted foul in her mouth.

Takara laughed, letting the sound fill the room before she spoke. "I am more efficient than Carlotta. I already have people in Kenya, and they're doing a fantastic job."

Imara swallowed, and the familiar sandpaper feeling trailed down her throat. How had she missed this connection? All of Safiya's problems started soon after the catacombs. This had been Professor Santini's plan all along? She blinked. When she opened her eyes, she couldn't tell how long they'd been closed.

"Answer my question," Takara said, lifting a toe to Imara's side.

She blinked back trying to muddle through the thoughts in her head. What question? She hadn't even noticed Takara talking. These blank spots in time were happening more and more. She shook her head again. "I don't know what you said. My brain is being weird, and I keep blacking out. Unless

I get water or some kind of food, I don't think I can help you."

The words came out of her much differently than when she asked for water the first time. That time she had used the soothing voice Professor Santini taught her. It usually calmed people, but it seemed to have the opposite effect on Takara. This new tone of voice came out direct and clear with no nonsense.

The new tone seemed to work much better for Takara. She nodded, then tapped her ring and sent a message. She stared at the door expectantly, but when nobody came, she clicked her tongue. "These people are so stupid," she said. "I'm the only one who seems to have any intelligence whatsoever. Once I get what I want, I'm never working with other people again."

"What *do* you want?" Imara asked, surprised the thought had never occurred to her. She always saw Takara as purely evil, killing anyone who got in her way. Power seemed like the most obvious goal. She wanted Egypt, Kenya, and maybe even the whole world. But if Takara could imagine a time when she didn't have to work with people, then maybe power wasn't her ultimate goal.

Takara grinned like it was her birthday, except the present she'd receive was mass destruction. "I want to murder Marco Santini with my bare hands," she said. "Preferably, I would tear him limb from limb, but even with all my strength training, I don't think my arms will be strong enough. But I do have some effective torture techniques I've been perfecting. I'll torture him for exactly one week, and then I will rip his body apart while he's still alive."

A shiver danced up Imara's spine. Every trace of warmth in the air froze in an instant. "Why? What did Marco do to you?"

Just then, the door opened. Takara rolled her eyes, but by the time she faced the tagger coming into the room, the reaction had vanished. The tagger handed her a cup of water and Takara took it with a short nod. When the tagger left the room and the door shut behind him, Takara pushed the cup to Imara's lips.

She gulped it gratefully even though it was warm. With each swallow, she expected the cup to be stolen from her lips. Instead, she was able to drink it down to the last drop. After Imara drank it all, Takara threw the cup at a wall with a grimace.

Imara shifted her mind to Marco Santini. She knew he was Carlotta Santini's brother, and he had built dams inside the catacombs but used shoddy workmanship. That workmanship led to deaths. Her eyes narrowed. "Did you know someone who drowned when the catacombs flooded?"

"Someone?" Takara said with a sneer. "It wasn't just anybody; it was the love of my life!"

"Keiko's father?" Imara asked.

She knew instantly that was the wrong thing to say. She remembered that Keiko's father was still alive, but also, Takara ground her teeth and slammed a fist against the wall. "Do not speak to me about Montu! That man is the stupidest being to ever exist. He could never come anywhere near the perfection of my Riku. Montu has only ever found fault with me. He deserves the life he has now. I gave him everything, and all he ever does is tell me I'm wrong to want revenge."

Takara's entire demeanor had changed in this exchange. She clenched her fists and huffed through her nose. Her cold indifference had burned to a seething passion. The most interesting thing was how completely she had changed the subject. Apparently she would happily go off on a tangent as long as she felt enough passion for the topic. That could be a helpful thing to exploit when needed.

Takara sneered again but with a weight in her eyes. Her shoulders quaked, and her chin trembled—all signs of grief, whether because of Montu or Riku, it wasn't clear. For a moment, Imara had to remind herself how this woman had murdered freely over the last few months. She may have been beyond forgiveness at this point, but it was interesting that she wasn't beyond sympathy.

Takara let out one last huff and slumped to the ground next to Imara. She tapped her ring and scrolled through the screen until she found a video. She skipped to the middle of the video and said, "Which one of these people is lying?"

The video showed the inside of the council chambers. The sixteen council members sat behind a semi-circular table. Takara had the sound muted, which made it difficult to detect any lies. One of the men stared straight forward and didn't blink the entire time he spoke. Imara lifted her hand to point him out, when the woman next to him covered her mouth and changed the position of her head. Another obvious tell. Several more seconds into the video, seven other council members exhibited obvious signs of lying. When the video ended, she couldn't help any more than when it had started.

"Lying about what?" she asked.

Takara lifted her hand as if to slap her. Imara merely lifted her chin and said, "Every council member is lying in that video. If you want a more specific answer than that, you have to tell me what this is about."

Takara reacted by balling her hand into a fist with a pointed stare at Imara's rib cage. But she seemed to think for a moment and reconsider. "Are any of the council members working with Sef?" Takara asked.

"I don't know. Is that what this video is about?"

"No." She steepled her fingers and set them against her lips. "If I can't figure out which council member is lying, I have a plan that involves Sef. I'm going to get his list and trade it to the council for the information I want."

"That could work," Imara said. "They've been trying to catch Sef for years, and the list has everything they need. But it's on his ring in an un-shareable file."

"I know." Takara stared back her, running a thumb along the hem of her shirt as she thought. After a moment, she nodded to herself as if coming to a decision.

"The video is about Marco," she said. "The council members each say where they think he's been hiding for the past twenty years. I already know they're all lying because none of them said Alaska, and everyone knows he's in Alaska. One of the council members helped him hide twenty years ago, so I *know* one of them knows where he is. I just don't know which one."

"You're trying to find him? Why don't you just go—" The words froze in Imara's throat before she finished the sentence. Maybe she shouldn't give Takara any ideas.

It didn't matter. Takara guessed exactly what she almost said. "Go to Alaska and look for him myself? I tried that. Alaska is too big with too many tiny towns. I didn't even know he was still alive until six months ago. Carlotta lied to me. And then she convinced me that getting the location from the Egyptian Council would be the most efficient way to find him. Now that I'm so close, I actually agree."

Imara closed her eyes. Her chin fell, and she started to nod off. Again. She clenched her jaw, trying to keep herself awake. A thought tickled at the back of her mind, persisting until it roared to the front. There were too many tiny towns in Alaska. And if Takara knew the right town, she could probably ask around and find Marco in a matter of hours.

It was strange then that Takara spent so much effort trying to get Imara to find a liar, when all she had to do was ask which town Marco lived near. Because Imara happened to know that. She knew someone who lived close enough that he used Marco's name as an insult. The memory from the catacombs flashed through her mind causing a wave of panic to flip through her.

The question of whether or not she should protect Marco wasn't really a question at all. Takara wanted to murder him and Imara didn't want his blood on her hands. So, she'd have to play this game of searching for the liar and hope a more direct question never got asked.

"I don't understand," she said. "If you already knew they were lying, what did you expect me to see in the video?"

Takara went back to the video and this time, turned up the volume. "That's the trick," she said. "Most of them have no idea where Marco is. So, they're lying, but they're also lying about lying. Only one member of the Egyptian Council actually knows his location. *That's* who I want you to identify."

The video began again. With the volume turned up, it was even easier to identify lies. Even without her hila. She'd leaned on it for so long, and all that time she didn't even need it. Her eyes flitted from one council member to the next. They all displayed obvious tells, nothing special in any of them.

But then, she saw it.

A tiny woman who looked about ninety years old. She seemed vaguely familiar and had short gray hair and buck teeth. As she spoke, the old woman added extraneous details to her story, making it seem more believable. In fact, her story sounded more believable than anyone else's.

And then she scratched her nose.

Watching the rest of the video only confirmed Imara's guess. That tiny woman was the one Takara wanted. That meant she needed to be protected.

When the video ended, Takara stared expectantly.

"I got eraserfalled. I can tell they're all lying, but I can't see what you want me to see."

For a long time, Takara did nothing but stare back at her. Her cold and hardened expression had returned. Without warning, she pulled a knife from her pocket. Before Imara could cower at the sight, the cords around her ankles and wrists had been cut. She stared at her wrists and then looked up at the woman, too surprised to react.

The black-haired woman forced Imara onto her feet. The moment she stood, she collapsed again. After spending so long in a crouched position, her muscles were unable to support her body. Coupled with the pain in her ribs, she could do nothing but clutch her side and gasp.

Takara's eye twitched at the sight. Rather than exhibit a shred of sympathy, she tapped her toe and rolled her eyes.

After a huff, she opened the door and snapped her fingers. Rajesh appeared in the doorway a moment later. "Carry her," Takara said. Without further explanation, she left the room.

TWENTY-FIVE

RAJESH LOOKED DOWN AT THE BROKEN
cords in front of Imara and then looked back at the doorway.
He knitted his eyebrows together, clearly straining in thought.

"I think Takara wants you to pick me up and follow her,"
she said. "I can't walk."

He bounced his head with a nod while wrapping one arm
under her knees and one around her shoulders. Her ribs
jarred as he lifted her from the ground, causing a gasp to
escape her. Each step felt like another pummel to her side.
Rajesh took careful steps at first, but the farther ahead Takara
got, the more hurried and pain-inducing his steps became.
When they started down a flight of stairs, she groaned each
time his foot touched down. When they reached the bottom,
a mixture of sweat and tears caked her face with saltwater.

At last, Takara had stopped in front of a door. She set her
palm on a bioscanner, and the door opened. After pointing to
a padded chair with restraints, she headed for the large
hologram covering one wall.

Rajesh dropped Imara onto the chair in a move that was
probably meant to be gentle. He quickly glanced back at
Takara. While she scrolled through the wall hologram, he
snuck a chunk of bread into Imara's hand. She stuffed it into

her mouth and swallowed it in one gulp to get rid of the evidence as soon as possible.

When Takara turned away from the hologram, she scowled at Rajesh. "Leave now. Stand outside the door, and I'll tell you when I need you again."

As he plodded away, Imara searched around the room. A short cart hovered next to her padded chair. On top of the cart sat two plastic trays: one empty and one littered with syringes. She tried to ignore the shiver that thrummed through her as she looked along the back wall. On a short shelf sat a small collection of knives. Next to that was a box of magnets. The longer she stared, the more sinister they looked.

How could Takara use magnets? And for what?

When the door shut behind Rajesh, a corner of Takara's eye seemed to glisten. She had gotten distracted earlier when confronted with a topic she cared about, and now might be a good time to use that. It took a moment to recall the name, but when she did, Imara said, "Tell me about Riku. Were you married before the flood?"

Takara's face fell. Whatever had been on her mind seemed to be erased completely. She swallowed, and the glistening in her eye grew. Looking down, she said, "Our wedding was less than a week away. Even though we were from Japan, we were getting married in Alexandria because Riku always wanted to live there." She looked down, and her breath trembled as she tried to swallow. "We both drowned in the catacombs."

Imara's lips parted in surprise.

"Riku held my hand while the water filled our lungs. He looked me straight in the eye and said, 'I love you. In life and in death.' Well, he only mouthed it because we were underwater, but I knew what he was trying to say. He said it to me a lot."

She turned away and let out a little sniffle. "I remember exactly what it felt like to drown. The blackness that surrounded me. The dark taking over. I was scared but at peace because I knew Riku would be there in death." A long puff of hair escaped her nose. "But then, suddenly, I was waking up. The water had been removed from my lungs, and I lived; but Riku was nowhere to be found."

She turned around, and her cheeks flushed with heat. "We had drifted away from each other after I blacked out. It was too late for Riku by the time they got to him." Her fist reeled through the air until it crashed down on the corner of the empty plastic tray, sending it flying. "Marco stole away the love of my life less than a week before our wedding. On that day, I vowed I would get revenge if it was the last thing I ever did."

Before Imara could react, Takara stuck a syringe into the skin under Imara's ear. A tight pain contracted every muscle in her body. As her muscles seized, she started shaking. Shards of glass seemed to scrape through her veins. She heard a voice screaming for at least four seconds before she realized it was her own. Her eyes rolled back into her head, and she screamed even harder.

A small pillow got stuffed into her mouth. In a split-second glance, she could see Takara standing by with perfect indifference, neither taking delight in her pain nor being bothered by it.

Ten seconds later, the seizing stopped, and Imara sucked in gulp after gulp of air. While she gasped, Takara removed the pillow and shoved something new into her mouth.

After the disorienting pain, it took a moment to realize what sat on her tongue. She noted the soft texture and delighted in the taste. Food. Stuffed squash seasoned with curry. Not just food, but delicious food. She chewed ravenously, and savored the taste as it slid down her throat. After she swallowed, Takara placed another chunk of the squash into her mouth. She chewed without question, enjoying every moment.

After ten delectable bites, she wanted to sing Takara's praises. But that thought made her pause.

Takara narrowed her eyes and leaned forward until their noses almost touched. "Remember," she said. "I can help you or I can hurt you. If you give me the information I want, I'll give you more food. If you give me anything else, I'll use you to practice torture techniques."

Imara gripped the sides of her padded chair as she gulped. "What if I can't help you find the liar? You said you might trade Sef's list to the Egyptian Council for information, right? Do you have it already?"

"You have a lot of nerve asking a question like that since the only reason you're here is because you lied about having the list. Why would I capture you if I had it already?"

Imara ignored the question. She needed Takara to go off on a tangent again. She needed to keep her talking, and a good ego stroking might do it. "Keiko says you're the best hacker in the world. Is that how you plan to get the list?"

The woman let out a soft chuckle. Rolling her shoulders back, she said, "It did take some of my most brilliant hacking, but yes, I already have something in place. I put a virus on

Sef's ring that already located his infamous list. The file is still un-shareable, but if he accesses the list from a wall hologram, my virus will create a copy of it, and the copy will download to the wall hologram. I just have to trick him into accessing the list from a wall hologram, and then the list is mine."

"The Egyptian Council might not give you Marco's location even if you have the list. Despite the corruption in Egypt, they're still morally strong."

Takara raised an eyebrow and tilted her head to the side. "How do you know so much about Egyptian politics?"

"Because of my..." Imara stopped before she said anymore. If Takara knew about Abe, she could use it against either of them.

Takara waved a hand through the air. "Yes, yes," she said. "Itafe Nazari's son. I've had both of you followed for weeks. You seem to like him, but I still don't understand why you're here all the time. Carlotta was so sure you wanted to save Kenya."

"What I want is to be a good person."

The woman pushed her silky black hair over her shoulder in a movement so familiar, Imara could practically see Keiko staring back at her. "You're not a good person now?" Takara asked.

"I'm trying to be." Imara shifted on the chair, which only sent a burning sensation through her rib cage. She grimaced, and only part of it was caused by the pain. "I used to be cynical and hurtful, especially to my sister. All I want is to make things right with her."

Takara let out a short laugh. "I doubt that."

"Why?"

"*All* you want is to make things right with your sister?" Takara asked.

187

"Yes," she said bobbing her head up and down.

This only caused Takara to roll her eyes. "If that's all you want, then why are always in Egypt? If you want to make things right with your sister, then shouldn't you go home and make things right with her instead of spending all your time here?"

"You don't understand," Imara said as she clenched her jaw. Things are crazy right now because of Sef and because of you. But it won't be like this forever. Soon I'll have time for my sister."

"Stop," Takara said, holding her palm up. "I don't care. I want to know which Egyptian Council member knows where Marco is. That's it."

Imara folded her arms over her chest and forced her eyebrows as low as they could go. "Then I can't help you."

Without a word, Takara lifted another syringe and stabbed it into Imara's neck. Within seconds, she was screaming.

And screaming.

Pain washed through her, even greater than before. Fire burned through her ribs and through her arms. When the worst effect of the syringe had worn off, her shoulders shook with sobs.

Takara plucked another syringe from the tray, but Imara cried out, "Don't. Please don't. I can't take it again."

"Then give me what I want," Takara said simply.

Tears streamed down Imara's cheeks as her chest bounced with hiccups. Each one felt like a cricket bat to her ribs. "I don't know any more than you, please just let me go." She never intended to resort to begging, but the pain had become too much.

Another syringe punctured through her skin, and the shooting pain seized her muscles yet again. Her heart fluttered when the pain finally stopped. Gasping for breath, she begged for a second time. "Please. *Please* don't do it again."

Takara lifted another needle, and it was too much. She had to give in.

"I have…" Imara hiccupped as more tears poured down her cheeks, "I have an idea."

Takara paused, pulling the syringe back. "Go on," she said.

Her breath shuddered as she tried to take in air without jarring her ribs. Finally, she said, "You want information from the Egyptian Council, and Sef wants to be a member of the Egyptian Council. You both have control over half the city. Instead of fighting each other, why don't you just work together?"

Takara brought a hand to her chin as she thought. "Interesting. The taggers wouldn't like it because we're supposed to hate criminals, but if I found a way to get the taggers to agree…" She tapped her chin. "How could I get the taggers to agree?"

"I don't know," she said as she panted. "Please, I can't think with all this pain."

Takara jabbed another needle into her neck, and finally Imara understood. The woman didn't care whether she lived or died. She would to squeeze as much information out of her as possible and then discard her like some broken drone.

The searing pain seized through her again. The world swirled around like whips and jerks. Her body shook so hard, she worried it would break another rib. Her vision went white. Prickles scratched under her skin while fire seemed to erupt from every pore. Sweat poured down her neck, and all she could think was that she finally understood how a person could want to die.

And that's when she felt it.

A choice.

Each thump of her heart was more labored than the last. If her head stopped fighting, her heart might stop too. If she wanted to end this, she could.

But… Naki.

She couldn't leave before they fixed things. Not yet. Not when they were so close.

And Abe.

He had believed in her when no one else did. If she could fight for anything, she could fight for him.

And her parents too. And maybe even Kenya. She couldn't give up now.

With that thought, the pain inside her changed. It still hurt more than anything she had ever experienced, but it was no longer a death wish. Now it was a triumph.

She squeezed her fists and screamed out. Not a strangled cry, but a war cry. Nothing could stop her now. She would leave this place and fix things with Naki.

This wasn't over yet.

It was hard to tell how long the pain lasted after that, but when it finally subsided, a smile tugged at her lips. She sat up in the chair and took in deep gulps of air, ready for anything.

Takara stared at her without blinking. Her face showed awe, but she wasn't necessarily inspired by it. Mostly curious.

"What happened?" Takara asked.

The smile on Imara's lips grew, and, somehow, her muscles seemed stronger than they had in days. "I'm not helping you," she said.

For awhile, Takara did nothing but stare. Again, she asked. "What happened to you?" She pulled Imara's shirt down to reveal a monitor button attached to her chest. Tapping it, Takara said, "Your vitals dropped. You almost had a heart attack, but then something changed. Did you have a thought? Or remember something?"

Before either of them had a chance to speak, a man with drooping earlobes entered the room. He tugged at one of his earlobes and reluctantly said, "Your daughter is here."

Takara flashed her teeth and threw one of her syringes at the man. "What are you talking about?"

He threw his hands in front of his face and gasped. When the syringe clattered to the ground without puncturing him, he straightened. Now, he seemed to fear Takara's anger over his silence. He tapped his hologram ring, and a security video displayed. Keiko stood in front of a mansion, probably the one they were all inside of. Her face burned red, and her mouth opened and closed with wide movements, making it clear she was yelling.

The sound must have been directed straight to Takara's earphones because the room stayed silent, but she seemed to be reacting to the words. A moment later, Takara slapped a third tray which caused a knife to soar through the air and slice through her hand on the way down. She screamed and batted the knife away, causing a splatter of blood to burst from her hand. She shoved the man out of her way and clenched her fists as she ran from the room. He winced and reached again for his earlobe.

"Help me," Imara said before he could leave.

He dropped his hand and gave her a look that almost looked liked sympathy. Almost. But then he turned toward the door.

"Do you agree with Takara's actions? The drone attack, the murders?" she asked.

The man paused, but only for a moment. His hand hovered over the door opener, not quite ready to close it. "Do you?" Imara asked. "Is this what you wanted to accomplish when you came to Cairo? Did you want taggers to be known as murderers?"

Dropping his arm to the side, he let out a long breath. "Taggers are not murderers. We want to protect the world from villains." He looked down. "We weren't supposed to become the villains."

She sat up in the chair, doing everything she could to ignore the fire in her side. "Please help me," she said. "I am not your enemy."

His face twisted up into a grimace as cold as ice. "You killed Carlotta. You *are* the enemy." Without a word, he left the room and locked the door behind him.

With a deep breath, she pushed herself off the chair to stand. The pain dropped her to her knees at once. He was right. She was partially responsible for Professor Santini's death. The guilt of it might never fade completely. Her ribs rattled as she sucked in a breath.

But, she hadn't survived torture just to give up now. She tore the monitor button off her chest and eyed the door. Pain or not, she was going to escape.

192

TWENTY-SIX

IT HAD BEEN TWO DAYS SINCE IMARA GOT kidnapped, and Abe was ready to personally rip out the throat of anyone who got in his way. He could imagine plenty of things Takara might have done to Imara in that time, and only a few of them seemed better than death.

He balled his hands into fists and paced the room. They'd taken a day and a half to locate the taggers' base. Five hours to sleep. Two to gather supplies. None to make a plan. All this time, and they still only had four people and a half-baked idea.

Four people to break into Takara's mansion. Four people to rescue Imara.

Him, Husani, Keiko, and Siluk. Edrice would do remote work as usual. Keiko wasn't even supposed to help since she was under the global working age. But she said she wasn't going to leave so Abe might as well stop arguing about it.

Husani walked in and raised an eyebrow. "You're pacing again."

"Really?" Abe said. "I had no idea."

Husani leaned his shoulder up against a wall. "What are you so nervous about? We go on rescue missions all the time. This is literally our job."

Abe flashed his teeth with a sneer.

Husani moved from the wall and gave him a comforting pound on the back. "Imara can take care of herself. She'll be all right."

A glare was the only response he could muster. They had absolutely no guarantee Imara would be all right. They didn't even know if she was still alive. The sooner they got to work, the better.

Just then, Siluk came in through the door. "Finally," Abe said. "Let's go." They followed him to the main room where Keiko and Edrice argued over whether or not they should risk contacting the Egyptian police.

At this point, if the decision hadn't been made, it wasn't going to be made. He plucked his bag from the ground and said, "We're leaving. Forget the police."

Keiko nodded with a look of triumph. She grabbed her own bag, and soon all four of them were out the door. Once in the bubble car, Abe went over the plan again.

"This is a classic distract and grab. Avoid physical contact at all costs. All of you will cause a distraction that's hopefully big enough to draw out Takara and anyone else in the mansion. While you're busy, I'll slip in and find Imara."

Husani rubbed his knuckles. As usual before a mission, his eyes were shifting from playful to serious.

Siluk pulled a handful of glass balls from his pocket, each one a little bigger than a marble. "Here are the fire bombs," he said. He handed half of them to Abe. "Just smash them on the ground, and once the scent spreads out, it will smell like there's a fire nearby. Hopefully that's enough to get some taggers to go and investigate."

"Won't the smell get on our clothes?" Keiko asked as she leaned in to look at the glass balls.

Siluk nodded. "Yes, if you're too close. Make sure to smash them at least five feet away from your body, and then get to another room as quick as you can."

Husani rubbed his knuckles one last time before giving Abe a little punch on the shoulder. "Why are you so quiet? Where's our rousing speech?"

Abe jerked his body away with a frown. "I'll feel better when I know Imara's safe."

Luckily, Husani got distracted by a call from Edrice. He pushed his hologram back and increased the size so all of them could see her clearly.

"The mansion is only two levels," Edrice said. "It looks like most of the bedrooms are upstairs. The main floor is mostly the kitchen and living area. There's also a bathroom and conservatory, but it's doubtful you'll find Imara there. There's also a large utility room that might be worth checking out after you go through the bedrooms."

Siluk sat up and leaned toward the screen. "Do you have the blueprints? Can we see them?"

"No," Abe said. "Anyone can look at the blueprints through the city database, but you can't download them."

Siluk's expression soured. "So, we're relying solely on Edrice's memory?"

"She has photographic memory," Husani said.

"Oh." Siluk sat back in his chair, relaxing his shoulders. "Never mind then."

"Do you need directions on the safe house again?" Edrice asked.

"We know," Husani said. "It's the usual safe house with food, water, and medical supplies. We'll take Imara there to hide out from the taggers and to assess if she needs to go to the hospital."

They spent the rest of the car ride discussing strategies, but Abe only contributed small grunts and nods. He'd spent so much time getting ready, this was the first time he had a chance to really think. Of course his mind went to a conversation he wanted to forget.

Just before Imara had been kidnapped, she called him healer. *Ugh*, again. Why couldn't she let it go? And she said he feared responsibility. That was ridiculous. He wasn't the perfect boyfriend, but at least he tried. What would she say if she found out about…

He clenched his jaw to shut the door on that thought. He'd worry about that if, and only if, it ever came up. It wasn't that big of a deal anyway.

Thinking back on the conversation, he clenched his jaw tighter. Imara also said he only saved people who didn't expect to be saved. That was even more ridiculous. He was on his way to save her, wasn't he? Didn't she expect him to do that?

But no, of course she didn't. Twice in the catacombs Imara saved herself. If he knew anything, it was how Imara was sitting in that mansion trying to figure out how to free herself. She never expected anyone to save her.

He loved that about her, but did that mean she had been right? That he only saved the people who didn't expect it?

His fingers curled tighter into a fist until his fingernails dug into the palm of his hand. Whether she expected it or not, he wouldn't rest until he held her safe in his arms. He'd worry about his nonexistent hila later.

They arrived around the corner from Takara's mansion only a minute later. Seeing it looming in front of them sent a rush through every limb in his body. They kept the bubble car out of sight and then crept toward it on their tiptoes.

Keiko glared at the mansion for a solid thirty seconds before she finally spoke. "I can see a lot of sounds coming from inside, but they're all on the main floor. I'm a sound seer," Keiko said, pointing at Siluk before he could ask.

He nodded in return.

Keiko narrowed her eyes again and licked her lips. Finally, her expression softened. "I think there are only three people in the front room. We won't know for sure until they open the door. The good news is, there's a security camera on the porch just like I hoped. I should be able to draw my mom out if I scream loud enough."

"What about the upper level?" Abe asked.

"I can't see any sounds coming from up there," Keiko said. "But sometimes it's hard to tell through windows. And there could be people up there who aren't making any noise."

He nodded and dug through his backpack for his rope ladder. It had a mechanism on the end that would automatically attach to any surface. "I'm going in on the second level then. Keiko, don't start yelling until I'm at the window."

She nodded in reply, and they all waited as he threw the ladder with the mechanism hitting on the window ledge. As usual, it landed exactly where he wanted it.

Just as he started climbing, Keiko held out her hand and glared at the security camera. "It's beeping," she said. "I think you set off an alarm."

Just then, his phone started buzzing, and he accepted a call from Edrice. "That team of taggers by the warehouse just started moving. You have about seven minutes before Takara's backup arrives."

Abe nodded and ended the call. "A backup team of taggers is coming," he said to the others. "They'll get here in about seven minutes. Husani, I need you to keep me on track with time, so you're coming with me. Keiko and Siluk, distract the brains out of these guys. And remember: distract and run; don't engage."

Husani was right on his heels as he started up the ladder. A moment later, Keiko started screaming. "HEY! I know you're in there, Mother. I want my money!" She banged on the door and raised her voice several notches. "HELLLLOOOOOO? I KNOW YOU'RE IN THERE! If you don't come out here, I'm going to call a news reporter and get her to broadcast all the nasty things you've done to Dad and me. Do you think the stupid taggers will listen to you after they've heard all that?"

Abe had climbed to the window now. He used a metal rod to smash it open. "How long?" he asked.

"Six minutes, thirteen seconds," Husani replied.

Abe climbed into the dark room. Empty. Not just empty of people, but empty. No furniture. No wall hangings. Nothing. Nothing except a long rope and an awful stench. He clutched his stomach to keep from gagging.

"Time?"

"Five minutes, fifty-eight seconds."

He nodded and pressed the door opener. When the door whooshed open, they walked into a long hallway with at least five more doors. A staircase led to the downstairs, and someone at the bottom must have heard them because she started heading up.

Abe pulled a fire bomb from his pocket. He shifted his body closer to the staircase until he could toss the fire bomb over the banister and down the stairs. The tagger was halfway up the stairs before she paused and started back down again.

He let out a breath of relief and looked at Husani.

"Five minutes, twenty-three seconds," Husani whispered.

They tried the next door, but this room looked the same as the last. Empty hardwood floors, empty walls. Nothing but a rope and a stench that induced nausea. Before leaving the room, Abe looked closer at the rope. This one had been cut with a knife. He bent down to examine it and found a few black hairs on the ground next to it. Short, but curly. He'd recognize them anywhere. Imara's.

She had been here, but where was she now? Why had only her hairs been left behind?

"Four minutes, forty-five seconds, Abe. We need to move."

TWENTY-SEVEN

IMARA FORCED HERSELF TO HER FEET AND slammed a hand against the door opener. Locked. Of course it was. She searched for a heavy object and grabbed a metal pitcher sitting on the shelf. She slammed it over and over into the door opener, but it did nothing. This door opener must have been more advanced than most. *Of course it was.*

She closed her eyes and tried to think. Adrenaline flooded her veins now, but she didn't know how long it would last. Picking through her brain, she remembered Edrice had told her about these door openers a few weeks ago. The scanner checked either the hand print or the DNA, but usually not both.

Placing a hand over the scanner, she watched the light glow, and a tingle went through her palm.

DNA dependent then. If she could just find some of Takara's DNA, she might be able to trick the scanner.

She went straight to the splatter of blood from Takara's cut on the wall. Imara rubbed her palm across the blood until it covered her hand.

She went back to the scanner and held her breath as she tried again. The door sputtered, opening just a crack. She tried to shove her shoulder through the opening, but she didn't have enough room. Instead, she grabbed a tray from the ground and jimmied it into the crack.

Once she had the right angle, she pulled back on the tray to use it as leverage to push the door open more. She gained another few centimeters. That would have to do. With the pain in her ribs and the adrenaline fading, this was her only chance.

She squeezed herself through the opening, holding her breath as her ribs brushed the door frame. Once outside the door, she panted hard, immediately noticing the smell of fire. No smoke filled the air around her, but she heard several shouts and shuffling of footsteps back near the staircase she had come done earlier.

With no one in her immediate vicinity, she tiptoed down the hall until she found the front door. Takara stood in the door frame. Imara turned on her heel and sprinted down another hall. She spotted a window that looked easy enough to open and climb through. As long as she could do it without being too loud.

Her bloody handprints adorned the window as she struggled with the lock. But soon, she had it open and pushed her body outside. When her feet hit the ground, a nearby figure started toward her. She raised her hands, ready to fight, only to have them fall to her side a moment later.

"Siluk?" she asked.

She shook her head. Maybe she was seeing things. Her brain had been acting funny all day. "Where's Abe?" was all she could think to say.

His eyes widened at the blood on her hand, but he tore them away to glance down the road and back up again. "He's supposed to be rescuing you. How did you get out?"

He was at her side before she could respond. He squeezed her shoulder, probably in an attempt to comfort her, but after the torture she had endured, it did nothing but cause a shooting pain throughout her body.

She gasped and doubled over in pain, her knees scraping against the road. The adrenaline that helped her escape was fading fast, the pain in her ribs nearly blinding her. Siluk's lips parted in horror, and he reached for her again, trying to help.

"I can't walk," she said through a gasp.

Siluk nodded and lifted her to her feet. He wrapped her arm around his shoulder and guided her down the road. After they rounded a corner, he helped her into a bubble car. He tapped his ring and typed in a message to Abe.

I have Imara. I'm taking her to the safe house in the bubble car. Meet us there.

She clutched her side as the car began to move. After a few small coughs, she asked, "Why are you even here, Siluk? Am I hallucinating or something?"

He laughed, but it didn't erase the fear etched into his eyes. "You know, one of these days you should let someone rescue you instead of rescuing yourself."

She dug her fingernails into her knees, trying anything to get her mind off the pain. "I only escaped because Keiko made Takara leave the room. And there was a fire that distracted the taggers."

With that, Siluk smirked. "Not a fire, just the smell of a fire. And you can thank *me* for that."

She looked up to thank him, but got hit with a wave of nausea instead. She squeezed her eyes shut and wrapped her arms over her stomach. Not too tight, or it would only make things worse on her ribs. "Are we almost there?" she asked.

Abe tossed another fire bomb over the banister before they moved to the next room. He could hear frazzled shouts from downstairs. Good. He didn't want the chaos to let up anytime soon. In the next room, things looked exactly the same as the other room, except this one didn't smell quite as bad.

It still worried him though. How many people was Takara holding hostage? And what exactly was she doing with them? And how long had she been doing it?

Just as he prepared to open the last door, he got a message from Siluk. He saw Imara's name and barely had a chance to register the rest.

Husani spouted off the time, but Abe had already run down the hall back to the first room. He was climbing down the ladder before Husani caught up. Once at the bottom, he sprinted toward the safe house, completely unaware of Takara, the taggers, or even the mansion. All he needed now was to see Imara.

ಜಿಜಿಜಿಜಿ

Imara lowered herself onto the velvety couch in the safe room. When Siluk handed her a pillow, she gently positioned it against her side. It didn't help. Nothing seemed to help with the pain, not even the pain killer Siluk had found in one of the kitchen cupboards. He propped another pillow behind her head, and then left to get her a glass of water.

He returned with a glass filled to the very brim. The sight of it almost made her cry. She took tiny sips, but even that caused too much pain in her side. She sighed and pushed the cup back into his hands. Just as she fell back on the pillow, the front door opened. An instant later, Abe vaulted himself to her side.

For one strange moment, all she could think about was saltwater caking her face and the stench seeping from her skin. What would he think of her? She should have asked Siluk to spray the smell away.

Abe pressed one hand to her cheek and wrapped the other around her shoulders. He stared into her eyes as if nothing in the world existed except her, and all those silly thoughts melted away. "I thought you'd be dead," he said. "I thought—" But then his voice broke, and he buried his face in her neck while a sob shook through him.

She squeezed him back, suddenly not caring how much it hurt. Everything would be okay now. She breathed in deeply, enjoying the spicy smell of him. A trace of the milky, musk layered scent lingered on his clothes, but the spicy, sweetness of cinnamon and cardamom overpowered it.

His hand slipped down her back and around her side until he brushed a thumb across her ribcage. "Broken ribs?" he said through his teeth. "Three of them!" He set his forehead against hers until their noses touched. "What did she do to you?"

"I'm fine," she said. She wasn't, but he knew that.

He huffed and pulled her into a tighter hug, but one that gripped her shoulders instead of her stomach. Somehow, he knew just where to set his hands to make the pain feel better, not worse. He kissed her forehead three times as he brushed his thumb along her ribcage. With each brush, the searing pain began to dull. He opened his mouth to say something, but before he could, Husani spoke loudly.

"Oooooh," Husani said, drawing out the syllable so it lasted a few seconds. Abe flinched and immediately dropped his head into her neck until his lips pressed against her collar bone.

"You guys are dating *each other*," Husani said.

Imara tilted her head to the side, but Siluk voiced the question in her mind. "You didn't know that?" He narrowed his eyes while his hand curled into a fist. "Why didn't he know that, Abe?"

Abe turned his face away from all of them. He closed his eyes and stroked her arm. Little pockets of anger and mistrust bubbled up inside her, but she pushed them all away. She'd had enough surprises for one day. All she wanted now was to soak in as much of Abe as she possibly could. Everything else could wait.

"Does Edrice know?" Husani asked quietly.

This made Imara sit up in surprise, which she immediately regretted. Abe's eyebrows rose to the top of his head as his hand settled over her ribs. He rubbed ever so gently over them while his other hand massaged her shoulder. Already, the pain from her jolt began to fade. She winced and leaned back into the couch. "You said it wasn't against the rules for us to date each other," she said.

One of Husani's eyebrows twitched upward as he stared at Abe.

"It's not against the rules," Abe said. He stroked her cheek while a tear fell away from his eye. "Don't worry about that right now."

Before anyone could say another word, Keiko burst through the front door with a scowl that could have made snow fall in the Sahara desert. "Thanks for waiting for me, guys. I thought we were all going back in the bubble car together."

"Imara could barely stand," Siluk said simply. "I decided not to wait."

Keiko's scowl dropped as she clapped a hand over her mouth. When her eyes wandered over to the couch, her eyebrows jumped up in surprise.

"Did *you* know they were dating?" Siluk asked.

"Enough," Abe said. "We can deal with that later. I'm taking Imara to a hospital, so the rest of you can go home. We'll make new plans in a couple days after she has time to recover."

TWENTY-EIGHT

SEVERAL HOURS LATER, IMARA ALMOST FELT good enough to dance. Her ribs were set and secured with dissolvable nano bots. She'd had enough food and water to make up for her time in Takara's mansion. In a few days, she'd be as good as new. They just had to make a quick stop back at headquarters to grab her jacket. Then, in less than an hour, she'd be home.

Abe took her hand as they entered the familiar building. The moment she stepped through the door, the air hung thick with a sense of dread. She tried to ignore it as she followed him into the office. Soon, the search for her jacket was forgotten.

Edrice stood at her desk with both her fists clenched tight. A vein popped out of her forehead, the purple matching the ribbon in her hair.

After four straight hours of Abe picking the goop from her eyes, Imara saw tiny wisps of angry blood red flames snaking off Edrice's skin. The excitement of getting her hila back got smothered by the tension around them.

Edrice slammed her fist onto the desk, and Abe gripped tighter on Imara's hand.

"Is it true?" Edrice asked. "You're dating her?"

"I'm allowed to date whoever I want," he said.

She shook her head. "Are you serious, Abe? That's the best you've got?"

He took in a deep breath and held it, releasing neither words nor air.

"How did you think this was going to turn out?" Edrice asked. "Bringing her here? To work with us? How could you possibly think that was a good idea?"

Imara rubbed her foot along the back of her leg. She tugged the hair on the back of her neck, trying to decide if she wanted to know what was going on or not. She decided not, but that wouldn't make the problem go away. Biting her lip, she turned to face Abe, making sure he could see she wanted answers too.

When her eyes met his, he looked down with a frown. A sign of shame. Even his shoulders hunched. And now a drop of mustard yellow guilt dripped off his skin. "Edrice is my ex," he said.

She gulped because somehow she knew. The signs were there all along even though she had done her best to ignore them. Even still, she wasn't prepared for Edrice's reaction to Abe's words.

"Your *ex*?" Edrice said with a scoff. "Don't say it like that, Abe. She deserves to know the truth."

Imara turned to Edrice with an eyebrow raised. The pain in her ribs may have been healing, but another kind of pain sprouted in her heart.

Edrice folded her arms in front of her chest. "We were together for over two years. And we broke up less than a month before your little escapade in the catacombs. I don't know what you think is happening with him, but I can assure you, it's nothing serious."

Abe dropped Imara's hand, leaving a chill between her fingers. He took a step forward and said, "I'm allowed to date whoever I want. Don't blame this on Imara."

Edrice laughed. "Blame it on Imara? Why do you think I'm blaming her? I love Imara. No, I'm putting the entire blame on you, *Abraxas*." She slammed her fist onto the desk again. "What were you thinking? We're trying to run a business. One that happens to be falling apart if you haven't noticed. So what do you do? You bring your rebound girlfriend to work with your ex, and then you decide not to tell anyone? How long did you think the charade would last? Did you consider the consequences for one second? Even one tiny little second?"

His nostrils flared as he coiled his hands into fists. "Imara needed a job. Plus, we needed someone with her skills. I made a business decision."

"A business decision?" Edrice said, forcing out a laugh. "That makes complete sense. Because we've never had anything personal affect employees. We haven't had three girls quit *in a row* because of how Husani treated them. Oh wait, yes we have. This is probably the stupidest thing you have ever done in your entire life."

He flexed his jaw so hard, the veins in his neck strained. "Imara is brilliant at rescue missions. Her skills have been critical."

Edrice rolled her eyes, and her shoulders went back with them. "You're trying to make this about Imara, but it's not."

Imara swallowed, trying to ignore the tightness in her chest. She spotted her jacket on a nearby chair and began taking tiny steps toward it. Once she had it, they could go. Maybe some space would be good for Edrice.

"Do you think I'm stupid?" Edrice asked. "I know you just did this to make me jealous. It's completely obvious and not fair to her at all."

Abe grabbed a chair and pushed it so hard, it fell on its side. When it landed, he kicked it to the wall. "She needed a job. How would you like it if you lost your dream job because of an eraserfall?"

"You think that's worse than what I actually have to deal with?" Edrice asked. "Which is probably losing my entire business because you thought it was a good idea to bring your rebound girlfriend to work with your long term-girlfriend."

"I got my jacket," Imara said suddenly. Her voice came out higher than she expected, but at least she'd gotten the words out.

He nodded, and the tension in his shoulders relaxed for a split second.

When he turned toward her, the vein in Edrice's forehead throbbed and blood red flames of anger shot out through her skin. "What am I supposed to do now?" she shouted. "Fire her?"

"No," Abe said, immediately turning back to Edrice.

Her jaw set, and she spoke through her teeth. "Should I fire you instead? Do you want to sell me your portion of the business?"

His entire body twitched, but then a strange calm came over him. It started at his shoulders and soon swept through his body until all his muscles had relaxed. He sighed and tilted his head to the side. Watching him, Imara could see that he was annoyed, and yet, comfortable. This was an argument he knew how to have. That alone made the tightness in her chest grow. So much history, and maybe it couldn't all be forgotten.

He let out a short sigh. "Don't do this, Edrice. We can work it out."

In a shrill voice, she asked, "How? How did you think—"

Abe turned away from her and put his hand on Imara's shoulder. She almost shrank away from his touch but managed to keep herself steady enough to look him in the eye.

"You can go," he said. "I'll message you later tonight to see how you're doing."

She opened her mouth to protest, but Edrice started talking before she could let any words out. "We might have to fire her. You know how stupid it is to date employees. And don't argue with me about it; you know I can get your dad on board. I already called him, and he is fuming."

"Abe," Imara said. She knew Edrice wanted to fight with him, but she wanted to fight with him too. Alone. And since she was the one currently dating him, she deserved to have higher priority.

But all Abe did was reach back and squeeze her hand. He didn't even turn to look her in the eye. "I'll message you later," he said quietly. But then, he nudged her into the hallway and shut the door.

TWENTY-NINE

IMARA STARED AT THE DOOR WHILE A nagging lump grew in her throat. She had just endured torture, starvation, and pain. Inexplicable pain. She only survived knowing Abe would be there for her if she ever escaped. And now, she stood behind a closed door with absolutely no idea whether her job or her relationship would last the night.

She slunk out the front door and climbed into the bubble car still waiting to take her to the airport. Before the car started moving, Keiko waved her down and climbed in next to her. "Where's Husani?" Imara said.

"Don't ask," Keiko said as she pressed the button to get the car moving.

Her mind reeled as she stared at Keiko. She sought the colors with her hila, but they were already starting to fade. Maybe removing the goop wasn't the only thing that helped with her hila. Maybe Abe's presence did something too. Without the colors, she turned to body language.

Keiko slumped in her seat with a vacant expression. Her hands rested against her knees with the palms up as she sighed. Defeat.

When the bubble car started moving, Imara saw Husani around a nearby corner. Keiko flinched, and her hands curled into fists. Anger.

"What did he do?" Imara asked.

"Nothing out of the ordinary," Keiko said through her teeth. Her fists relaxed as she made eye contact. "How are *you* doing? Abe told us you got tortured."

"Yes," Imara said while a frown weighed her lips down. It wouldn't do any good to water down the truth. And if anyone deserved the whole truth, it was Keiko. "Takara wants to kill Marco Santini because of Riku. Do you know who Riku is?"

Keiko rolled her eyes and leaned back into her chair. "Yes," she said. "Her fiancé. The man my dad could never live up to apparently." Keiko shook her head. "Sometimes I wonder about him. Did they really love each other as much as my mother thought? Did she deserve it?" Keiko rubbed her arm with a frown. "I don't know, sometimes I wonder. Was there a time when my mother wasn't so evil?"

Imara stared into Keiko's eyes searching for more body language cues. She was definitely defeated and angry, but those had more to do with Husani. Her chin kept quivering too, and she kept rubbing her nose. Both signs of guilt.

Imara's new instinct was to search for a positive emotion, but even that didn't seem right. Maybe instead of ignore the negative, it was better if she helped with it. Maybe she could turn the bad into good. Searching through her mind, she finally pinpointed what she hoped was making Keiko feel guilty. "You aren't doomed to turn out like your mom, you know?"

Keiko swiped her wrist across her nose. "Obviously," she said.

But the confidence in her voice couldn't mask her body language. Prodding, Imara said, "You don't have to be like her."

In a flash, the façade fell away, and Keiko dropped her face into her hands. "Not according to Husani," she said.

Imara lowered her eyebrows as a protective surge shot through her. "What did he say to you?"

Keiko lifted her chin just high enough that her words wouldn't be muffled by her hands. "He said you can't rewrite DNA."

Another protective surge shot through Imara, ready to slap Husani across the face. But the anger dissolved a moment later. Husani was a hopeless flirt and selfish maybe, but he wasn't cruel. "Maybe he wasn't talking about you."

"Yeah, that's likely," Keiko said while rolling her eyes. "Whatever. Husani means nothing to me. I only liked him because he compliments me every five seconds, but he does that with everyone so it's not like it means anything. It doesn't matter to me anymore. He can go flirt with every single girl in the world for all I care, as long as he stops flirting with me."

Keiko did care, but maybe it was best not to push it. "How much do you know about viruses?" Imara asked suddenly.

"The sickness kind?" Keiko asked. "Not very much. Do you have one?"

"No, sorry," Imara said. "Not the sickness kind, the computer kind. Takara said she put a virus on Sef's ring that located his list."

Keiko scoffed and pushed her knees up to her chin. "What good is that to her? He's still the only one who can access it since it's un-shareable."

A grin started forming on the edge of Imara's mouth. "That's not all the virus does. If Sef ever accesses the list from a wall hologram, the virus creates a copy of the list and downloads it to the wall hologram."

Keiko's knees dropped as a gleam appeared in her eye. "That's brilliant," she said. "If I made a virus like that, we could get..." she trailed off as she tapped her ring and began working on her hologram.

"Do you think you could recreate the virus?" Imara asked.

"Maybe," Keiko replied. She tapped away on her hologram for several seconds, then said, "Takara is way better at hacking than me because she has more experience, but also because she's a pattern sensor and can see patterns in the code that most people can't. Even if I do create a virus, hers is bound to be a lot better."

She chewed on her bottom lip as she tapped her hologram screen. Her eyes flitted from one corner of the screen to the next. Awhile later, a smile curved onto her face. "I bet I don't have to recreate the virus. I'll make a virus that piggybacks on top of hers. Then, our virus doesn't have to do anything but track Takara's virus." She tapped a few more times and said, "I'll start it tonight."

Imara sat back with a smile. At least one good thing had come from getting kidnapped. They didn't get Takara arrested or stop the taggers, but at least they were one step closer to Sef's list. "Are you going to start coming on missions all the time?" she asked Keiko. "I've liked having you around."

Keiko flinched and tapped off her ring. She stared out into the night and said. "No. I'm—" She looked down at her hands as she clasped them together. "That's why I wanted to come with you to the airport. I came to say goodbye."

"What?" Imara asked. The question came out in a strangled breath. "Are you leaving Cairo?"

Keiko dug her knuckles into her leg as she spoke. The frown on her face kept rising and falling, as if uncertain whether the news was good or bad. "Some rich dude in Alexandria wants to hire my dad to paint a mural in his house. My dad's an artist, by the way. I don't know if you knew that. If my dad takes the job, it could take months to complete. So, it makes sense for us to move there during the job."

Imara tried to swallow over the lump in her throat but failed miserably. It also did nothing for the re-emergence of the tightness in her chest. She wanted what was best for Keiko, but she didn't want to say goodbye either. She only had five friends. Maybe four since Edrice might hate her now. And if she got fired, she could count Husani out as well. She didn't even want to think about whether or not the list included Abe.

At least she still had Naki.

She shook her head, trying to clear those thoughts from her mind. Keiko's dad needed a better job, and this one sounded perfect. How could she be selfish enough to want Keiko to stay in Cairo. "That will be nice," she forced herself to say. "You can see all your old friends in Alexandria again."

"Yeah," Keiko said, forcing a smile on her lips. It fell away a moment later. With a sniff, she said, "I sort of lost all my friends. Last year was really rough for my dad and me, and I took it out on them. I was jealous and mean." Tears suddenly welled in her eyes until a few spilled over onto her cheeks. "They all left me, and now I'm stuck wondering if I was that horrible to my dad too, and he just never said. I love him the most, and I may have hurt him the most too."

It felt so natural to wrap an arm around Keiko as she cried. Imara cared about that girl a lot more than she had cared about anyone during her teenage years. But the truth of those words stung in her heart. Apparently they shared the fear that they had hurt their family most of all. But maybe that was the point of families. To be there through the worst and still love you anyway.

"I'm sure your dad understands," she said. "If you're worried about it, just show him how much you love him instead of only telling him. But I bet you weren't as bad as you think."

"Yeah," Keiko said with a nod. She looked up with a half smile. "You know, I always liked being an only child because I got all the attention." She squished her mouth up in thought. "But I would have liked having a sister like you."

Imara's head dropped just as her heart sunk. "You wouldn't say that if you knew how I treated my sister."

Keiko laughed. "All sisters fight. Maybe you weren't as bad as you think either."

Just then, the bubble car arrived at the airport. As Imara climbed out of the car, Keiko said, "Will you message me to let me know how things go over the next couple of days? I might be too busy to make it to headquarters."

Imara nodded and hopefully hid most of the despair that had washed over her face. How *would* things go over the next couple of days? She didn't know, and she wasn't excited to find out.

THIRTY

THREE DAYS LATER, EDRICE CALLED. IMARA never expected to hear from Edrice before she heard from Abe, but that didn't stop her from answering. She tapped Edrice's picture and tried to clear all emotion off her face.

"Do I still have a job?" she asked.

Edrice sighed, and a genuine look of guilt swept over her face. "Yes," she said. "I thought Abe told you already." She glanced down, looking ready to apologize, but then seemed to think better of it. Instead she took a deep breath. "We just got an anonymous tip with two things about Sef. One, he's actively trying to get onto the Egyptian Council so he can take control of the city. And two, he's receiving a huge shipment of dangerous items. Don't ask what the dangerous items are because we don't know. Abe and Husani are going to try to intercept the shipment, remove anything dangerous, and then let the rest of the items go to Sef as planned."

She cleared her throat slightly. "I know Abe hasn't asked you to help because he insists you're *still recovering*. But I know those nano bots work fast, and I thought you'd be eager to get back to work. Do you want to come?"

"Yes!" she said, nearly jumping out of her bed. She had done enough recovering to last the rest of her life. And she needed to see Abe. Her only contact with him in the last few days had been through Naki. Which was weird. She still had so much to tell him about Takara and Sef. And the virus.

"Oh," Imara said, leaning back against her pillow. "I asked Keiko to make a virus."

Edrice's eyes lit up with a smile. "Yes, she told me about it. We might actually get the list; it's amazing!" But then her face fell, and they both seemed to remember the last time they had seen each other.

Silence stretched between them while Imara scratched her nose. "I didn't know," she said after awhile. "About you and Abe. I would have told you we were dating, but…"

Edrice's lips pinched into a thin line. Her eyebrows twitched, but she steadied her face a moment later. "Here's the thing. Abe has commitment issues. I'm sure you've noticed. He always does stupid stuff, like he says 'I love that you're so smart,' or 'I love it when you arrange meetings' but he never *ever* says 'I love you.' He can't bring himself to do it."

The truth of those words jarred through Imara until her toes curled. She'd only just noticed the same thing. In the bubble car, before she got kidnapped. He said he loved her curls. It seemed like a fluke at the time, but then she had way too much time to think during her three days of recovery. It had finally occurred to her that Abe never actually told her he loved her. Was it worse he also never told Edrice? She didn't know.

Edrice stared for several seconds with her lips parting, and then closing again. Finally, she let out a big sigh. "I'm sorry you got involved in this. I really am." She frowned, but then she gave a little nod to herself. "What I'm about to say… it's going to sound like I'm trying to hurt you, but I'm not. I'm only telling you this because I like you, and I think you deserve to know the truth."

She sighed again and grabbed the corner of her teal blue hair ribbon. It would have been great if Edrice showed any body language signs of lying or scheming. But she didn't. The only thing her face exhibited was deepest sincerity.

With one last clench of the jaw, Edrice spoke again. Quickly, as if trying to get a bad taste out of her mouth. "The truth is, Imara, you're nothing but a rebound. Abe is a really great guy, and in other circumstances I might even be rooting for you two. But he and I were together for two years straight. We broke up because of this stupid deal I made with Sef. Abe was really angry about it. Honestly, I think he started dating you to get back at me."

Edrice dropped her face into her hands and covered her eyes. "He's going to get back together with me, and everyone knows it. I'm sorry you got in the middle of this. If I hated you, I wouldn't say anything, and I'd be glad you got hurt. But you're my friend. I'm furious with Abe for hurting you like this, and I'm even angrier that he's oblivious to it. You deserve better than that."

Imara ran her thumb across the short hairs on her neck. They bristled against her thumb like a feather. It only made her worried. And angry. And hurt. Abe was the first one to believe in her. She tried to see the best in people because of him. She was trying to be better. Yes, she could probably do it without him, but she didn't want to.

"I'm sorry," Edrice said again. "We're meeting at headquarters in a few hours. I'll message you the details. If you change your mind and don't want to come, that's fine. Just let me know."

Mercifully, Edrice ended the phone call a moment later. Imara had braved a smile at the end, but that was a mistake. The smile only hurt. Everything hurt. Everything inside and all over.

But maybe Edrice was wrong.

No. Not maybe. Definitely. Edrice had to be wrong.

Imara had something special with Abe. She couldn't give up on him yet.

"Who was that?" Naki asked as she came into the room with a box of tissues.

"Edrice."

Naki's nose wrinkled. "She's lucky I wasn't in here because I would have told her all the reasons she needs to keep her grimy hands off Abe. And if she tries to fire you, I'll—"

"She didn't fire me," Imara said, cutting her sister off. "She called to invite me to a job today."

"Oh," Naki said as her arms went limp at her side. "So soon?"

Imara pushed herself out of bed and headed for her closet. "It's been three days since I left the hospital. My body is fine, but I'm dying of boredom."

Staring down at her hands, Naki said, "Just promise you'll come with me to the concert tomorrow night. They're supposed to play a new song, and there might be a special guest."

"Of course," Imara said, bobbing her head up and down. "I wouldn't miss it for anything. I promise."

Naki flicked an empty tissue box off Imara's desk and replaced it with the one in her hand. Flopping herself onto the bed, she said, "Oh, I almost forgot. Abe messaged me a few minutes ago. He says 'Keiko told them about the virus. And also he hopes you're feeling better, and he can't wait to see you once you recover.'"

Imara pulled a coral pink shirt from the closet as she shook her head. "Did you tell him I need to talk to him?"

"No. I'm not doing your dirty work for you."

Smashing the coral pink shirt into a ball, Imara said, "He won't answer my messages or my calls. I have important things I need to tell him. I don't know why he keeps messaging you and acting like everything is fine."

"It's because he's an idiot," Naki said as she laced her fingers behind her head. "I've told you this a thousand times. Just get rid of him while you have the chance."

Imara dropped the coral shirt onto her shoulder and dug through the closet to find a pair of black leggings. "I don't want to get rid of him." Her chin dropped to her chest. "I love him."

Naki let out a snort. "And I thought I had relationship problems. You can do what you want, I guess, but if he doesn't come to Kenya soon, I might have to sabotage your relationship. Oh, and by the way, Mom and Dad already hate him."

Imara tore her head from the closet, smacking it against the door frame in the process. "Why?" she asked, rubbing her brand new goose egg.

"You've been together for months, and he hasn't been here once. Not once!"

222

Still rubbing around the bruise on her head, Imara ducked back into the closet. "It's just busy right now."

"Puh-lease," Naki said, heading for the door. "Enough with that lame excuse. If you really mattered to him, he'd make you a priority no matter how busy he was. He's in love with his business. The sooner you realize that, the better."

Naki huffed as she left the room. Maybe she was complaining about Imara's priorities too, not just Abe's.

But what was she supposed to do? Give up on him? Give up on her job? Give up on Egypt? Sef was still there. The taggers were still there. She couldn't walk away now with so much at stake.

THIRTY-ONE

SOMETIMES THINGS HAVE TO GET WORSE before they get better. That's what Abe kept telling himself. The taggers killed more in the last three days than they had since their first day here. In the same three days, Sef's gangsters seemed more powerful than ever, which didn't make any sense. Why weren't the taggers killing the gangsters anymore?

He gripped his bag as he stomped into the office. Edrice and Husani's whispers stopped the moment they saw him. They'd been doing that a lot lately. Edrice sat down at her desk and said, "Imara is coming, so don't leave until she gets here."

"What?" He turned on his heel to face her. "When did you talk to her?"

Edrice wore a smug expression as she scrolled through her hologram screen. "She's fine, Abe. She didn't even know she still had a job, by the way. You might want to work on those communication skills."

Before he could retort, Imara walked into the room. Her hair looked freshly trimmed, and her cheeks were bright. He plastered on a smile, hoping it would help. But how could it help? He'd practically ignored her for three days, so how could he expect her to not be mad?

He wanted to talk to her. He did. But he was so afraid of what she would say. Keeping his distance had seemed like the safer option.

His smile didn't have any effect on her. She merely nodded at Edrice. "Are we leaving immediately?" she asked.

"Yep," Husani said, and then he and Imara started for the door.

Edrice hadn't even yelled at Imara. If anything, they both smiled at each other. Smiled? How had Edrice done more to repair her relationship with Imara than he had?

His gut clenched as they climbed into a bubble car. Husani seemed more than happy to keep the conversation in his hands. "I love your hair, Imara," he said. "When it's short on the sides and back, it makes the curls on top extra fun. It looks especially gorgeous on you."

She gave him a tentative smile and then turned to the window. "What's the plan?"

Again, Husani supplied the answer. "We go to the shipping warehouse and wait for the boxes to arrive. After they've been delivered and before Sef's gangsters get there, we open them up and steal anything dangerous so the gangsters can't use it."

"How long do we have?" she asked.

Husani stared off to the side and squinted one eye. "Based on my internal clock, which is perfect, we should have ten minutes between drop off and pick up. We'll have to work fast."

She nodded, which made the curls topple over onto her forehead. Abe felt he should probably say something. *Sorry I ignored you for three days? Sorry I didn't tell you about my ex girlfriend? Sorry you're working with her?* No, it was best to stay quiet. Once the conversation started, it wouldn't end for awhile. Best to wait until the right time.

"Are you okay, Imara?" Husani asked as he set his hand on her forearm. "Are you sure you're ready to work after everything Takara did to you?"

"I'm fine," she said, turning away. She reached up to pull on her hair and let out a sigh. "The taggers are in Kenya. I think they're the ones who framed Safiya."

"What? In *Kenya?*" Abe's insides reeled. He moved closer to her, trying to catch her eye. She kept it firmly focused on the window. At least he knew Naki had passed along his messages. Imara couldn't have known about Safiya being framed otherwise.

"Apparently it was part of Professor Santini's plan. The taggers are supposed to take over Egypt first and Kenya second."

Abe shook his head and sat back in his chair with a scowl. "When did you find out? Why didn't you tell me?"

Imara glanced back long enough to give him an icy stare. It probably wouldn't have hurt so much if it wasn't so well deserved. "You've been surprisingly unreachable," she said through her teeth.

Before he could respond, Husani jumped in. "Better taggers than gangsters, if you ask me. How bad could they be?"

She turned to face Husani with a glare. In words that sounded sharper than usual, she said, "I jumped through an eraserfall trying to stop the taggers. I don't want them here, and I definitely don't want them in my home country. They're worse than you think."

Abe gripped his knee to keep himself from smacking Husani.

After a tiny gulp, Husani said, "I shouldn't have said that. I'm sorry."

When they arrived at the warehouse, Abe looked at Husani and asked, "How long?"

"I timed it so we'd arrive at the same time as the... and there they are." He pointed out two huge delivery drones that dropped five wooden boxes onto the delivery pad.

Abe glanced around, but no employees came to retrieve the boxes. He shrugged. Might as well take advantage of the opportunity.

Before they could get to the delivery pad, two employees came out of the warehouse, seeing him and the others immediately.

With no time to hide, Abe started walking with a swagger and punched Husani in the shoulder. "That was crazy last night, right?"

Husani let out a laugh. "Yeah it was. That was fresh when Bast started singing. I didn't know he could sing. Did you?"

Imara seemed to catch on that they were putting on a show so the employees wouldn't suspect them. She shook her head with a smile, and it was the happiest face he'd seen on her all day. That thought made his gut clench with guilt.

Soon, the employees had the boxes loaded onto a hover cart to bring into the warehouse. Abe tapped his ring and said, "I have a video, if you want to watch Bast again."

Instead, he started recording a video just as the employees came to the door of the warehouse. He zoomed in far enough to record the first employee's fingers as he typed a code into the door opener.

When the employees disappeared behind the door, Abe played the video back again.

He watched until he knew the code by heart. "How long until they unload the boxes and leave the room?" he asked Husani.

Husani scratched his ear as he looked to the side. "About sixty-two seconds."

They spent the time in silence. He kept turning to Husani expectantly, but Husani would only shake his head. He dared a glance at Imara at one point, but she speared him with a look that cut through his heart. Best to not try that again until after they'd had a proper talk.

When sixty-two seconds had passed, he played back the recording one last time as they strolled to the door. He typed in the code, but an error notification chimed a moment later. He huffed at the screen and studied the video one last time. When he typed the code in again, he knew for certain he did it the same as the employee had. But the error notification chimed again.

"Maybe they reset the codes after each use," Imara said.

He nodded with a frown. "I was afraid of that."

Husani scowled and crossed his arms over his chest. "Too bad Keiko's not here. She could probably hack it open for us."

Imara shot Husani a filthy look, and Husani shrank back. What was that about?

Turning away, Husani said, "But Keiko is a free agent. She can do whatever she wants. If she doesn't want to help us rescue orphans or stop her evil mom, I guess that's up to her. I mean, it's a little selfish and all, but—"

"Husani!" Imara said with a scold.

Husani's shoulders dropped, and he rubbed the back of his neck. "Yeah, yeah, I know. It's not really selfish of her. She's under the global working age and all that. I just thought she'd want to see us."

Imara shot him another glare, but Husani seemed to be avoiding her eyes. How had they done so many missions without an ounce of interpersonal issues, and all the sudden things were falling apart? Abe shook his head. It was probably his fault. Or definitely his fault.

He waved the thought away. "Maybe I can hack into it. Keiko taught me a couple tricks while we were trying to figure out how to get Imara out of the mansion." He tapped the screen on and then slid his finger across the top until the control panel menu displayed. He tapped into the grid system when suddenly Imara stepped forward, gazing at the door opener.

She whirled around to face him and said, "Can you get this stuff out of my eyes?"

He drew his eyes to her slowly and raised an eyebrow. Then he looked back at the door opener. "Now?"

She stepped in between him and the door opener. "Yes, now. Just do it."

He sighed and looked into her eyes. Sure enough, the familiar goop sat in the corner of each eye. She stood patiently as he picked it out, apparently unaffected by his touch. That was a sour thought. Once he cleared the big pieces away, he noticed small strings of goop that slid out over her irises. Wherever this stuff came from, it was getting worse.

He let his hand linger on her face for one extra second, but she pulled away seeming to sense he had finished. She bent down over the screen and tapped on an app. Her eyes narrowed as she reached for the hair on her neck.

He couldn't help the grin that formed on his lips. She always looked cute when she was thinking like that. But the more she concentrated on the door opener, the more familiar her stare became. He remembered it from the catacombs.

Before the eraserfall.

For a moment, a spring of hope burst through him, and he almost laughed with glee. Was she getting her hila back? But the moment he had that thought, he remembered what he had just done.

Picked the goop from her eye.

His heart sunk. Maybe she had stopped bothering him about it, but she obviously still thought he was a healer. Which was impossible. Now his gut clenched knowing he had inadvertently given her false hope. He couldn't bring her hila back any more than he could bring his mom back.

As his gut twisted, Imara's face fell. Whatever she thought she could do or see, it obviously wasn't working. She tapped the screen and bit her lip, but she kept shaking her head while puffs of air came out her nostrils.

Time for a new plan. He scanned the area for another entrance to the building. A window sat a few feet from the door. It had worked at Takara's mansion. Maybe it would work again. He tried opening it first, but the lock was secure. Imara was still staring at the door opener, and Husani was checking around the other side of the building.

Abe spotted a large rock on the ground. Without thinking, he grabbed it and chucked it at the window as hard as he could. Even as the rock left his fingertips, he knew it was a bad idea. Not because they could get caught, but because the window most likely had impact-proof glass.

As he suspected, the rock bounced off the glass and back toward him with even greater velocity. He took a step to the side to swerve away from the rock, and it just barely missed him. When his mind relaxed, he realized Imara was gripping his shoulder.

"Be careful," she said breathlessly. "I don't want you to get hurt."

He felt his lips twitch into a smile. He turned toward her, letting his arm briefly brush against hers. He flashed her with a smirk. "So, you still care about me then?"

She pursed her lips, but it didn't hide the grin she tried to suppress. "I'm thinking about it," she said. "But only partly because you smell so good right now."

He would have kissed her right there except Husani gave him a death glare once the idea hit his mind. Still, he reached for her waist, and she didn't pull away. They shared one brief look, which Husani ruined less than a second later.

"We have five minutes and eighteen seconds, Abe. We need another plan."

Once again, Imara slid her hand to the back of her neck so she could pull on her hair. Her eyes narrowed in thought, which made the gold flecks in her black irises stand out even more. She really did look cute doing that.

Suddenly her hand dropped to her side. "Why don't we just go in the front door?"

"No," Abe said.

When he didn't elaborate, she turned to Husani.

"You can get arrested if they catch you tampering with a package," Husani said.

"How would they know it's not mine?"

"They scan your identification if you do anything suspicious," Abe said.

She shrugged, not looking as frightened as she should have. "Then I won't act suspicious. I'll walk in like everything is normal. If they scan my identification, I'll just play dumb and act like I went to the wrong warehouse on accident."

Tension shot through his shoulders as he clenched his fists. "It's too dangerous."

"I think it's a good plan," Husani said.

Abe huffed and stuffed his hands into his pockets to keep himself from smacking Husani over the head. "It's *not* a good plan. It's too much of a risk."

Imara quirked her head to the side with an air of confidence. "It's too much of a risk for plan A, but we're on plan B now. Or plan C if you count you throwing that rock at the window. We're running out of time, and we have to do something."

Husani nodded making a stupid face that was probably supposed to look thoughtful. "We definitely have the best chance if you're the one who goes in there, Imara. Your magical powers of persuasion are unstoppable."

She snorted, but started to round the corner toward the front door. Why did everyone suddenly think they could go over his head? Imara was good at what she did, but he didn't like putting her at risk. Especially so soon after she'd been tortured. Even if he was going to lose this argument, he wouldn't go down without a fight. "What if you get arrested?" he asked.

She put on a sweet smile and fluttered her eyelashes twice. "You can bail me out, can't you?"

With that, she rounded the corner and he could do nothing but wait.

Husani smirked. "I've never seen someone convince you as easily as Imara does. She'll be able to pull this off easily."

Husani was right. She did have a power over him that he'd never been able to control. Whether or not he had a similar power over her was yet to be seen.

"You know another reason she's so good at persuading?" Husani asked. "She is extremely hot."

"Really?" Abe said with his eyebrows lowering. "It's 2121. I hope the human race has evolved past helping people just because they're hot."

"But she *is* hot."

"Shut up, Husani."

The tease in the boy's eyes fell away, and in an instant, his face grew serious. "She is, and you know you aren't the only one who's noticed. Plus, she's smart and kind. I know looks aren't everything, but she has both inside stuff and outside stuff. She's the perfect package."

"Do you have a point?" Abe said through his teeth. He checked around the corner of the building to see if Imara was coming back yet.

"Yeah," Husani said. "The point is, maybe you should have thought things through before you lied to the two most important people in your life."

Abe hit his fist against the wall with a scoff. "*Most* important?"

233

Husani rolled his eyes. "Besides your dad, obviously."

For a moment, a glare seemed to be the only response he could muster. "They are not *both* the most important."

Husani stepped forward, crossing into his personal space. He lifted his chest, standing as tall as he could. "The only way I'm wrong is if you're counting your mom too. Your business is your life, and like it or not, that means Edrice. You can try to pretend Imara is more important, but the only one you're fooling is yourself. You met her a few months ago. I don't care how intense things got in the catacombs, she can't erase two years of history."

"Maybe history isn't everything."

Husani laughed. "If you believed that, maybe you wouldn't have kept the secret."

Abe massaged a sudden knot growing in his shoulder.

Husani glanced around the corner then looked back at Abe. "After we finish this mission, you need to let Imara go. She'll be all right."

"That's what I'm afraid of," Abe said under his breath.

THIRTY-TWO

ABE GLANCED AT THE WAREHOUSE entrance again right as Imara came out of the building. A moment later, she joined them around the corner. Her forehead beaded with sweat, and a deep crease ran between her eyebrows. "The taggers are here," she said. "They're taking the packages."

He blinked for a moment before her words sunk in. When they did, he rolled his shoulders back. "Okay, plan D. We distract the taggers until Sef's gangsters get here, and then we get into the boxes while they're fighting with each other."

"That won't work," Imara said.

"It might. If we make sure they know the taggers were stealing their boxes, they'll be angry."

"No, Abe, you don't understand."

"Just use your powers of persuasion, Imara," Husani said. "You can convince them."

"The gangsters are working *with* the taggers now," Imara said abruptly.

"What?" Husani said as he took a step back. "Since when?"

Abe let out a long sigh and rubbed circles into his temples. "How did they think of this?"

235

"They didn't," Imara said. She dropped her head down. "It's my fault. I don't know if we can stop either of them now. The taggers or the gangsters." She buried her face in her hands. "I've been trying to tell you."

Abe gulped, and his chest tightened with the pain of her emotional wound. She was devastated. Heartbroken. All he could think was how badly he needed to fix this. "It's not your fault," he said, hoping it would provide some sort of respite.

"Yes, it is," she snapped back. "I told Takara to do it. She wanted information. It was the only thing I could say to get her to stop torturing me."

"To stop torturing—" Abe stopped mid sentence and pinched the bridge of his nose. "It's not your fault." This time when he said it, he knew it was true. "She was torturing you. I don't care what you had to say; I'm just glad you're okay. And it's fine. We'll figure it out. Maybe they win this round. We'll win the next one."

She swiped a tear off her cheek and his arms itched at his side, wanting desperately to reach for her. She let out a little huff. "All I want is to be a better person, but I've done nothing but make things worse. Takara used my speech to get followers. Now she's using my idea to join the gangsters. Every gain she's had is because of me."

Before Abe could say a word, Husani jumped to her defense. "You were only involved in two things that helped Takara get ahead. She's done tons of other things besides that, and so has Sef. And besides that, even counting those two things, you've helped a lot more than you've hurt."

Those words didn't cheer her up, but they did seem to calm her. Now it was Abe's turn. He only hoped he could make thing better because the frown on her face caused him physical pain. He considered words, but went straight for physical contact instead.

He reached for her hand and interlaced their fingers. Her breath hitched, but her shoulders relaxed, and she looked up at him with a softer expression.

"Uh, hey," Husani said. "Where's your professionalism? No flirting on the job. Or holding hands."

Abe swatted Husani's chest and said, "Go away." Husani rolled his eyes, but didn't protest again.

Abe cupped Imara's cheek, and even though her breathing got heavier, her eyes seemed to be magnetized to his. He looked deep into her gold flecked eyes, choosing to ignore the goop that had somehow reappeared. "I promise you. We will stop Sef and Takara. They're ahead right now, but we won't give up. We can do this."

He brushed his thumb over her cheek. With as much determination as he could muster, he said, "No matter how bad things get, they can always get better. They can get worse too, but if we spend all our energy thinking about what can go wrong, we lose the chance to help things go right."

She stared back at him, then did a tiny nod. His words hadn't really been an apology, and her nod wasn't exactly forgiveness, but it sort of felt like it anyway. The past few days seemed to melt away, and in that moment, things were back to normal. It took everything in him to not kiss her right there.

He almost did it anyway, even though they were on a job. But before he got the chance, Imara's eyes sparked like they always did when she had an idea.

"What if we destroy the boxes instead of trying to find the dangerous things in them?" She pulled away and peeked around the corner. Her voice lowered to a whisper. "A long time ago, Siluk showed me how to arrange a hologram screen to catch the sunlight and start a fire. You know how you can do that with a magnifying glass? You two distract them and I'll start the fire."

Husani clapped his hands and rubbed them together. "All right, gang. What are we on now? Plan E?"

"We can do this," Abe said just as the taggers came out of the building.

He and Husani rounded the corner, and Husani immediately raised his voice. "Hey losers," he said. The two taggers stopped pushing the hover cart and looked up with scowls. "You're out running meaningless errands for the boss, huh? How does it feel to be so unimportant to the team?"

Abe strutted past the hover cart, drawing the taggers' eyes away from the warehouse so Imara could sneak up to the boxes without them seeing. He puffed out his chest and said, "I hear you're working with Sef now. Do you like being on the same team as him or are you just too afraid of Takara to do anything about it?"

Both taggers balled their hands into fists. But in the end, he was the one who swung a fist first. Imara worked too close to the taggers, and he worried one of them would notice her. A fist rammed into his stomach, so he used both hands to shove the tagger to the ground.

Before the tagger fell, he jabbed his toe into Abe's shin, which caused a shooting pain through his leg. He lifted his fists again and felt a very different sensation in his jaw. It wasn't pain, but more like the awareness of pain.

It probably would have escaped his notice entirely if he hadn't seen Husani getting punched in the jaw at the exact same moment.

Abe shook his head and swung another fist at the tagger who was coming at him. Not pain, but the awareness of pain. Husani's pain.

Impossible.

He lost track of time as the fight went on. It all muddled together until one of the taggers said, "Hey! That girl started a fire."

Abe felt the heat before he saw the cause of it. When he turned, he saw one of the wooden boxes engulfed in flames. Imara glared over her hologram, trying to start another fire. But both of the taggers saw her now, and they were both trying to get to her.

"Time to go," Abe said.

Husani turned to leave and inadvertently swung his arm into the fire. He let out a shout as he ripped his arm away. At the same moment, Abe felt the same strange sensation along his forearm. Not pain, but the awareness of it. He could feel where Husani had been injured.

That meant nothing. He still couldn't see a thing. Most healers were seeing healers, weren't they?

He ignored the sensation and started running, but stopped again when he saw Imara stubbornly trying to light a second fire. He ran back and wrapped his hand around her wrist and she finally started moving at his insistence.

Soon, they were all running. Down three alleys and into an abandoned building the taggers wouldn't think to check. Hopefully.

"I got a picture," Imara said as soon as she had caught her breath. "I opened the box and got a picture before I set the box on fire. It was full of a bunch of electronic and metal parts. I don't know what they're for, but we can probably figure it out with the picture I took."

Abe grinned at her just as Husani let out a grunt. Without thinking, he grabbed Husani's arm and pulled it closer to his face. The burn didn't look bad, but he could feel that it went deeper than it looked.

Yes, he could *feel* it.

As soon as he admitted it to himself, the feeling became even easier to pinpoint.

"How'd you know I got burned?" Husani asked.

Abe ignored the question and dug through his bag for ointment. While he slathered it along Husani's arm, he asked, "How's your jaw?"

Husani grabbed his chin. "Is it swelling. Can you tell I got hit?"

"No," Imara said.

"Your jaw will bruise, but it won't be too bad. And it should be gone in a few days. Your arm will take longer to heal, but it should be fine as long as you put ointment on it every morning and night."

Husani nodded without question. Apparently, he didn't think it was strange at all that Abe seemed to know those things with complete certainty. Imara, on the other hand stared at him with one eyebrow raised.

He rubbed more ointment into Husani's arm. At the same time, he pressed a pressure point in Husani's palm. He did it so automatically, he probably wouldn't have even noticed he was doing it. Except, Imara was staring at him with that same look of excitement she always wore when she was trying to convince him about being a healer. "I know," he said to her.

A smile spread onto her lips, which almost made him chuckle. All along it had been so easy. Once he believed it, then he could feel it. The awareness he always had became more than just a gut feeling. Now it was a real, physical feeling.

"What do you mean? You know what?" Husani asked.

Abe let out a puff of air and shook his head. In one moment, everything he knew about himself had changed.

And all it took was acceptance.

THIRTY-THREE

THE NEXT MORNING, IMARA WOKE UP WITH the corner of a desk digging into her shoulder. A blanket drifted off her arm as she shifted away from the desk. She pulled the blanket up to her nose and sniffed it. It hadn't been there when she fell asleep.

Her muscles creaked as she pulled herself to a sitting position. She decided to never sleep on a floor again. The crick in her shoulder reminded her too much of Takara's mansion.

She glanced over the room, the office at Abe's headquarters. Keiko was curled into a ball on the floor next to her. Abe laid on his stomach with his arms and legs splayed out around him. Husani slept next to him, but Edrice was missing. She must have woken up already.

After failing to retrieve any dangerous items from Sef's shipment, they all stayed up late pouring over the picture Imara took. They spent hours gazing at the contents of the box, trying to figure out what could possibly be made with the items. And how they could be dangerous. None of them wanted to give in to the possibility that Sef and Takara might actually take over Cairo.

Each of them helped in their own ways. Edrice found blueprints for all sorts of electronic devices. Imara, Abe, and Husani studied the blueprints trying to find a device with the same items that had been in the box. Keiko spent the time perfecting her virus, hoping to get it finished before she left for Alexandria.

The hours had ticked by, but none of them wanted to leave.

When they got too tired to think, Abe brought pillows and blankets. They had all nodded off one by one while spouting off theories, each more ridiculous than the last.

A few minutes later, Edrice came in with plates of taameya, a breakfast falafel, from a nearby restaurant. Soon, they were all awake and back to deciphering the contents of the boxes.

And still they had nothing but a few wild guesses.

They spent an hour, then two, then ten. Still, they had nothing.

Around dinnertime, they all took a break. Keiko, Husani, and Edrice all went home to shower and eat, but Imara and Abe went back to headquarters. It was the first time they'd been alone since she left the hospital. It probably wouldn't have taken so long to find a spare moment alone, but Abe seemed to be avoiding the conversation.

With their backs pressed up against a wall of the office and with plates of food in their laps, she was finally ready to make him talk. He smiled nonchalantly, making small talk and pretending everything was fine. She allowed him a few minutes of this before she put her plate of food on the ground.

"Abe," she said slowly. "We need to talk about Edrice."

The smile he'd been wearing for the past twenty-four hours ripped away from his face and got replaced by a grimace. "I assumed you didn't want to talk about it," he said, pushing his food around with a fork. "Because you haven't brought it up yet."

She tilted her head to the side. "When was I supposed to bring it up? With everyone standing around?"

"No."

"Before that then?" she asked. "When I was still at home? Because I tried that. You spent three days sending messages to Naki instead of me."

"You were recovering," he said, leaning away.

"You were avoiding me."

He flinched and stared at his plate. After a moment he crossed his arms over his chest. "You have to see things from my perspective. You got eraserfalled, and you didn't have job. You were devastated, and I couldn't handle it. I knew Edrice would freak out if she found out we were dating, but I also knew you'd be great at this job. And you are. You and Edrice were even friends. Everything was better without anyone knowing; so can you really blame me for keeping it secret?"

She let out a scoff and didn't try to hide the patronizing look in her eye as she tilted her head. "You should have told me," she said. "You should have told Edrice too. You should have told all of us. Don't pretend you did the right thing."

"I—" he said as he raised his hands in defense. "I," he said again. But then his hands fell and he let out a sigh. "Yes, I should have told you. I'm not convinced Edrice had to know, but I should have told you." He flinched, and a wisp of a wine-colored fear spike grew out from his skin.

Another fear spike grew, followed by a cobalt blue drop of sadness. He looked down. "I was afraid you'd break up

244

with me if you found out I was working with my ex. I know it was wrong to lie, but… I was afraid of losing you."

The sincerity in his eyes went a long way toward helping her forgive him for this whole thing. "I get why you did it," she said. "I'm not excusing it, but I get it."

His fingers twitched as if to grab her hand, but she snatched her plate off the ground to keep her hands out of reach. "After the hospital, you were supposed to come with me to Kenya. You still haven't come. But then we met Edrice here, and the truth finally came out. She was mad, and I was mad. We both deserved an explanation. We both deserved your attention."

She lowered her eyes until she was staring at a lone sesame seed on the edge of her plate. She took in a sharp breath. "And you chose her."

Abe swallowed and pulled at his shirt collar. He swallowed again and closed his eyes. "I'm sorry." He started to speak again, when a notification chimed from his ring. He shook his head at the distraction and said, "I never should have—"

But then his ring chimed again, and this time Imara's did too. She wrinkled her nose at it, and he opened his mouth one more time. As if on cue, they both got a series of three notifications in a row.

Imara let out a huff and tapped her ring. "It's Keiko," she said. She skimmed through the messages as quickly as she could. By the time she read the last message, she was already on her feet, heading for the door.

Within seconds, she and Abe were rushing down the road.

Imara tapped her ring and moved her hologram screen to the side so she could see Keiko as she ran. Once on the phone with her, Keiko said, "I'm sending you the virus now."

Imara kept her eyes on the road as her feet slapped the pavement. Abe tapped on his hologram when suddenly, his face fell. "Husani isn't answering. He's probably still in the shower."

Keiko waved her hand at that. "It doesn't matter. Imara has to do it; she's the only one he won't recognize."

"Sef did see me once," Imara said. "It was my very first night here."

"That was months ago. He won't remember," Abe assured her.

Imara nodded, scanning the buildings for the restaurant Keiko had mentioned. The same restaurant where her dad worked.

"The file I sent you has the virus and a program. You have to open the program to plant the virus. Just minimize your hologram screen so it's too small for Sef to see. Then, bump into him or do whatever you have to do so that your ring makes physical contact with his ring."

She felt the curls bounce over her forehead as she nodded. She already knew the next part. After the rings made contact, she had to pretend to be a waitress and offer to let Sef use the private conference room. One that conveniently had a wall hologram in it.

They'd been waiting for an opportunity like this, but never expected it to come so fast.

"Everything should be set," Keiko said. "Sorry to rush you into this, but my dad and I are leaving for Alexandria tomorrow, and I wanted to be sure I finished this for you before we left."

Imara nodded and ended the call. But before she turned off her ring, another phone call came through.

"Who is it?" Abe asked, leaning toward her screen.

She moved the screen so he could see, then tapped Naki's picture.

"Where are you?" Naki asked.

"I'm in…" Imara started. "Oh. Oh no, the concert. What time is it right now?"

Naki's lips pursed as she tried to hide a sniff. "If you're still in Egypt, it's too late. I'll just have to go without you."

Imara's heart sunk, but she couldn't go home right now. This may be their only chance to get Sef's list. Yet again, she'd have to disappoint her sister. Imara frowned. "I'm sorry, Naki. Something came up."

"Just like always," Naki said as she turned her head away.

Heat spread through Imara's cheeks. "This is time sensitive. Sef is at a restaurant and Keiko's dad is working there, and Keiko finally finished the virus. It's the perfect opportunity to get his list."

Naki waved her hand through the air. "It's fine. I'll just go with Basara instead. He's been calling me a lot lately. See you later."

Her gut twisted as the phone call ended, but she shoved the feeling away. This plan wouldn't succeed unless she had complete focus. They arrived at the restaurant only a minute later.

Abe squeezed her hand and said, "I'll be right outside if anything goes wrong. Just be careful."

Imara barely nodded as she walked through the doors.

THIRTY-FOUR

A MAN WITH OLIVE SKIN AND DARK HAIR approached Imara the moment she entered the restaurant. "I'm Montu," he said. "Keiko's father."

She nodded as she took the apron and nametag he handed her. The other waiters wore all black. The coral pink shirt she'd been wearing since yesterday would stand out against their uniforms. And she hadn't showered since yesterday morning. She hoped no one would notice.

Montu ushered her into the dining room where he pointed out Sef's table. The portly man sat with three other people Imara didn't recognize.

She tapped her ring and opened the program, just as Keiko had instructed. After shrinking her hologram screen as small as possible, she strolled over to the table with arms swinging and a wide grin on her lips.

Stopping at their table, she opened her mouth, but Sef started speaking first. "We already ordered. What are you doing here?"

Her stomach twisted in a knot as she blinked. But the moment passed, and she slapped her hand to her forehead. In her most soothing voice, she said, "I went to the wrong table again." She let a tittering laugh escape through her lips. "That's the third time this week."

Sef narrowed his eyes at her. She leaned forward and asked. "Did you want anything else? Might as well use me if I'm already here, right?" She playfully touched her hand on top of his. Her breath froze as her focus turned to his ring. Just one brief moment of physical contact. That's all she needed. A moment later, she felt their rings touch.

But Sef refused to match her playful attitude. He pulled his hand away and glared at her. She tried another smile and said, "It was my mistake, I'm so sorry. Would you like to be moved to our private conference room to make up for it?"

"Why aren't you wearing black like the other waiters?" a woman at the table asked.

Before she could respond, Montu appeared and wrapped an arm over her shoulders. "You're needed in the kitchen," he said.

Once they were out of earshot, she whispered. "Why did you pull me away?"

A second later, she had the answer. Abe waited for her in the hallway. The color drained from his face as he panted. "Takara is coming. We have to get out of here now. We'll have to get Sef to use a wall hologram another time. At least we planted the virus."

She huffed but didn't protest. Montu helped them slip through the back door while the pain of yet another failure gnawed at her insides.

"I chose my business," Abe said once they were safe in the alley.

She jerked toward him as they walked out to the main road.

249

He ran his thumb along his chin before he spoke again. After a careful breath, he said, "I didn't choose Edrice. I chose my business. Maybe that was still wrong, but I thought you should know."

She nodded, not really sure what to say. They were quiet for a long time. Finally, Imara said, "I should probably go home."

"No." Abe turned on his heel until they stood eye to eye. "Naki said you were already too late. Just stay here. I want to spend time with you."

His words melted through her, but she forced herself to think about more than his russet brown eyes and bouncy hair. "I have to make Naki a priority," she said. "I can't keep spending every second of my time here. What if I go home right now, and I'll come back tomorrow morning?"

"Please stay." He took her hand and stared until his look warmed her from head to toe. "I've barely seen you these past few days, and it's been awful. I need to be with you. Especially after everything I..." He looked down with a gulp.

"Why don't you come with me?" she asked cautiously.

He pressed the palms of his hands into his eyes and shook his head. "Imara, I can't. If Sef gets on the Egyptian Council, he'll destroy my business. Everything I've worked for."

"He'll probably destroy all of Egypt while he's at it," Imara said. "Plus, the taggers will come to Kenya once they have Egypt in their control."

Abe dropped his hands and cupped them around hers. "Yes, see? You have to stay here so we can stop them. We're so close."

She chewed on her lip as she stared at her shoes. "I guess Naki did say it was too late for tonight."

"Exactly." He interlaced their fingers together. "You got the virus on Sef's ring, right?"

She nodded.

"See. We just have to figure out what was in those boxes, and we'll have a way to stop them. You have to stay."

THIRTY-FIVE

THE NEXT MORNING, IMARA UNLOCKED THE
door to her apartment, still rubbing the sleep out of her eyes.
They had all spent the night at headquarters again and finally
had a list of three possible devices the items in the box could
be made into.

Imara was home to shower and change, and then she'd be
off to Egypt again. She meandered into the kitchen and
jumped when she saw Naki standing in the corner holding a
mug.

"I wondered if you were ever going to show up."

Imara tried to rub the sweat off her palms as she
remembered their phone call yesterday. If only Sef had been
at the restaurant a tiny bit earlier. She could have been home
in time to go to the concert.

"I'm sorry," she said, curling her fingers around the hem
of her shirt.

Naki folded her arms across her chest and jutted out her
chin. "You're always gone. I thought it would be different
now, but it's not."

With her chin quivering, Imara tried to find the words to
explain. It all seemed so clear last night when Abe asked her
to stay. But having to face her sister, she realized any excuse

would be empty. Her thoughts kept circling back to the same thing. The thing she'd been desperately trying to ignore. Tears pooled in her eyes, and they started falling before she could even breathe.

Naki lunged forward and wrapped her in a hug. Naki's own eyes had tears spilling out of them. "I miss you, baby sister," she said. "When are we going to be friends again?"

Sobs shook through Imara as she pushed her eyes into her sister's shoulder. All this talk of being a better sister, and it turned out Takara was right all along. If she wanted to make things right with Naki, she had to stay *here* and make things right. She couldn't keep flying away to Egypt to spend every spare minute of her time.

It didn't matter if she was saving Abe's business. It didn't matter how much Cairo needed help. It didn't even matter how perfect Abe was for her.

If she wanted to make things right with Naki, she had to put her first.

Her body trembled as she held onto her sister. The only solution sat in the front of her mind as clear as day. But just because she knew what she had to do didn't mean she wanted to do it.

She wanted two things, and both were good; but one was better and she couldn't have both. She could have Naki or she could have Egypt. In the end, she'd always have to choose.

Her knees buckled out from under her, and Naki fell with her to the ground until they were nothing more than a huddled mass of limbs and tears. After allowing herself to cry for a few more minutes, she untangled herself and sat against a cupboard, brushing away her tears.

Naki looked at her. Waiting. Whatever she expected, Imara knew it wasn't what she was about to say. Maybe Naki wanted an apology or a promise. She'd get neither.

Imara dropped her chin into the palm of her hand as she pushed the words out. "I have to break up with Abe."

Naki flashed her teeth. If Abe were here to clean the stuff out of her eyes, she might have been able to see blood red flames of anger coming off Naki's skin. Another thing she'd have to lose. Abe's healing on her hila only seemed to last when he was around. Without him, she'd lose it all again.

She felt a weight in the pit of her stomach, but it didn't change her decision. She loved Abe, but she couldn't choose him over her family. She *couldn't*.

Naki folded her arms across her chest as anger flashed through her eyes. "Serves him right after all the stupid lies he fed you about his ugly business partner. Eddy or whatever her name is."

Imara sniffed. "Edrice. And she's not ugly."

Naki pulled her arms tighter over her chest and put her nose in the air. "She's not breathtakingly beautiful like you. Abe doesn't deserve your face after what he did. He doesn't deserve your smarts either. Or your tenacity."

A slice of sorrow cut through Imara, causing her eyes to droop. "Can we please not insult Abe? I know he messed up, but that's not what this is about."

Naki snorted. "You can think whatever you want, but I hate him."

Imara stood and tried to shake away the anxiety running through her veins. If she was going to go through with this, it needed to happen sooner than later. The longer she sat here thinking about it, the more she lost her resolve.

She turned back to her sister and attempted a smile. "I don't know when I'll be back tonight, but this time I'm coming back for good."

THIRTY-SIX

ABE DROPPED HIS DISHES INTO THE SINK just as he heard a knock on his apartment door. He opened it with a huge smile, which immediately dropped when he saw Edrice standing in front of him.

"Oh," he said.

"They were drones."

"What?"

"In the boxes," Edrice said.

"Oh," he said as the words finally sunk into his mind. "Sef's shipment, you mean. They were drones?"

She nodded. "Husani figured it out right after you left headquarters this morning. He was on the phone with a manufacturing plant asking about the list of items, and they said it must it drones. Takara used delivery drones when she first got here, but the Egyptian Council locked them so she couldn't hack them again. Then, they put an alert on her bank account so they would know if she ever got the parts to make her own drones. She was smart enough to not buy the parts herself, but now she's working with Sef, and apparently he bought all the parts instead."

"But Imara set one of the boxes on fire. That had to do something. Maybe we ruined their plans."

Edrice shrugged. "Maybe. Or maybe it just prevented them from making as many drones as they wanted. They haven't done anything yet, so I guess we'll see."

Abe nodded and leaned against his doorframe. But then he stood up and raised an eyebrow. "Is there a reason you came to my apartment to tell me that? You could have just messaged me."

"I have something else I need to say."

He rolled his eyes. "If it's what I think you're going to say, then don't."

She stomped her foot and clenched her jaw. "Stop messing around. You know you aren't going to be with Imara forever, so just get it over with already." She swallowed and stared at the ground before she said, "I miss you."

He shook his head and let out a sigh. "Edrice."

But before he could say another word, she grabbed him by the shoulders and kissed him.

ဩဩ⬥⬥

Imara turned the corner to Abe's apartment, and her mouth dropped when she saw Edrice kissing him. Kissing. Him!

He pushed her away immediately. His eyes grew wide when he saw Imara just down the hall. It was obvious the kiss was neither his idea, nor his desire. It didn't matter. That didn't make it any easier to see their faces pressed up against each other like that. Edrice crossed her arms over her chest in a huff. She turned to leave and let out a squeak when she saw Imara.

"We'll finish our talk later, Abraxas," she said as she ran off.

Imara stomped up to his door, not sure if she should punch something or vomit.

Abe looked like someone had knocked the wind out of him. "Uh," he said awkwardly. He ran his fingers through his hair. "Uh, you can…" He shook his head and let out a breath. "Just come inside."

"I don't think that's a good idea." She had to do this fast, and then she had to leave. If anything else happened, her resolve would crumble to dust.

"*She* kissed me," he said grabbing Imara by the shoulders. "I didn't kiss her back. I was about to tell her it's over for good, and then she was just on me. I didn't want it. You have to believe me."

"I believe you."

A palpable relief washed over his face. He didn't ask her to come in again. Instead, he dropped to the ground and pulled his knees up to his chest. "Things are so messed up right now. Sef and Takara are working together. My business is falling to pieces. And then Edrice comes and kisses me. Everything's falling apart."

With a deep breath, Imara closed her eyes and tried to still the fluttering of her heart. Abe's desperation was the last thing she needed to be confronted with. But then again, nothing about this was ever going to be easy.

"I'm going home," she said.

"You just got here. You can't leave yet."

No, *nothing* about this would be easy. This next part would be worst of all. She rubbed a finger across her eyebrow and opened her eyes. "I can't keep going back and forth between Egypt and Kenya. It's not working for me. I know things are bad here, but I have to make Naki a priority. I can't do that while I'm here. I have to leave."

It didn't seem possible, but his face fell even farther than it had before. "What about Sef and Takara? What about my business?"

A pit of guilt festered inside her, but she couldn't change her mind now. She had made the decision and had to stick with it. "I can't do this," she said. "I can't keep going back and forth. I have to go home."

He blinked at her without saying anything. He looked to the side while the words seemed to settle in his mind. And then his eyebrows furrowed. "That's not fair," he said.

A flash of anger ran through her as her muscles tensed. "Why not?"

"You're making me choose between my business and you?" His jaw flexed, but his eyes held pain. Anger.

"No," she said in a softer voice. Her head fell with a sigh. "I could never ask you to choose. I'm just telling you; I can't do this anymore."

He curled his hands into fists and blew hard breaths out of his nose. But before the second breath was finished, his face contorted. Every trace of the anger vanished. "Wait a minute," he said, jumping to his feet. Such a strong energy radiated off him, it seemed solid enough to touch. He took a deep breath, and it shuddered as he sucked the air inside. "You're breaking up with me?" he asked.

Her hand found itself at the nape of her neck. Picking at the hairs was always easier than answering. "I'm sorry," she said.

"No." His voice came out in a tragic, strangled burst. The soft tone was fragile and so vulnerable. "Don't do this," he said. "I'll come to Kenya. I'll fly my jet down to you every night after work. I'll come every weekend."

Tears started forming in her eyes for what seemed like the thousandth time in the past week. She never expected Abe to fight like this. She thought he'd be angry. She thought he'd threaten to get back together with Edrice. All of that she had prepared for.

But now, his eyes glistened, and she couldn't bear to see it. She turned away and spoke to the ground. "That won't work, and you know it. Your business means everything to you. You spend almost every waking hour on it. *And* a handful of hours on the weekend. You can't focus on me unless I'm here."

"Then don't go," he said as his voice broke. She chanced a look into his eyes, and the moment they met, he pulled her into a tight embrace. "Please don't go. Please don't make me choose."

She hugged him back. She hugged him hard and long, and he hugged harder. Their tears mingled together as their cheeks brushed up against each other. And then they hugged tighter. Because they both knew what was going to happen, and they both wanted to avoid it.

A sob shook through Imara. She had to force herself away. She had to get this over with now or she might never manage it. Already her determination wavered. Abe's tears had hurt worst of all.

"It's because of Edrice, isn't it?" he asked as soon as she escaped his arms. "I know I should have told you. I'm sorry about that, but I don't have feelings for her. I promise I don't."

"It's not because of Edrice." Imara swiped her nose with the back of her hand. "It's because your heart belongs in Egypt." She clutched her stomach, trying to ground herself. It all hurt much worse than she ever imagined. "You can save Egypt without me anyway." She turned on her heel and sprinted down the hall before he could protest.

THIRTY-SEVEN

ONCE SHE ROUNDED THE CORNER, IMARA slowed to walk. A sense of dread surrounded her, threatening to draw her back to Abe's door. Maybe this was the right thing but why did it have to hurt so much?

A moment later, Abe called out to her. "Imara, wait."

She flinched and kept her back turned firmly away from him.

He sprinted down the hall until he was at her side. When she glanced at him, he said, "No, it's not..." he shook his head, flustered. "All Egyptian citizens just got a message, and... you have to see this." He shifted the hologram screen already projecting from his ring with the volume high enough for her to hear.

She turned to face the hologram screen completely once she realized what was on it. It showed a live video broadcasting the Egyptian Council chambers. Imara's mouth dropped at the sight.

Standing in front of the Egyptian Council with her chin held high was Takara. Sef stood next to her rubbing his hands together while he eyed the members of the Egyptian Council.

"As I was saying," Sef said. "You are all going to resign, and I will appoint new people in your places, including me. Does anyone have something to say against that?"

One of the council members stood and slapped his palms against the semi-circular table he sat behind. "You have no power here. Why would we resign?"

"I'm glad you asked," Takara said, turning to grin at the camera recording her.

Sef nodded and tapped his ring. He synced it to the wall hologram, and Imara nearly jumped out of her shoes.

"The list!" she said. "He just synced to the wall hologram. If we can get to the council chambers, we can get the list."

Abe nodded so fast, his hair shook, but soon they both froze with their eyes on the live video.

On the wall hologram of the council chambers, sixteen separate videos appeared. At the sight of them, each of the sixteen council members gasped.

Takara looked straight into the camera and narrowed her eyes. "I hope you all remember my drones and what they're capable of. I had to build new ones, but I installed cameras in them this time. I wanted everyone to see what they see."

She approached the wall hologram. Once there, she enlarged one of the sixteen videos so it covered the others. The video bobbed up and down slightly as the drone flew through the air. It closed in on a young woman walking down the street. "Now," she said. "Who does this one belong to?"

Imara's eyes flicked back to the Egyptian Council members. One man's eyes widened, and every muscle in his face went slack.

With a smirk, Takara pointed at him. "This is your daughter, correct?"

The man gulped.

Takara tapped her personal hologram screen, and the drone recording the man's daughter suddenly reached out its arms and zoomed toward the girl. Remembering the prison attack, Imara could picture the blue shock of electricity traveling through the drone's arms. The girl would be dead in seconds.

"Stop!" the man said, clutching the edge of the table.

"Then resign." Takara said simply.

The man brushed the sweat from his hairline. He gulped and hung his head. "Yes. I… I resign."

Takara nodded and waved a hand toward one corner of the room. "Sef, draw up the paperwork. Now, who's next?" She enlarged a video of two boys playing with a ball. She didn't have to say another word before the next Egyptian Council member resigned.

Imara watched in horror while the next thirteen council members all resigned without a fight. The only Egyptian Council member left was the tiny woman with gray hair and buck teeth. Imara recognized the old woman immediately. She was the same one who was keeping the secret about Marco Santini's location. Her video showed a man who looked as old as her.

The tiny woman rolled her shoulders back. "I will not resign. My Omari would never forgive me if I did anyway."

Takara rolled her eyes, but simply tapped her hologram until the arms of the drone wrapped themselves around Omari. She glanced at the old woman as if to give her one last chance, but the woman held her chin high. A moment later, electricity sizzled through the arms and shocked the man to his death. The old woman's eyes glistened as a tear fell away from her eye, but her chin never wavered.

"Now?" Takara asked.

"Never," the woman replied.

Takara shrugged and went back to her hologram screen. Suddenly, a new video appeared recording another woman who looked very much like the tiny council woman. Maybe her sister. The old woman turned away from the wall hologram and sniffed. "I will still not resign."

The drone electrocuted the second woman to death, but the council woman still would not budge. Exasperated, Takara tapped off her ring. She pulled a gun from her pocket and shot the council woman with no regard for the fact that she was being recorded. In fact, as soon as the woman slumped to the ground, Takara turned to the camera with a half smile. "You all saw that," she said. "Now watch as nothing is done. We have complete control of Cairo, and soon we'll have control of Egypt."

The feed suddenly went black, and Imara could do nothing but stare at it with her mouth open wide. After several seconds, she shook her arms out to alleviate some of the tension inside.

Abe shoved a hand through his hair. "Takara must have hacked the feed. She must have messaged every Egyptian citizen to make sure they saw that video."

Imara reached around for the hair on the back of her neck. As the hairs bristled across her thumb, she considered her options. She had to go home, but she couldn't leave Egypt now. Not like this.

She couldn't stand by and watch Egypt be destroyed. But after that, she wouldn't come back. Even if all of Egypt's problems were solved, Abe would always choose his business over her. So she'd help, and then she would leave.

They didn't have much of a chance, but there was still one thing they had that Takara wanted. Maybe the time had come to use it.

Abe sighed and shook his head. "I know you just tried to break up with me—"

"I did break up with you."

He waved his hand through the air. "We can talk about it later. And I know you have to go home. I respect that, but…"

"I'll help," she said before he could ask. "We have to get the real Egyptian Council members reinstated, and we have to get Sef's list from that wall hologram in the council chambers. I think we might even be able to get Takara arrested since she just murdered someone on camera. But as soon as we stop them, I'm going home."

Abe nodded, but his head tilted to the side. He rubbed his thumb along his chin, then shook his head again. "What can we do? We can't just break into the council chambers with Takara there. She's too powerful."

"I know what we have to do," Imara said. She took a deep breath and then let out a long sigh. It wasn't ideal, but they had to do something. She nodded to herself and spit the words out before she could change her mind. "We have to give her what she wants."

He scoffed. "She's on the Egyptian Council. She'll have control of Egypt by the end of the night. She just got everything she wants."

"No, she didn't. She only wanted to infiltrate the Egyptian Council to get information. And she just killed the person who had it."

He turned to her with the sweetest look of hope. She had to look away from him to keep herself from being sucked into it. She bit her lip. "Tell everyone to meet at headquarters. I don't have a plan yet, but I have the beginning of one."

THIRTY-EIGHT

IMARA WAITED UNTIL ABE WAS SHUT INSIDE A bubble car before she tapped her ring. She had asked him to gather everyone and meet her at headquarters in ten minutes, but she had something important to do first.

After tapping her ring, she scrolled through her contacts until she found Siluk. She wasn't sure what to expect when she called him, but he answered quickly enough. That seemed like a good thing, especially since she needed his help.

"Hey, Imara," he said. "How are you feeling?"

"What?" She quirked her head to the side and made a mental note of her head and stomach. "I feel fine." She shook her head. "What do you mean how am I feeling? What kind of a question is that?"

"Because you broke up with Abe. Are you doing okay?"

"Oh. I, uh… I'm—" She shook her head. "He told you already? It happened three minutes ago."

Siluk's eyebrows rose, but he quickly squashed them down. "Wow, that's recent. Um, no; he didn't tell me. Naki did. But you really broke up with him?"

She clenched her jaw as a rush of heat flowed to her fingertips. Siluk always thought he was privy to her personal life. That had always annoyed her. She'd barely talked to him

268

in months, and now he suddenly seemed to think they were good enough friends to discuss her breakup? A breakup that was currently ripping her heart to shreds no less. She pursed her lips and took a deep breath. "We are not going to talk about that."

Siluk raised one eyebrow but didn't protest. He just waited.

She took another deep breath and tried to start over. She jerked her head, trying to shake the fog of anguish growing in her mind. This day wouldn't be easy knowing she'd have to leave Abe at the end of it, but despairing over it wouldn't help anything. She sucked in a breath and pushed the words out, forcing herself to forget her personal issues. "Do you know where Marco Santini is? Could you drive to his house and talk to him in person?"

"Who?" Siluk asked.

More fog invaded her mind, and most of it consisted of memories of the catacombs. Things like Abe walking next to her. And holding her. And kissing her.

She shook those thoughts away and tried to focus on the part of the catacombs that she actually needed to remember. "He's the guy who built the faulty dams in the catacombs. You said he lives by you. He's Professor Santini's brother."

Siluk gave her a blank stare in return.

She snapped her fingers as she tried to remember any details. "I can't remember his name, but you said everyone uses it as an insult."

"Oh," Siluk said as he slapped his forehead. "Masud Ganim. I forgot he changed his name. And I totally forgot he was Professor Santini's brother. Yeah, I can get to his house. It doesn't take long with our new hover mobiles."

"Good. I didn't want it to come to this, but..." She let out a sigh. "Takara and Sef just took over the Egyptian Council."

"They did what?" Siluk said as his mouth dropped. "When?"

She rubbed her forehead and looked down. "A couple minutes ago. The taggers and gangsters are working together now. But if we can get Takara to leave Egypt, the taggers won't have leadership. Hopefully, we can stop the gangsters while the taggers are distracted. Plus, we have a way to get proof so Sef can be arrested."

"Okay," Siluk said while drawing out the syllables. "How exactly are you going to get Takara to leave Egypt? And what does Masud have to do with anything?"

She tapped her fingers against her thigh as she explained. "Takara was at the catacombs when it flooded twenty years ago. She and her fiancé both drowned. She was saved, but her fiancé didn't make it. She's been trying to find Marco, or Masud whatever, for years. She wants to kill him. Well, torture him and then kill him. She has these insane torture techniques."

Siluk raised one eyebrow, still looking unconvinced. "So, you're going to tell her where he is so she can come here to torture and then kill him?"

"No," Imara said. "Of course not. That's the next thing I needed to ask you. Do you have ideas for how to protect him? I don't want to get your family involved because it will put them in danger."

She snapped her head to the side. "Wait a minute. *We* can protect him. I can't believe I didn't think of this earlier. Abe can fly his jet to Alaska, and then the two of you can go get Marco. I won't give Takara his location until Marco is safe with Abe on the way back here to Egypt. Plus, that way she'll be gone for at least two hours while she flies to Alaska and back. Hopefully, by the time she gets back here, the real Egyptian Council will be reinstated and she'll get arrested."

When the ideas finished spilling out of her, she looked back at the hologram screen tentatively. "Well?" she asked. "You don't have to help. I realize it's dangerous."

He rolled his eyes. "I'm in, Imara. Don't worry about that. Do you want me to call Abe and explain the plan to him? Then you don't have to talk to him."

She reached for the back of her neck until she could firmly tug the hair. Even with a fresh haircut she could still grip it enough to hurt. It didn't distract her from the pain inside, however. She bit her lip as she let the hairs bristle under her fingernail. Finally, she looked up and said, "Yes please." She squeezed her eyes shut for half a moment before looking back at him. "And thank you."

He did a strange sort of half grin and nodded. She tapped her ring quickly because tears started forming in her eyes and didn't want Siluk to see them. But she was grateful he was willing to help.

Maybe she should have also been grateful that he gave her a chance to talk about it, but more than anything, it felt like an imposition. Who did he think he was, asking such a personal question? She needed time to let the feelings settle. She didn't want to talk to anyone about it— not yet.

Scratch that. She could think of one person who felt like the safest person in the whole world to talk about this particular subject. Unfortunately, she had just finished breaking up with him.

By the time Imara made it to headquarters, she barely had enough time to nod goodbye to Abe as he set off for his jet. He seemed completely engrossed in the task, with no feelings at all about losing his latest girlfriend. Her stomach twisted in knots at the thought. That's all she was now. Just another ex.

Edrice turned pink when Imara entered the office. Probably because she'd thrown an unwanted kiss on Imara's boyfriend last time they saw each other. But Abe had been at headquarters for awhile before Imara arrived. Was it possible that something more had happened? Had he and Edrice already gotten back together? Edrice insisted it was inevitable.

Imara shoved that thought down to the deepest, darkest part of her brain. The part that held the memory of Professor Santini rushing to her own death. The part she never wanted to remember.

She stood at the head of the room and wrung her hands as she stared at Husani and Edrice. Just as she opened her mouth to speak, the door whooshed open.

When someone burst through the door, she didn't recognize who it was until she saw the violin tucked under her elbow. But with a super short bob that had been dyed amber brown, it didn't fully register that it was Keiko until she collapsed onto the floor with a huff.

"Keiko!" Imara said. "I thought you were in Alexandria already."

Keiko glared at the floor and turned until her back faced Husani. "Yeah," she said. "Turns out that mural painting job for my dad was a trick set up by my dear mother. Shocker, right? Luckily, I figured it out before we got there."

Husani poked her in the head and asked, "What did you do to your hair?"

272

Keiko slapped his hand away. "Don't touch me," she said through her teeth. She stood up just to move several centimeters away from Husani before she sat back down again. "I was sick of looking like my mom. So, I hacked off my hair and improved the color. Before you say anything, I don't care if you like it or not. Keep your opinions to yourself."

Husani opened his mouth, but Imara jumped in to keep him from saying anything. "I'm glad you're here, Keiko. We really need your help."

Keiko took the opportunity to move even further away from Husani and then looked up expectantly.

"Do you think you can figure out how to stop the drones?" Imara asked.

Keiko screwed her mouth up as she thought. "I have some ideas, but I don't know for sure."

Imara nodded. "Good enough for me." She looked out at the rest of them. Keiko's return was perfect. To do the next part of her plan, it would be best to split up. Since Keiko had no desire to be around Husani, Imara would work with him. Which was doubly perfect since she had no desire to be alone with Edrice at the moment.

"Keiko and Edrice, you two stay here and try to figure out the drones. Husani and I are going to go looking for gangsters to help us get inside the Egyptian Council chambers. Once we explain that we can get Sef's list, hopefully some of them will be willing to help us. Any questions?"

There weren't any, and soon she and Husani were on their way.

THIRTY-NINE

HUSANI KICKED IN THE DOOR TO AN abandoned building. Imara peeked in but didn't see any people. Just plastic bags, broken knife hilts, and photos strewn over the floors. Another one of Sef's hideouts was officially empty. She didn't expect it to be easy to recruit gangsters, but she didn't think it would be this hard either.

"They're probably just in regular offices now," Husani said with a huff. He noticed a picture on the floor and let out a long whistle. "My, that is a fine looking woman. Too bad she's one of the bad guys because otherwise I'd be..."

He trailed off when she rolled her eyes at him.

"I'm sure she has other qualities besides her looks," he said, flipping his hair out of his face. "But I don't know them so why should that stop me from enjoying how attractive she is?"

Imara shook her head and marched toward the doors. "Come on, this one's empty. Let's try the next one."

Once they were out the door, she dug her nails into her palms. She never expected to be this angry at Edrice. Strangely, it had very little to do with Abe at all. She was already planning to break up with him before Edrice had planted that kiss. But Edrice didn't know that. And Edrice was supposed to be her friend. Was it possible to be friends with someone who had dated your boyfriend? Maybe, but the more she thought about it, the weirder it seemed.

"Yo, dreamer!" Husani shouted. "It's this way."

She shook her head and brought her attention to the road. Husani gave her a long glance, which would probably turn into a question. A question she didn't want to answer. So, she asked one of her own instead.

"Why don't you ever flirt with Edrice?"

He snorted. "Uh, Edrice is my sister."

Imara's eyes shot up to her forehead. "Excuse me, what?" She squinted as she thought way back to when she had first met them all. "Oh wait," she said. "Do you mean because you both lived in the same home for awhile? When you were in the care of the Egyptian Council? Abe told me that's how you and Edrice met. But just because you lived in the same house, doesn't mean you're actual siblings. And Edrice is beautiful and super smart. Plus, it probably would have annoyed Abe, and you love doing that."

Husani kicked in another door and let out a sigh of disappointment when the room came into view. Also empty. He shook his head and cocked an eyebrow up at Imara. "I see why you're confused because that *is* how we met, and we don't look anything alike, but Edrice is my literal sister. Half sister, anyway. We have different moms, but the same dad. We didn't even figure out we were related until a month after we met."

For some reason, this didn't make her feel better at all. Everything would have been much easier if Edrice someone else to run to besides Abe. But Husani wouldn't have been right anyway. He had a thing for Keiko, even if they were still in the middle of a fight at the moment.

"Yeah," Husani said. "Our dad is... how should I put it? Foul, loathsome, creature of the earth seems too kind, but it gives you the idea anyway. He has a disgusting number of children and somehow has escaped responsibility with all of them. I guess the Egyptian Council has been a little too busy with more important issues. Like Sef."

Her mouth dropped, and she blinked twice while the rest of her body remained frozen in place.

"Uh," Husani said as she continued to stare at the road ahead of them.

She didn't snap her mouth shut until after shaking her head several times. After another twelve seconds, she said, "So, when you said 'you can't change your DNA,' you were talking about yourself? You're afraid of ending up like your father?"

Husani's cheeks darkened with a blush as he turned away from her. With a gravelly voice he said, "How did you know about that?"

She rolled her eyes and pressed forward. They still had one last building to check before they went back to headquarters empty handed. If they could find even one person to help them, it would make a difference. Just one person.

Imara glared at Husani, hoping to make him feel some level of guilt. "Keiko thought you were talking about her. She thought you were saying she's doomed to end up like Takara. Is that what you think about her?"

"What?" Husani said, jerking his head to the side. His surprise seemed genuine. In fact, he almost seemed offended by her accusation. "Of course I don't think that. Keiko is freaking awesome. She's rebellious, but in the cool way, not the bad way. She goes rogue, but only to do the right thing. And she doesn't take crap from anyone. But she also plays the violin, and I don't know if you've ever seen her play, but she turns into this gentle, elegant creature, and she gets really into it, and you can't help but feel it's the most beautiful song ever created. Plus, she's gorgeous. Extremely gorgeous." Husani stumbled over the air and took a little cough to clear his throat. "What were we talking about?"

She didn't know when things had changed, but all the sudden, she felt like a big sister. For one brief moment, she was no longer a peer.

She sighed. "If you ever tried giving Keiko a genuine, well thought out compliment like one of those, instead of the stupid pick up lines you say all the time, you two might have a shot at an actual relationship."

"Whoa," Husani said throwing his hands in the air. "Who said anything about a relationship? I like being free and enjoying every lady. I don't need to settle down."

Imara snorted. "Please, that act won't work on me. Especially now that I know more about you. You flirt with every girl you've ever met because you're afraid if you don't, one of those girls might develop some actual feelings for you. And if you have actual feelings for her, then you have a chance to hurt her, just like your dad has hurt all the women he's ever been with."

Husani scoffed and opened his mouth to respond, but seemed to be stuck trying to come up with the words. He puffed his chest out, but his bravado was pointless now. They both knew the truth. With an angry growl, he said, "I don't need relationship advice."

Imara gave him a sideways glance.

Husani cocked one eyebrow up and asked pointedly, "Did you really break up with Abe?"

In an instant, the big sister feeling faded, and he had the upper ground. She sniffed and turned away from him as a flood of emotions overcame her. "I had to," she said in a whisper.

Husani laughed. "Oh, you had to? You didn't want to, but you had to?"

She marched forward on the street and tried to hold her head high. "That's exactly what happened."

She frowned. "You didn't know me before, but I wasn't very nice. I was judgmental and cruel. I saw the worst in everyone. It's because of Abe that I'm different now. I stayed here so I could help him like he helped me. But the thing is, the people I hurt most of all were the ones I care about the most. My sister and my parents. Mostly my sister. I resolved to do better and make things right with her, but…"

Husani nodded. "But you can't fix your past mistakes until you go home and spend time with your family."

It wasn't a question. What it was, was frustrating. How had Husani figured out in three seconds what it took her months to realize? Either way, it didn't matter now. Her shoulders slumped. "Abe needs to save his business. It's a completely worthy goal. I can't possibly ask him to give that up for me. But I can't give up my sister for him either. And since our goals require us to be in different territories…"

For the first time, Husani actually looked sad. He wasn't necessarily rooting for them, but he did seem to feel bad about it. For some reason, his sympathy did the worst thing of all. It made her say something she never would have under normal circumstances.

Imara bit her lip and let out a little sniff. "I'm sure Abe won't need long to get over me. He only broke up with Edrice a month before we met. And he kissed me within hours of meeting. If he fell for me that fast, I must not be anything special. Probably, I was just there and he was lonely."

She sniffed again, and it all sounded so pathetic. And yet so true. All these months she had been trying to convince herself they had something special. But if he cared about more than her looks, it should have taken longer for him to fall for her.

For his part, Husani seemed to be conflicted about what to say next. There was no way he couldn't tell how devastated she was. It was written plainly all over her face. Right in the middle of a mission. She was supposed to be the level-headed one who didn't let interpersonal issues get in the way of things. So much for that.

"I don't know..." Husani started. But then he didn't volunteer anything else. In fact, he tapped his ring, apparently to distract both of them.

Since the act wasn't convincing, Imara asked, "What? You don't know what?"

Husani shifted, turning his shoulder away from her. After a quick jiggle of the head, he said, "Abe's not that kind of a person. He's nuts about some things, but..." he shrugged. "He's loyal and... He's not that kind of guy. He wouldn't have kissed you if he didn't feel something."

279

She raked her fingers through the curls on top of her head. She didn't know if that should make her feel better or worse. It actually made her feel a little bit of both. She tapped her ring to check the map and scowled when she saw how far they still had to go. Another block and a half.

Another block and half to think, or maybe worse, talk.

Thinking seemed to be the better alternative for most of the trip, but too much thinking only brought more questions to her mind. Just before they reached the hideout, one question escaped her lips. "Do you think they're going to get back together? Abe and Edrice?"

She wished she could recall the question the moment she asked it. The look on Husani's face gave more of an answer than she wanted.

Her shoulders drooped, and she tried to swallow the lump in her throat. "Soon?" she asked, holding back a sniff.

Husani threw his hands in the air. "I don't know," he said. "Edrice is my sister. I have to hope they get back together because that's what she wants."

Imara's head fell as she tried to nod. Somewhere along the way it got stuck and came out as more of a twitch. At least they had reached the hideout. Husani lifted his foot to kick in the door, but dropped it again at the last second. He stood there without moving while her heart pounded in her chest.

At last, he took in a deep breath and swallowed. "But I do think you're better for him," he said.

FORTY

WHEN IMARA AND HUSANI ENTERED THE building, they heard voices from around a corner. They perched onto their tiptoes and crept down the hall. Once near enough, they peeked around the corner to see who was there.

About a dozen people sat at a table with heads lowered while hurried whispers bounced between them. They didn't wear red armbands marking them as Sef's gangsters. Instead, each of them had a lime green T stitched into their black shirts.

Taggers.

Not just any taggers. A man with a round scar on his forehead stood out to her. She recognized the others as well. The taggers from Alexandria. The same ones who had been at the graduation party. They all wore scowls as they whispered.

The man with the round scar on his forehead slammed his fist against the table. He raised his voice just high enough for Imara to hear. "She killed that woman on the council. An innocent woman! That's not what the taggers are supposed to stand for."

A woman with long, silver earrings said, "And I know she's torturing more people in that mansion than we know about. I hear the screaming."

Takara.

They were talking about Takara.

It seemed even the taggers weren't happy about everything she'd done.

"What can we do?" said a young woman with a squeaky voice and a plaid shirt. "She's stronger and smarter than all of us."

The young woman dropped her head into her hands, revealing the young man at her side.

Rajesh.

He noticed Imara in almost the same moment she noticed him. When their eyes met, she let out a small gasp and clutched Husani's wrist. They would have to run.

But Rajesh didn't move. He parted his lips, but shut them again and averted his eyes. Before she could imagine what that meant, another person at the table noticed her presence.

The man with the round scar on his forehead jumped to his feet. "Everyone back to the mansion. Hurry!"

The man reached for a small black box on the table and pressed a button on top of it. Instantly, a drone that had been sitting in the corner rose into the air and headed for Imara and Husani. The taggers scrambled to their feet while the drone flew.

Imara threw her hands over head. Not that it would make any difference. The drone could electrocute anyone, no matter what their hands protected. For a split second, she remembered how the man with the scar had complained about Takara murdering the council woman.

Maybe the drone was only a distraction, not a murder weapon. Maybe the taggers didn't want to kill an innocent person like her. But as soon as that thought came to her head, she shot it away. The taggers blamed her for Professor Santini's death. She wasn't innocent in their eyes.

She ducked to avoid the drone, just in time to notice Rajesh grab the black box that the man with the scar had left behind. Now the last tagger in the building, Rajesh went to touch the button on the black box. Husani pulled a stun gun from his pocket and aimed for Rajesh.

The blast from the stun gun missed, but it came close enough to make Rajesh jump. The black box clattered to the ground as he stumbled on his feet.

When the box hit the ground, the drone jerked, then dropped out of the air, landing on Husani's outstretched arm.

Husani let out a cry as the drone forced the stun gun out of his hands. It cracked into pieces the moment it touched the floor. He scowled and glared at Rajesh. "You're not good enough for a stun gun anyway."

He curled his hands into fists and lunged toward Rajesh. Since he had a significant head start, Rajesh made it out the door long before Husani reached him.

"Coward," Husani said at the door. He stomped toward it with murder in his eyes.

Imara grabbed Husani by the elbow and used every bit of her strength to pull him back. "If we try to fight him, the rest of the taggers will come after us."

"He was trying to kill us!" Husani shouted.

"We don't know that for sure. Maybe he grabbed the box to try and stop the drone from attacking."

Husani ripped his arm away from her and growled. "Since when are you as optimistic as Abe?"

"We're trying to find people who can help us fight against Sef," she said, kicking the drone to be sure it was still inactive. "We don't have time to get distracted by Rajesh."

"He betrayed us!" Husani said. "He betrayed you!" He let out a long scoff and pounded his fist against a wall. "He's the reason you got tortured. And got broken ribs."

She clutched her stomach. "Trust me, I remember." She shook her head. "He was selfish, but he wasn't trying to hurt me. He just wanted to take care of himself. I don't think he wants us dead."

Husani muttered several incoherent words under his breath before he said, "You should have let me punch him. At least once."

Imara rolled her eyes. Before she could respond, her ring chimed with a notification. She opened the new message, and soon a half smile twitched at her lips. "Keiko says she figured out how to stop the drones. Let's get back to headquarters and hope Abe gets to Marco soon."

FORTY-ONE

ABE LANDED HIS JET IN A FIELD OF SNOW next to a tiny town. Maybe the city of Noorvik was big by Alaskan standards, but it was miniscule to him who had lived all his life in Alexandria and Cairo. Siluk appeared, waving his arms.

When Abe got out of the jet, the cold air accosted him. Even with the coat he brought, the chill pierced through his skin and drove straight to his bones.

Siluk laughed and handed him a much thicker coat along with a hat and some other cold weather gear. "Now do you see why Egypt is ridiculously hot for me?" he asked.

Abe's teeth chattered as he tried to nod. "I'm getting it." He zipped the coat up before attempting to adjust his temperature controlled underclothes. Those would help warm him, but only the coat could shield him against the biting wind.

Siluk laughed again and pointed toward two hover mobiles. After quickly explaining how they worked, Siluk started his engine and set off for Abe to follow. It took a few moments for Abe to figure out the controls. It took another three minutes to drive it without jerking to the side every few seconds.

When he finally got the hang of it, he nodded at Siluk. "Piece of cake," he said.

Siluk nodded back. And then he tilted his head to the side. "So, Imara broke up with you, huh?"

"No."

The look on Siluk's face almost made the lie worth it.

Siluk narrowed his eyes, but finally shrugged. "I know she did, but if you don't want to talk about it, that's cool. We'll be there in a couple minutes."

Abe nodded and kept his mouth shut. He considered Siluk a friend, but that didn't mean he wanted to bear his soul to him. Besides, they had work to do. With everyone busy in Egypt, he didn't like thinking about the trouble they'd be getting into without him. The sooner they got back on the jet, the better.

The landscape was so full of snow, Abe wasn't sure how Siluk knew which way to go. But Siluk forged ahead with a look of confidence. The look only pounded a fist into the knot twisting in his gut.

Soon enough, a lone hut appeared on the landscape of snow. Two minutes later, they had parked and headed for the door.

Siluk knocked, and they didn't wait long before someone answered. His shoulders were hunched over and his face looked windburned. There was a droop to his eyes that must have taken years to be developed. The man saw Siluk and immediately said, "Are you here with my fish? If you have any extra, I'll…"

His voice trailed off when he noticed Abe standing there. His eyes paused at Abe's face as he seemed to take in the skin color and obvious Egyptian descent. The man's face fell, and his shoulders visibly dropped down further.

"Marco Santini?" Abe asked.

The man sighed and rubbed his forehead. "If you're here to bring me to Takara, could you please just kill me first?"

"Considering what she's planning to do to you," Abe said. "That's a pretty good suggestion. But no, I'm not here to take you to her. I'm actually here to save your life."

৪৩৪৩৵৶৵৶

Imara jogged back to headquarters with Husani. Maybe it was stupid to expend so much energy this early on, but her anxiety couldn't take the walking anymore. With two blocks to go, her ring started buzzing with a phone call.

A flurry of electricity went through her when she saw Abe's picture. She tried to settle her face into a neutral expression before she tapped his photo to answer the call. As soon as the screen came up, Husani had jumped to her side.

"Hey," Abe said. And then he stopped. Stopped and stared while their eyes met and thousands of unspoken words drifted between them. Was it always going to be like this? Every conversation so awkward she could scream?

No, she reminded herself. It wouldn't always be like this because she was leaving and wouldn't see him anymore. That thought didn't feel any better than the last.

"We saw Rajesh," Husani piped in from beside her.

Abe's nose twitched, and his eyes darkened with a visible rage. His head tilted to the side ever so slightly as he spoke through his teeth. "Did you strangle him?" he asked.

"Nah, Imara wouldn't let me," Husani replied.

287

Imara let out a *tsk* and pushed Husani away. "Forget Rajesh. We have more important things to worry about at the moment. Did you find him?"

A man leaned into view for half a second, then quickly pulled away. She didn't expect him to look as familiar as he did. It wasn't his facial features as much as his eyes. They looked exactly like Professor Santini's. Seeing them set her stomach into an explosion of remorse.

She took a deep breath. "Keiko said she can stop the drones. We'll contact Takara soon and give her Marco's location. Don't forget to send a picture for proof. And, can you drop a location tag before you leave?"

Abe didn't make eye contact as he moved his fingers to his screen. He nodded absently and said, "Sending it now."

She continued. "Keiko said we'll have to go to Takara's mansion to turn off the drones."

Saying the words out loud put a shiver through. It hadn't seem so bad in her head, but now the thought of going back to her place of torture seemed more than a little frightening.

"What?" Abe said, moving his face forward. His eyebrows furrowed until a crease appeared between them. "Husani." He waited until the boy made eye contact with him. Then, he pointed in her direction and said, "You keep an eye on her."

She put both hands on her hips and scoffed. "I can take care of myself, thank you very much."

"I know that," Abe said. "You can also rescue yourself, as you've proved multiple times. But this is Takara we're talking about, and you have a tendency to risk your safety for the sake of others."

"Like you're one to talk," Imara said under her breath.

288

"I want an extra pair of eyes on you, that's all," Abe said.

She let out an exasperated sigh. "We'll be fine," she said, and ended the call before anyone else could speak.

Why did Abe have to go be all gallant and worried about her safety like that? That's what boyfriends were supposed to do, not ex-boyfriends.

She stomped forward and didn't speak the entire rest of the way to headquarters. When they arrived, she still didn't want to speak. Not with Edrice. Not with anyone.

Luckily, the moment they opened the door, Keiko directed her back out of it. "Edrice is going to stay here and guide us through the city. Let's go stop those drones."

FORTY-TWO

AN ONSET OF NAUSEA GREETED IMARA WHEN Takara's mansion came into her view. She hadn't expected to feel anything since she only saw the inside of the mansion last time she was here. But standing in front of those doors triggered a painful reminder that burned in her ribs.

After tucking those memories neatly into the stack of things she never wanted to think about for the rest of her life, she traipsed up to the door and knocked.

Next, she looked straight into the security camera and said, "I have Marco Santini's location. If you want it, open this door."

It took eleven seconds before the door opened, and even that seemed surprising. Imara, Keiko, and Husani were ushered inside by silent taggers, different from the ones they had encountered earlier. The taggers motioned for them to sit on a couch, and then they stood guard at either end of the room.

Several minutes later, Takara burst through the front door with three drones hovering over her head like hummingbirds.

Her eyes fixed onto Imara's. Her arms shook while every vein in her hand popped out. "Did you know where he was when you were here before?" she asked.

Imara ignored the question and tapped her ring. "Do you want the location or not?"

At that moment, the silky-haired woman seemed to notice her daughter sitting on the couch with them. Her eyes narrowed at the short, amber hair that no longer matched her own.

Imara opened her mouth and pushed the words out, desperate to keep the woman's mind off her daughter. "The only thing we ask in return is our safety."

Takara's eyes jumped back to hers, and a throaty laugh bubbled out from her throat. "The only thing you'll get in return is your life, and even that isn't guaranteed."

Imara thought about protesting, but knew better than to argue with Takara. Rather than engage in more conversation, she tapped her ring and pulled up the location tag Abe had sent earlier. She scrolled through her contacts until she found Takara's face.

The woman's nose twitched with a smile as Imara sent the information to her. She nearly drooled as she gazed at the location tag. But then, her face warped, and she jerked her head toward them. "How do I know this is real?"

With a tap, Imara showed her the picture featuring Marco Santini and a little hut in a snow-filled landscape.

The expression that overcame Takara's face was difficult to describe. If she could have bottled the glee a serial killer felt at claiming a new victim, it would have been that times ten. Plus, a smattering of grotesque curiosity.

The look was so vile, Imara had to turn away. She wasn't surprised to notice Husani and Keiko had done the same.

Takara tapped on her hologram, scrolling through different apps as she mumbled to herself. She tapped her hologram screen one last time, and then turned off her ring. Just then, the drones above her crackled with electricity.

"Time to clean up," Takara said as she waltzed away.

The nearest drone reached out for Husani. He called out to Keiko, panic lacing every syllable.

Keiko tapped furiously on her hologram screen. "You'll have to dodge it for a couple minutes. I have to find the breaker box for the house," Keiko said.

Husani jumped off the couch, and Imara wasn't far behind. Two drones circled her while the third zoomed toward Keiko. She threw herself in front of the girl and waved her hands attempting to get the drone's attention.

Luckily, the drone turned toward her only a moment later. She dodged the second drone and threw a pillow, trying to hit it out of the air. Before she could search for the first drone, she noticed the two taggers who had been standing guard by the door. They covered their heads, each wearing a look of terror.

"She left us. The drones are on attack mode; they won't know not to target us," one of them whispered.

A black blob flying through the air pulled Imara's attention away. Husani had thrown a large, black blanket over the drone and was now trying to wrestle the drone to the ground.

It seemed like a pretty good idea until Keiko's voice rang through the air. "That blanket still conducts electricity, you idiot. Let go before it kills you!"

He dropped the blanket faster than a cobra strike just as a rush of blue sparks shot through it.

Imara's attention turned to the first drone, which she avoided by running and dropping to a crouch before the drone could react. It hovered for a moment, scanning the room to find her. A second later, the fight was on again. Most of her energy was spent dodging and weaving. She threw a vase at one point, but the drones were better at dodging than she was.

More taggers entered the room with eyes on the front door, probably trying to escape. She ducked to avoid the blanket-covered drone, but at the same time, saw another wrapping its arms around one of the taggers. The woman barely had time to register its presence before shocks jolted through her body.

"Stop it!" a man screamed. "She's one of us. She's a tagger!"

But then, another drone wrapped its arms around him, and he was dead on the ground a second later.

Screams broke out as they all realized what was happening. When Takara had said, "Time to clean up," she had meant everyone. Including the taggers.

Imara chucked a pillow toward the closest drone, which threw it off balance just long enough to protect another tagger. More taggers ran for the front door while the rest of them kept fighting.

Two drones headed for Imara. She ducked behind the couch to hide, searching for anything to use as a weapon. She jerked her head to one side and pulled back when she noticed Keiko centimeters from her face.

"I *need* the breaker box," Keiko said. "She's powering the drones through this mansion. If I can cut power to the entire mansion, it should cut off power to the drones. That's my theory anyway."

"On it," Imara said with a nod. She hopped over the couch and slapped a drone away with her bare hand. Soon, she was in a familiar hallway, which caused a shot of nausea through her stomach. Clenching her stomach, she headed straight for the door she wanted least to go inside. Even still, she knew that room would be her best chance at finding the breaker box.

A tagger woman stood outside the torture room with heavy tears streaming down her cheeks. Imara took careful steps forward, but as soon as the woman noticed her, she pulled a gun.

Rather than fight, Imara tried to think what Abe would do. "Help us," she said. "I need to find the breaker box in order to stop the drones."

The woman wrinkled her nose with disgust, but she didn't shoot either. "You killed Carlotta," she said through her teeth.

Imara locked eyes with the woman and tried a little smile. In a soothing voice, she said, "I didn't. I know you'll never believe me, but I promise I didn't. But even if I did. Is this what you want?" She waved a hand down the hall toward the whirring drones and strangled shouts. "Taggers are supposed to stop criminals like Takara and Sef, not be led by them. Is this what taggers believe in? Mass murder?"

They were both still for several moments. The woman's mouth turned into a frown, and she began to glare. But a second later, the gun clattered to the ground. The woman took in a deep breath and let it out slowly. She tapped a code into the door opener and pointed to a metal box built into the wall.

Before Imara could enter the room, the woman had disappeared. Imara tapped her ring as she marched toward

294

the box. When Keiko answered her call, she said, "It's in the room down the hall on the left. Can I do anything before you get here?"

Before Keiko could answer, a shower of sparks appeared out of the corner of Imara's eye. She turned and saw not one, but two drones coming straight for her. She backed up against the padded chair in the middle of the room, and a rush of heat tingled through her. She pivoted to back up more and promptly tripped over a box of magnets. She kicked it, ignoring the familiar shiver up her spine. What *did* Takara use those magnets for?

Imara ducked behind the padded chair as the drones drew closer. She grabbed a plastic tray off the nearby hover cart and chucked it at the drone.

When that didn't work, she tried the knives. The first knife hit against the drone with its hilt. She huffed and threw another. This one hit the drone with its blade squarely in the belly. Rather than damage the metal, the knife only bounced off, heading back for her.

She pulled her arm in front of her face and jumped to the side. Apparently, knives wouldn't work either.

She glanced down at the box of magnets near her feet. She grabbed a handful as she backed into the corner. The nearest drone stretched its arms toward her, but her eyes fell on the whipping blades keeping the drone aloft. She glanced at her handful of magnets, when an idea popped into her mind. But it was too easy. Surely the drones couldn't be beaten like this.

The mechanical drone arms reached forward until one brushed across her shoulder. The time to think had passed. Maybe it would work and maybe it wouldn't, but there was only one way to find out.

She threw a magnet, aiming for the drone's propellers. Within seconds, the magnet attached to the blade, which immediately threw the drone off balance. The arms reached for her again, but the drone veered to the left until it crashed into the floor in a puff of smoke. By the time she aimed for the second drone's propellers, it was already zooming back outside the door.

She stuffed as many magnets as possible into her pockets, then headed to the metal box.

"Here she is," Husani said through the doorway.

Keiko rushed in a moment later shaking her head. "We thought you were upstairs. We went through three rooms before we..." Her voice trailed off as her eyes landed on the breaker box. She had it open a moment later and tapped into the nearby keypad.

"How'd you do that?" Husani asked when he spotted the broken drone on the ground.

Imara grabbed a handful of magnets and dropped them into his hands as she explained how to throw the drones off balance with them.

Before she could finish, two drones zoomed into the room.

"Anytime now, Keiko," Husani said as he ducked behind the padded chair.

Keiko flashed her teeth and glared. "I'm working on it"

Imara gripped a magnet. She had just narrowed her eyes to aim, when the power in the house went out. The first sound she heard was Husani tripping over the box of magnets with a grunt. The next was the whir of the two drones.

"The drones are still active," she said. "Is it going to take a minute to work?"

"That should have worked," Keiko said with a growl. "They have an internal power source, but the attack command has to come externally. Once I shut off the external commands, the drones should have powered down. Without..." her breathed hitched and she whispered, "It's got me."

Without a thought, Imara lunged in the direction she had last seen Keiko. With the lights out, she wasn't sure it was the right way until her hands made contact with Keiko's face.

Imara ran her hands down Keiko's arm until she felt the drone's arm. She ripped it away as she blindly threw one of the magnets. "RUN!" she screamed.

With only the shuffling of feet to guide her, it was hard to tell where the others were. She waited until both of them seemed to be out of the room before she started running too. A line of metal brushed across her arm. She ducked and chucked a magnet over her shoulder, hoping it would hit a propeller.

Keiko screamed, but Husani must have saved her because she thanked him a moment later. When Imara finally got outside the darkened house, she noticed Keiko gripping Husani around the waist. He held her head against his shoulder. When Keiko noticed they weren't alone, she quickly pushed Husani away and said, "I'm fine now."

Husani looked ready to fight it, but there was no time for that now. "Look," Imara said, pointing to the nearby road.

People filled the streets, many of them screaming. At least half wore a tagger T on their chests. Every few feet, dead bodies lay unmoving. And just ahead, with its arms reaching for the next victim, a drone hovered.

Imara's feet pounded against the road as she pulled a magnet from her pocket. It was still too far to aim properly, but the drone was ready to electrocute, and she couldn't stand by and watch. She chucked the magnet, which fell short and bounced against the road.

She had been so focused on grabbing another magnet that she didn't hear the drone behind her until it gripped her around the shoulder. Maybe it was stupid, but she aimed and chucked another magnet at the other drone first. Then, she grabbed another magnet and aimed for the propeller of the drone now gripping her.

A shock began to go through her, causing her body to seize. But her magnet pulled the drone off balance, and it disconnected from her body a moment later. She dropped to her knees and gasped for air.

"Careful!" Husani said as he helped her to her feet a moment later. "Abe will skin me alive if anything happens to you."

She nodded absently as she turned to check on the other drone. It was gone, and its victim lay on the ground, completely still. She clenched her jaw and felt a sting in her nose as tears started forming.

A man leaned over the victim with tears in his eyes. Both the man and the victim wore a tagger T on their chests.

Her breath hitched as she tried to swallow. Tingles danced in her fingertips, and fear gripped her. But she knew what she had to do.

She glanced toward Husani and Keiko and said, "We have to work with the taggers."

FORTY-THREE

ABE WAS TEN MINUTES AWAY FROM LANDING his jet safely in Cairo when his ring buzzed with a phone call.

He tapped it and answered the call, then let Siluk adjust the screen so both of them could see.

"What's up, Imara?" Siluk asked.

With his eyes focused on flying, Abe couldn't look at her for too long. Even still, he felt right away that she was hurting. Not physically, though there seemed to be some of that too. No, this was more emotional.

"We have to join the taggers," she said.

Siluk laughed.

Abe would have joined in if he hadn't noticed Imara's face first. She pursed her lips as she let out a sigh through her nose. Her serious face. Exactly the same face she wore hours earlier when she'd told him she had to go home.

"Why?" he asked.

She shook her head. "Takara sent the drones after the taggers—well, after everyone. The drones are attacking anyone they see, and the taggers aren't happy about it. But they were unhappy before too. They hate what Takara has done." She gave a little sigh, and it made the curls on her forehead rustle. "We couldn't find any gangsters to join us, and we don't have enough people to break into the council chambers. We need more people, and I think we have to ask the taggers."

Siluk shrugged. "Sounds good to me."

The fact that Siluk agreed so easily made Abe want to smack him. Abe had spent a lot of effort in the catacombs to help Imara realize how harmful the taggers were. He wasn't about to let all that go to waste. "They want to brand people," he said. "Ruin them."

"I know." She brought her hand over her heart and pulled the fabric of her shirt into a fist. "I know, Abe," she said with a small shake of her head. "I'm not saying we should agree with them."

Her head fell into the palm of her hand. When she looked up, she had a spark in her eyes. The special spark he only saw when she had her best ideas. "This is the only way we can take Cairo back. But I think…" Her voice trailed off.

For a brief moment, she made direct eye contact with him, and the tiniest hint of a smile tugged at her lips. She looked at him exactly the way she had when she finally let herself fall for him completely.

"We have to believe we can help them understand why tagging is wrong," she said. "With Professor Santini, everything was gray. She hid all the bad things underneath good things. At least with Takara, they can tell she's evil. It's black and white again. We have to believe they'll listen to logic now that Professor Santini isn't here to muddle it."

Marco's head popped around Abe's shoulder, and he spoke the first words he had said the entire trip. "You're right," Marco said. "My sister's hila was truth seeing, but her greatest strength was manipulating the truth. Her followers would probably follow her to the end of the earth if she asked. She always gave just enough truth that no one questioned the lies."

Siluk squinted one eye before he shrugged. "I guess, in a way, it's better to have Takara than Santini. Either way, I'm in."

Imara ignored him, keeping her eyes on Abe. He had to focus on the sky ahead of him, but he felt her eyes searching his face. He kept his mouth shut mostly because he couldn't figure out what to say.

Finally, she asked, "What do you think, Abe? I know working with the taggers seems stupid, but we have to believe they can change, right? If you convinced me, maybe together we can convince them. Do you think it's worth it?"

The fact that she asked him specifically did lift his spirits a little. Although, maybe it wasn't because his opinion meant more to her; maybe it was just because she knew he was the one she had to convince.

After chewing on the thoughts, he decided she was right. "Do it," he said. "And don't go for the council chambers until we get there. We'll be there in five minutes."

ಐಐಬಬ

Imara tapped off her ring and gave a little nod to Husani and Keiko. Now, they just had to find a tagger and hope her idea wasn't as crazy as it seemed.

The crying man was gone now, but a tagger woman stood near a store opening, her eyes shifting up and down the road.

A moment later, a drone zoomed toward her, and the woman screamed. Before the drone could extend its arms,

Imara threw a magnet into its propellers. The drone veered to the side and crashed within moments. The tagger woman was left with her mouth dropped open.

"Here," Imara said, handing her a magnet. "Just aim for the propellers. It throws them off balance and causes them to crash. Once it's down you can pull the magnet off and use it again."

She stooped down and pulled her magnet off the broken drone. When she stood up again, the tagger woman's mouth was closed, but now she was glaring. The woman said, "You killed our leader."

Imara sighed and shoved her hands into her pockets. "I actually didn't. I tried to save her, but she wouldn't let me. Do you want to help us?"

The woman took a step back. "Why would I ever help you?"

"Look," Imara said pointing down the street at the chaos. "Is this what you want? I disagree with you about a lot of things, but I know we both think this is wrong."

The woman looked down, but there was something about it that almost seemed like a nod. "Takara will kill us if we help you," she said.

Keiko snorted at that. "She's trying to kill you right now. What difference does it make at this point? Besides, Takara is gone. She's not even in Egypt. As long as we get to the council chambers and reinstate the real council members in an hour or so, we can have control of the city before she gets back."

The woman looked at them both with widened eyes.

Imara stepped forward and used the most soothing voice she could find. "Inside the council chambers, there's evidence against Sef and his gangsters. If you can help us get inside, we'll reinstate the real Egyptian Council and finally be able to take down Sef for good. If you and the other taggers help us, the council won't be looking to arrest you."

It took almost a full minute, but eventually the woman swallowed with determination in her eye. She tapped her ring and started a phone call. When a face appeared on her hologram screen, she said, "Takara left Egypt. We're going to break into the council chambers and take down Sef and all his stupid gangsters before she gets back."

Hope spread out from Imara's heart. She pulled a handful of magnets from her pocket and said, "Keiko, take these to headquarters and give them to everyone there. Husani and I will round up any taggers that want to help us. While we're at it, we'll use the magnets to take down as many drones as we can—hopefully all of them. And then, we're going to the council chambers and end this."

FORTY-FOUR

ABE ENTERED HEADQUARTERS WITH SILUK and Marco. For the first time all day, he felt like they might actually have a chance. He planned to drop Marco off with Edrice and hoped he could convince Siluk to stay as well. He did not expect Imara's sister to appear a few minutes after they arrived.

Just as he prepared to explain the plan to Edrice, Naki marched into the room. "What are you doing here?" he asked, taking a step back.

Her eyes narrowed as she jabbed her pointer finger toward him. "I hate you," she said.

He grimaced. "That's not wholly unexpected."

She jabbed her finger toward Edrice and said, "I hate you too."

Edrice furrowed her eyebrows. "Who are you again?"

"That's Naki, Imara's sister," he said.

Edrice's face fell, and she averted her eyes to the floor. "Oh."

Unaffected, Naki turned on her heel until her finger pointed at Marco. She raised one eyebrow and said, "I have no idea who you are, so I'm neutral on you." She turned a final time and her finger pointed again. "Siluk, as usual, you're good. Also, the news in Kenya has been going nonstop about the mess here, which leaves me with only one question. Where is my sister?"

Abe tucked a stun gun into his belt. "Did you want to help us fight? Because that's what we're about to do."

"Fight?" she said with a shriek. "I thought I told you to keep her safe."

At that moment, Keiko burst through the door. This door opening thing was starting to get old.

"I have magnets for you," she said. "They'll protect you from the drones."

As she explained how to use them, Naki's face twisted at every new word. "What is going on here?" she asked. She turned on him again. "I thought I told you to keep my sister safe. I don't care if you aren't dating her anymore; she's still your responsibility."

He dragged a hand down the side of his face as he rolled his eyes.

Keiko passed around the magnets but stopped in front of him with arms folded over her chest. "I just barely found out you guys were even dating. Since when did you break up?"

"Since never," he said with a scowl.

Naki scoffed. "Imara broke up with him earlier today."

"Oh yeah," he said with a nod. "She broke up with me. Sort of."

Naki turned in on him and glared. "What do you mean *sort of?*"

He shoved both hands through his hair at once. "We have more important things to worry about at the moment. Namely, reinstating the Egyptian Council before Takara gets back from Alaska."

"Right," Keiko said as she slammed a fist over the door opener. "Let's go. I'll explain everything else on the way."

He glanced back at the others as he ran after her. "The rest of you stay here. Siluk, explain everything to Naki. Edrice, you keep Marco safe."

FORTY-FIVE

THE CREAM WALLS OF THE EGYPTIAN
Council building stood out against the blue sky. The rows of
windows had green shades blocking the inside from view. A
metal gate protected the grounds, but one of the taggers had
a digital key, and soon they were inside.

Imara marched up to the wooden door of the building,
ignoring the pounding in her chest. Abe had said to wait, but
she wasn't very good at that. Especially with the fate of so
many people at stake.

At least Husani was with her, along with a group of ten
taggers. Rajesh was among them. Husani didn't like it, but she
had gotten him to stop threatening him at least. The worst
part of the whole thing was the tagger T on her chest.

She said she didn't want to wear it, but the taggers refused
to help them otherwise. So, she had pinned the T to her chest
and vowed to remove it as soon as she could.

At the door, the same tagger who opened the gate used
her ring to open the door's lock. Imara took a deep breath
before she pushed it open. Just like the gate, she left it ajar so
Abe could get in without a key whenever he arrived.

This was it.

Win or lose, whatever happened would happen now.

The moment she walked through the door, a gangster jumped to his feet. He must have been standing guard. She curled her hands into fists, but the gangster took one look at the *T* on her chest and let out a sigh of relief.

"Finally," he said, pulling her down the hall. "Takara left, and we've been waiting for instructions for over an hour. Sef doesn't know what she wants us to do next."

"Uh, yes," Imara said, clearing her throat. "That's right. That's exactly why we're here. To give Sef instructions."

She drummed her fingers on her thigh as she tried to take an inconspicuous glance back at Husani. The gangster might not have recognized her, but many of the gangsters knew Husani's face. Luckily, he had moved to the back of the group and walked with his head down.

"Where are the old Egyptian Council members?" she asked. Might as well get what she needed while she had his trust.

"Down there, second door on the—" The gangster stopped in his path and cocked his head at Imara. "Why do you need to know that?"

She tried to glare at him, though it was hard when her insides twisted. "*I* don't. But Takara has a message she wants delivered to them. Those two have it." She waved her hand toward Husani and another random tagger at the back of the group.

The gangster narrowed his eyes at her, which she countered by lifting her chin. He shrugged and pointed down the same hall as before. "It's down there, second door on the left."

She nodded at the back of the group and watched as Husani and the tagger left to head for the room. Hopefully they could release the real council members and get help before things got too out of hand.

A minute later, they entered the council chambers. Sef paced the floor while scratching his freckled nose.

"We have word from Takara," the gangster said when they entered the room.

Sef stopped mid stride and marched toward Imara. "What took you so long?" he said. Just like the gangster, he seemed to ignore her face and only saw the *T* on her shirt. All she could think about was that time at the restaurant when she planted the virus on his ring.

Yesterday.

Was that really only yesterday? Would he remember her face?

"What does Takara say?" Sef asked as he lowered himself into one of the council chairs.

"Uh. Yes, I have news. Uh, Takara says…"

Sef glanced back up at her and seemed to see her face for the first time.

She swallowed and threw her shoulders back, hoping to convince him with confidence alone. "She says we need to act. She wants us to go into the city and prove we're in charge."

That was too much. Too obvious. He'd know she was trying to get him to leave. The instructions didn't make any sense.

The man rose from his chair and took a step toward her. He looked down at the *T* on her shirt, then at the other taggers, and then back at her again. Recognition seemed to flutter at the corners of his eyes.

She needed a new idea, and she needed it now. Eyeing the rest of the room, she noticed two dozen gangsters. She could practically feel Rajesh twitching at the sight of them. The new Egyptian Council members were also there. They'd probably fight for Sef since he gave them their new positions, but she wouldn't know for sure until the fighting started. Either way, they were outnumbered.

Sef opened his mouth. Before he could say anything, Abe tore into the room with Keiko at his side. "Imara," he shouted. "Are you okay?"

It took less than a heartbeat for everything to dissolve into chaos after that. The gangster nearest to her jumped on her back, and she became unaware of the room. She whipped out her stun gun and held it out, but the gangster plucked it from her hand before she could shoot.

She dropped to the floor, and the stun gun blast hit another gangster who was coming up from behind her. Before the gangster in front of her could aim, she lunged for his legs.

He toppled back a few steps before he caught his balance. She took the moment to glance side to side to assess the room.

She first noticed Abe lying face down on the ground. Already? Her stomach dropped at the sight. She had no time to search for blood so all she could do was hope he'd been hit with a stun gun and not a real gun.

She noticed three of the fellow taggers also on the ground. They were more than outnumbered, and if she got stunned, it would all be over before it began. That meant one thing.

She couldn't get stunned.

She spun on her heel and tried to slap the gun from the gangster's hand. She felt his fingers squeeze the trigger as their hands brushed against each other. The blast from the stun gun rustled her hair as it whipped by.

It wouldn't be pretty, but she had an idea. She barreled her head toward the gangster's lower body. As soon as his body started to fold over hers, she stood up straight with as much force as she could muster.

The trick wasn't as efficient as it should have been, but it still worked. The gangster leaned on one foot until his body teetered at a forty-five degree angle to the ground. He tried to regain his balance with his other foot, but she kicked it out from under him as she plucked the stun gun from his hand.

While the gangster toppled to the ground, she readied herself to face the man standing behind him. Her heart skipped a beat when she saw Abe's brown eyes staring back at her.

His mouth had settled into an attractive smirk. "I should have known you'd be able to rescue yourself from danger," he said.

His grin was infectious, and soon a matching one found itself on her face. "I thought you got stunned."

He shrugged and ducked behind an overturned table. "I was faking it so I could get the slip on that guy."

She ducked down behind him and had to fight the sudden urge to wrap her arms around him.

"Where's Husani?" he asked.

"He's getting the real council members." She scanned the room again and noticed more taggers stunned on the ground. But she also noticed that even more taggers came in through the door and had joined the fight. She said, "There should be an access port to the wall hologram in the other room. Do you know where Keiko is?"

He nodded and pointed her out. Keiko held her fists out in front of a gangster whose arms looked as thick as her legs. She seemed to be holding her own with an impressive strategy of kicking him in the shins and punching him in the gut.

But then, the gangster grabbed Keiko by the shoulders and lifted her off the ground. That didn't stop her from kicking every inch of his body as she went.

The gangster seemed to notice a concrete statue in the corner of the room at the same moment Imara did. If he threw Keiko's head against that statue, she'd be knocked out and possibly have permanent damage.

Imara didn't realize she had jumped back into the fight until a shoe whipped past her head. It took seven steps until she reached Keiko and the gangster. Rather than go for the gangster, she simply held her arms out and caught Keiko from the air as he tossed her.

Keiko shook her bobbed hair out of her face then turned back on the gangster as soon as Imara set her down. Imara stunned him before either of them could move. "Go find Husani," she said.

Keiko scowled, but Imara gave her a scolding look. "He's freeing the council members and might need help. When that's done, we need you to access the wall hologram and find Sef's list. Abe and I can handle this."

After showing her how to find the room, Keiko stomped off with no small amount of huffing.

"You people are supposed to be on my side," Sef shouted through the chaos of the room.

More taggers had arrived. Abe was tackling a gangster to the ground while a tagger helped him. The fight had finally started to sway in their favor.

Sef must have realized the same thing because he grabbed a handful of gangsters, plus Rajesh, and bolted out of the room.

FORTY-SIX

IMARA BOLTED AFTER SEF WITHOUT TAKING a moment to think. Down a hallway, she passed a room on her left which seemed to be full of frantic shouts. She heard Keiko announcing updates on some hack she was performing. Half the council members were cheering her on and the other half were muttering about the use of hacking inside the council chambers.

Imara clutched her stun gun as she pressed on, keeping both eyes on Sef and the group of gangsters surrounding him. They'd all sacrificed too much to let him get away.

Willing her feet to move faster, she burst through the doorway to the outside. Once she spotted him, she rammed into Sef's shoulders and tackled him to the ground.

One of the gangsters pulled her away and held her arms behind her back. Just as she pulled herself out of the gangster's grip, another gangster took hold of her legs. Then, another gangster grabbed her around her stomach. The first gangster had her arms behind her back again.

She struggled against them, but soon they forced her onto her knees and no amount of pulling would get her free. Someone yanked her by the curls so her head was forced up to stare at Sef.

"I recognize you now," he said. "You're with that Nazari kid." He spat on the ground so near her body, some of the spittle landed on her knee. "He's been a thorn in my side for two years. I'll never forget what you've done here today."

"Good," she said with a rush of courage. "I hope no one forgets. I hope you all remember that fighting for the right thing is worth it. I hope you—"

Someone wrapped a hand over her mouth and her words were swallowed up in a palm.

"You may have won this time, but I'll start over in a new city. In a few years, I'll be just as powerful as I was." He leaned in close and poked her in the forehead, making her feel like nothing more than a child.

As he moved his hand away from her, a musky fragrance filled her nose. Her head drifted forward trying to capture more of the scent.

Intoxicating.

"You won't tell anyone which direction I went," Sef said. "I deserve to get away."

Her muscles had been straining against the arms holding her back, but now they relaxed. Sef didn't deserve to get away. He deserved to... To... He deserved something, right? Something important.

Punishment? Yes.

Or was it no?

The smell lingered around her as Sef backed away. He grabbed the closest gangster, Rajesh, but nothing seemed more important than taking another whiff of the musky air.

Something nagged at the back of her mind. Someone about this was wrong, but she couldn't quite put her finger on it.

All that effort thinking only meant less time for smelling.

Before she could sniff again, two figures appeared from around a nearby corner. Naki's face had hardened to a rigid fear, but she'd never looked so determined.

Naki? Where did she come from?

Her sister waved a stun gun around her head, shooting blasts in every direction.

"Naki, aim!" Siluk shouted as he tackled the gangster running toward him.

Imara jerked her head and blinked several times. Sef. She had to stop Sef. Not let him go. What was she thinking?

Sef ran past Siluk and Naki, waving his arms at them. "I am not in the wrong," he shouted. "I am not a criminal."

Naki aimed the stun gun, but her finger paused while a dazed look spread over her eyes.

"That won't work on me," Siluk said as he shoved his hands into his pockets. "I'm a smell master too."

He pulled out three tiny spray bottles and spritzed the air with three sprays from each bottle. Naki started shaking her head immediately, then she and Siluk ran toward the rest of them.

As Siluk's sprays wafted over to Imara, the intoxicating musky scent in the air neutralized. The gangsters around her blinked. The glazed looks in their eyes fell away. They seemed to realize where they were and what was happening and at once, all of them ran the opposite direction down the alley.

Sef managed to grab Rajesh before he could run. He wrapped an arm around Rajesh's shoulder and said, "I need to use your ID to get out of the country. You want to come with me."

Rajesh struggled against him, but Sef held him tighter and soon the struggling stopped. Sef glanced up at the building next to him and Imara followed his gaze. A security camera.

"It's coming from his wrist," Naki said. "I can taste mist. He must have some hose or something under his shirt."

All at once, Imara, Naki, and Siluk broke out into a run, heading for Sef.

Sef glanced up at the security camera again and pulled a gun from his pocket. He put it into Rajesh's hand, nodded toward Imara, and said, "Kill her."

Rajesh took the gun as he sniffed Sef's wrist. He aimed the gun at Imara, and the rest of them froze in place.

"Do it," Sef said.

As she ducked, Rajesh pointed the gun to follow her body. Steady. Until. His finger trembled when she made eye contact with him. Pleading with her eyes. *Don't do it.*

He looked down at the gun, and a muscle seemed to flex in his jaw. "No," he said.

Siluk fumbled with his spray bottles while Naki bit her lip whispering at him to hurry.

Imara took a step forward, maintaining the eye contact she had managed to get. "It's just a smell. Don't trust a smell that tries to control you."

Even without Siluk's neutralizing spray, the glaze in Rajesh's eye seemed to clear as he blinked and shook his head.

Sef held his wrist directly under Rajesh's nose and said again, "Kill her."

"NO!" Rajesh tried to throw the gun to the ground, but Sef stole it from his hand before he got the chance.

Imara charged toward him. Better to act now than wait around for Sef to aim.

Rajesh grabbed Sef's arm, attempting to pull the gun's aim away from her.

A moment later, she tackled Sef just as the gun went off. Her head slammed into his gut. He stumbled back, gasping for breath. Siluk barreled toward him from the side. Naki slapped him across the face, which didn't help, but it did bring a smile to their lips.

Within seconds, the three of them had Sef pinned to the ground. Another second later, Husani entered the grounds from the council building door. He had with him two women: one in a police uniform, the other a medical one.

When their faces slackened with horror, Imara followed their gaze. Sef's bullet had missed her, but it found another victim.

Rajesh.

He lay on his back, gasping for air. Blood seeped through his shirt as it gushed out of the wound in his chest. Her hand flew to her mouth while she jumped to his side. She pressed both hands over the wound. She had to stop the blood flow.

"You were right," Rajesh whispered.

She blinked and swallowed, then swallowed and blinked. "Just be quiet. We'll get you some help."

When he coughed, blood splattered over his mouth. He swallowed and said, "It does feel better to do the right thing."

His eyes fluttered closed, and a lump caught squarely in the middle of her throat. The woman with the medical uniform knelt down beside him and checked his pulse.

Ignoring her, Imara glanced around until she met Husani's eyes. "Get Abe," she said through her teeth.

The medical woman pulled the bag from off her back and unzipped it. "It's too late," she said. "I'll do everything I can, but—"

"GET ABE!" Imara screamed. "Husani, go find him!"

Husani clutched his heart as he stared at the pool of blood. His voice made a strangling sound as he tried to clear his throat. "She's from the hospital," Husani said, pointing to the woman in the medical uniform. "Abe only has basic medical training."

"If I have to ask you again…" Imara started.

Husani huffed, regaining some of his control. "Why do you think Abe can do more than someone from the hospital?"

"Because I'm healer." Abe appeared through the door of the council building, and Imara let out a sigh heavier than her entire body.

The medical woman's eyes flicked up at Abe's declaration. She immediately moved back and made room for him. "I'm so glad you're here," she said. "Can you tell if the bullet went through his heart? If it did, we've already lost him, but if not, I have some procedures. But it's so hard to tell without an x-ray."

She continued rambling as Abe knelt down at Rajesh's side. It took everything inside Imara to not latch onto his arm and bury her face in the soft cotton of his shirt.

A look came over Abe's face as he stared at Rajesh's body. No just concentration, but acceptance. He held this life in his hands, and for once, he was willing to bear the responsibility.

She held her breath as he worked. He let one hand rest gently over the bullet wound and he closed his eyes. He kept them closed for ten seconds, but she could tell he had the answer after only three. His body tensed, and a frown tugged at his lips. But he kept his eyes closed and breathed harder with each second.

When he opened his eyes, he stared at the ground. "It went through his heart," he said. He swallowed. "Then it ricocheted off a rib and went back through it again."

The medical woman's lip curled as she let out a curse.

Imara dropped her head into her hands. Why did the air suddenly seem so thin? Abe wrapped an arm around her shoulders and whispered, "I'm sorry."

A sob shook through her, and she pushed herself into his arms exactly where she didn't belong. But she didn't care. He embraced her without question. "He tried to save me," she said with a shivering breath. "Sef was aiming for me, and Rajesh pulled the gun away, and it hit him instead."

As Abe pulled her tighter, she heard Naki's light steps coming to their side. "He was trying to do the right thing," Imara said. She turned her head and rested her cheek against his shirt. Soft. She saw Naki trying to bore holes into Abe using only her eyes. He never relaxed his grip, no matter how Naki stared. Since Imara wouldn't let go either, he didn't deserve all the blame.

"What happened out here?" Keiko said from the council building door. Her eyes went wide when she discovered Rajesh's body a few seconds later. She gulped. "The Egyptian Council has been reinstated. They're finishing up the paperwork. The police are rounding up the last of the gangsters, and they're arresting the cops that were working for Sef. And they have an entire team at the airport ready to arrest Takara when she gets back. I see you got Sef also."

More officers had arrived, and Sef got hauled off to a police car. Everything they'd fought for was theirs. The victory might have been sweeter if the ground weren't littered with Rajesh's dead body.

FORTY-SEVEN

IMARA DIDN'T LET GO OF ABE UNTIL THEY were back inside the building. The council members tapped on their holograms with their noses practically touching the screens. The taggers cleaned up the room, a look of pride filling their faces. This reminded her to take the *T* off her shirt, but it also made her a little proud too.

The taggers had done the right thing. Just like her, they only needed someone to believe in them. She had been right that they could change.

She smiled at that, possibly the first smile she had worn all day.

Naki still glared at Abe, but he was too deep in conversation with Husani and Keiko to notice. Edrice had arrived and chatted with some police officers. Siluk wandered through the room, picking up bits up trash and righting overturned chairs.

Naki smooshed herself in between Abe and Imara and wrapped her arms around her sister's shoulders. Abe stepped away with a frown, but Naki only scowled at him and pulled Imara away. "I'm so glad you're safe, baby sister."

Imara returned the hug and let out a chuckle. "When did you fly to Egypt?"

Naki whipped a cluster of tiny braids over her shoulder. "I saw on the news what was happening here, and I didn't trust Abe, the *loser*, to keep you safe. So, I decided I better come here and do it myself."

"Um," Imara said. "That's… that was brave."

Naki squeezed Imara one last time. "See, you're trying to be better, and so am I. You inspired me."

Imara smiled. Another real one. These smiles felt good. "It's going to be different now, Naki. I promise."

Naki grinned and gave her another squeeze. "You know what? I believe you this time." Suddenly, she turned on her heel. "Ooh, I forgot. I promised Siluk I would remind him to call Darius when this was all over." She gave one final glare to Abe, then skipped off toward Siluk.

The space between them that Naki had been occupying somehow slipped away and Imara found her shoulder brushing Abe's a second later. She needed to get away before anything too drastic happened.

"Excuse me, Miss?" said a young woman in a pink hijab. She wore a news reporter pin on her chest. "Can I get your picture for the news?" Her jaw slackened as she made eye contact with Abe. While awestruck wonder filled her eyes, she said, "You're the orphan rescuer."

"Uh, excuse *me*, Miss," Husani said. "But all of us have rescued orphans. And we all helped take down Sef and Takara. You're welcome."

The young woman blushed and held up her hologram screen. She said, "Excellent. Then I'll get a picture with all of you. Move close together please."

Husani called Edrice over, and they all squished together for the picture. The entire time, the only thought in Imara's mind was how perfectly Abe's shoulder had tucked behind hers. And how easily she could drop her head onto the familiar spot. If only.

The moment the young woman finished taking the photo, Edrice disappeared back into the crowd. Husani held out a hand to the news reporter, and said, "Thank you, my…"

Knowing a ridiculous pick up line was about to spill from Husani's mouth, Imara started to roll her eyes.

But then, he curled his hand into a fist and snapped his mouth shut. "Thank you," he said again. "Have a good day."

And then he turned away.

As soon as the young woman left, Keiko raised one eyebrow and stuck a hand on her hip. "What? You're not going to flirt?"

"Not with her," Husani replied.

Keiko snorted. "Well, that's a first."

"I have to tell you something important, Keiko," he said. "I need to apologize."

Imara pushed Abe away before they could hear any more. They were halfway across the room before she realized her hands were still all over him. She tore them away and stuffed them into her pockets. "Sorry," she said. "Husani was about to apologize for something awful he said, and I thought they could use some privacy."

Abe responded by staring at his chest where her hands had been moments ago. Then, he looked back at her with a grin. She probably would have kissed him, but luckily Edrice spoiled the moment by appearing at Abe's side.

"I just sent you the paperwork," Edrice said.

"Oh." His face hardened to a serious stare that seemed unnatural on him. He tapped his ring and brought up the paperwork.

Edrice's eyebrow twitched as she eyed Imara. She clenched her jaw, but then seemed to force out a sigh. A moment later, she gave Imara a half smile. "Are you okay?" she asked. "You're not hurt or anything?"

"No, I'm fine." Imara held her breath, trying to control the emotions swirling inside her. Anger. Jealousy. Confusion. But the longer she stared, the more she realized how pointless they all were. She started to see her, not as Abe's ex girlfriend, but as Edrice. Her friend.

"What about you?" Imara asked, fiddling with the hem of her shirt.

Edrice put a hand over her forehead and sighed. "Obviously I'm fine physically. I've been coordinating with the police, and everything's been a little stressful." She shook her head. "But I guess it has been for all us."

Edrice bit her lip and stared at the floor. She rubbed her hand up and down her arm as she took in a deep breath. "I know you're leaving Cairo, and it's probably for the best." Her chin dipped further down as she stared at the floor. "But you were a really good employee. I just thought you should know."

"Thank you." Imara said. And she meant it. "You were a good boss. A really good one." She meant that too.

Edrice looked up with a smile, and they shared a moment of peace. Maybe they couldn't be best friends considering the history between them now. But at least they were a different kind of friend. The kind that still cared.

"Edrice," Abe said with a surprising sharpness in his tone. "Where do I sign this thing?"

Edrice rolled her eyes. "You are impossible."

He glared at the paperwork blinking back at him from his hologram screen. Edrice scrolled through it and pointed out a blank line in the middle of it. "Sign here," she said as she scrolled down further to a box. "Initial here," she said. "And sign next to the big X at the very bottom."

Abe nodded without taking his eyes off the screen and scrolled back up to the first spot. When he started signing with his finger, Edrice took a step back. "You're signing it now? Don't you want to think about it first?"

"I've thought about it plenty," he said as he finished his signature and scrolled down to the box. "This is happening, so get over it."

Edrice scoffed and turned on her heel. She stomped away without looking back.

"What was that about?" Imara asked. But the moment the words left her mouth, she closed it back up again. She didn't get to ask him questions like that. Not anymore. She turned away so he would know he didn't have to answer.

Abe, however, seemed unfazed by the question and offered the answer without question, even as she turned away. "I'm selling Edrice my portion of the business."

A second ticked by before the words sunk in. When they did, she grabbed his arm to stop him from signing the last line. "What did you say?"

"I'm selling my business. So I'm not tied to Egypt anymore."

She didn't really do it on purpose, but suddenly both her hands were gripping Abe's wrist making sure he couldn't sign that last line. "You can't do that," she said.

With his other hand, he popped a curl down over her forehead. "Thanks for your input, but it's my business. I can do whatever I want."

She held his wrist tight hoping maybe her words would sink in better that way. "I won't let you do this. You can't sacrifice your business just to be with me. You have to stay here."

To her surprise, Abe responded with a laugh. Next, he ran his fingers through his hair. "And what exactly is supposed to happen if I stay? My ex girlfriend owns half the business. Maybe I don't have feelings for her, but we have tons of history, and it's super awkward. So yeah, selling it sucks, but I'll just start a new business."

She pulled her hands back as if Abe's wrist were on fire. After carefully wrapping her arms over her stomach, she stared at the ground and asked, "Are you sure you don't have feelings for her?"

"Imara," he said cupping her chin. She turned away from his hand. He sighed. "Edrice made that deal with Sef, and I refused to forgive her for it. We fought about it constantly, and finally, *she* broke up with me."

He glanced to the other side of the room long enough for them both to see Edrice stood far out of earshot. Even still, he lowered his voice. "I guess she thought I would miss her once we weren't together anymore. Maybe hoping I would realize how much she meant to me. But instead, I realized she has never been who I thought she was. She's a genius business woman and an amazing person. But she's never been the person I wanted or actually needed."

He looked down and curled his hands into soft fists. "She didn't start the business to save orphans, she started it to make money. Which is honestly fine; making money isn't a bad thing. It just wasn't what I was looking for."

He touched Imara's face again, and this time she let him. His hand slid back until he was running a finger through the hair on the back of her neck. "And then I met you. You were everything I ever dreamed of. At first, you were just this gorgeous girl staring at me during a party, and I thought, *I should probably talk to her.* Then I followed you and watched you throw yourself in front of a hover cart to protect a random boy, and I thought, *Wow, she's pretty selfless to risk herself for someone else like that.* And then your sister got kidnapped, and the police were too afraid to help. So, what did you do? You decide to go after her yourself, willing to help your sister without one single thought about what you'd get in return."

He looked down at the ground with a chuckle. "Basically, it was all over from that moment on. I was smitten, and nothing could change that. I knew I was moving fast after Edrice, and I tried to slow down, but I couldn't. After every second with you, I wanted more. And because I'm an idiot, I did stupid things like lie to you and pretend everything would be fine. I messed up, but it doesn't mean I care about you any less."

"Abe." She pulled his hand away from her neck and held it out in front of her. It physically pained her to say the words, but they had to be said. "You can't sell your business for me. Maybe you want to do this now, but what about later? This business is everything to you. What about in a year?

328

What about in ten? At some point you're going to regret it, and you'll resent me for it."

He scoffed, and even though his eyes were soft, a fire burned inside them. "You don't understand. You said I wouldn't accept the responsibility of my hila. You were right. I am a healer, and I refused to see it. But it's more than that, and I didn't realize it until you broke up with me. I feared a real relationship too. And before you ask, yes, it was obviously because of my mom. I didn't want to get hurt so I never let myself get close enough for anything real. It was easier with Edrice because she wasn't right for me. But you?"

He stepped forward until their toes touched, and she could feel the heat coming from his skin. The spicy cinnamon smell clung to his shirt with a milky musk wrapping around it. He brought his head down until their foreheads touched, and she felt the lightest trace of moisture on his brow.

Then, he whispered the words she thought she'd heard so many times, only to realize he hadn't quite said them. But this time was different. This time, he spoke the words with no fillers. This time his conviction burst through the air with unmistakable clarity. He put his hand on her waist and traced circles over her hip bone. Soft, but full of yearning. "I love you, Imara," he said. "And I'm finally ready for everything that goes with that."

She couldn't help but kiss him after that. On her tiptoes, she wrapped her arms around his neck and kissed him like she never had. He met her lips with equal intensity, then pulled her body so close it nearly lifted her feet off the ground. With his arms around her, she realized it didn't matter what happened with her job or with the taggers or even with his business. Now they would face the world together.

Breathing in the smell of cinnamon and cardamom, she curled her fingers through his hair and almost forgot they stood in a crowded room full of people.

When they pulled apart, his lips stayed only a whisper away. She stared into his eyes, admiring the rainbow of colors running through them. Russet brown on the outside and olive green in the center. Tiny dots of maroon dotted through the center where the colors converged. All encased in the thickest eyelashes she had ever seen.

"Here comes the announcement," someone shouted through the room.

Abe snuck in one last soft kiss before he settled his chin on top of her curls. They both turned so they could see the wall hologram on the other side of the room.

"This should have the photos from that news reporter who was here earlier," one of the Egyptian Council members said.

As they turned to watch it, everything from the past twelve hours started settle. Things were going to be okay. The police would arrest Takara. She and Abe would convince the taggers to stop tagging. Soon, she'd be back in Kenya, and this time Abe could come with her.

As the hologram changed to a new screen, it showed a face that didn't belong to the news reporter. Imara's muscles shivered.

Wavy brown hair that had once been long and shiny was now matted and stringy. The brown eyes accompanying it looked hollow. A familiar puncture of holes lined the skin under the woman's ear. Imara had matching holes in her own neck caused by Takara's syringes.

It wasn't until the woman started speaking that the reality of her identity settled in. Her voice scratched as she spoke as if dehydrated.

It was obvious this woman had suffered at Takara's hand. That didn't make the sight of her any less gut wrenching.

Carlotta Santini began her speech with six simple words. "As you can see, I'm alive."

It's not over yet!

Lie Maker, Book 3 of the Truth Seer Trilogy, comes out July 1, 2019!

If you want to stay up to date on the release of *Lie Maker*, please join Kay L Moody's email list. You will also get free access to her exclusive short story, *Cloned*.

www.KayLMoody.com/collection

Author Bio

Kay L Moody is proud to be a female science fiction author. Her books feature cool science and technology, strong female leads, and a dash of romance. There's a strong focus on character development and societal conditions. She lives in the western United States with her husband and children. Visit her website to learn more.

www.KayLMoody.com

Author's Note

As always, I have to start by giving a huge thank you to my readers. You truly make this writing thing worthwhile. I have always been a writer, but for so long, I would horde my stories and not let anyone read them. I always thought they would never be good enough for the world.

Each time I get a new reader, I'm reminded that stories are meant to be shared. Thank you for reading my book and enjoying it in your own special way.

This book took me on a journey. It changed so much from my very first draft that it's hardly recognizable now. At times, I felt like a sculptor, trying to dig out the beauty I knew existed in there somewhere.

Now that it's finished, I'm so happy about how it turned out. Sometimes the characters surprised me and sometimes the hilas surprised me even more. Thank you for staying with me through this second book.

I can't wait for the third book and I promise it will be the best one yet!

Acknowledgements

I'm always amazed at the number of people it takes to finish a book. First, thank you to Kristy for once again being an amazing beta reader. Your support, insight, and encouragement were all necessary to completing this book.

Thank you also to my incredible editors. Deborah, your notes are always so helpful. You allow me to see my book through unbiased eyes. Emily, you are the best. Thank you for all your words of wisdom throughout this process. And thank you for dealing with my comma problems.

A huge thank you goes to my writers group. Alaura, Catherine, Emily, Jamie, Marissa, Nicole, and Stephanie, you have all been there when I needed advice. Thank you for not sugar coating my weaknesses and for being a catalyst for improving my writing. I have learned so much from all of you. I'm lucky to be among such talented writers!

I have so many family members that deserve a thank you as well. From my children, siblings, aunts and uncles, and more. You all believe in me so much. Your never ending support was a great source of strength to me during the writing of this book. Thank you!

I couldn't go without thanking my readers as well. You are the reason I write and the reason I keep dreaming up more book ideas.

Finally, the biggest thanks of all goes to my husband. I will never understand how you can believe in me without question. Thank you for laughing when I said I couldn't do it. And thank you for cheering with me when I finished. I never could have done it without your constant support.

Kay L Moody